Playing Games

PLAYING GAMES

Copyright © 2013 by Jill Myles

www.jillmyles.com

Playing Games

JESSICA CLARE

MYLES | SIMS | CLARE

Chapter One

"Why do I want to be on the show? Because the label told me to be here? It's not like I begged them to slap my face on TV. I'd rather be sitting in the studio." —Liam Brogan, lead guitarist for Finding Threnody, Pre-Game Interview Footage

"STAND IN FRONT OF THE CAMERAS, SWEETHEART, AND TELL US YOUR name." The assistant's voice rang out in the casting booth.

Nervously, I stepped forward into the bright lights, clutching the covered pan in my hands. I resisted the urge to shield my eyes from the light that was glaring right into my face and settled for only squinting a bit. "Hi there. My name's Katy Short."

"Tell us how old you are, Katy, and what you do." The voice behind the lights sounded utterly bored.

"I'm twenty-three and I recently received a degree from culinary arts school. I started a business. A cupcake business."

"Cute. And why do you want to be on *Endurance Island*?"

"Funny story," I said with a grin, trying to make myself seem as cutely approachable as possible—not something I'm good at, since my nickname is usually 'Cranky Katy.' "I'm actually not here for myself. I'm here because my brother, Brodie, really *really* wants to be on *Endurance Island*. And I'm here to show him some support. We figured he'd have a better chance if we both auditioned on his behalf." I gave the cameras my best cheerful smile and uncovered the enormous pan I held. "And so I brought a few presents so you wouldn't forget us, courtesy of Katy's Short Cakes."

At the unveiling of my pan, there were a few oohs and ahhs from the crew, which pleased me. It was early and they were probably hungry, so I'd banked on bringing some of my infamous 'Short Cakes.' I'd stayed up late into the night crafting them so they'd be fresh and delicious, and I had to admit that they looked delectable. Delicate yellow icing was piped atop perfect Dutch chocolate cupcakes in an ice-cream swirl design, and each one was drizzled with a gleaming chocolate ganache and topped with a cherry. The cupcakes in the center were missing the cherry, and I'd crafted marzipan letters, spelling out Brodie's name using the same font that *Endurance Island* used for their logo.

It was all part of our plan to get my brother on *Endurance Island*. He talked about nothing else, and I figured if my cakes could help him, it was worth spending a Saturday morning down here at the casting call. Brodie had dressed in yellow and dark brown to match the cakes, and I'd worn a matching outfit—brown leggings under an oversized yellow t-shirt that read 'Pick Brodie.' My blonde pigtails were decorated with cherries. We were totally ready to sell Brodie to the casting directors.

I held out the pan. "I brought this since I figured you guys might be hungry."

Someone in the crew immediately stepped forward and grabbed the pan, and a half-dozen hands reached into it, plucking out cupcakes. I grinned as a few exclamations of delight hit my ears, and a woman with a clipboard stepped forward, cupcake in hand. She licked a bit of frosting from her fingers, then set the cupcake down and picked up her pen.

"These are amazing. What did you say your name was?"

"Katy Short," I repeated cheerfully. "And I'm here for my brother, Brodie—"

"What do you do for a living, Katy?"

I hid my frown. Jeez. Did they have the attention span of gnats or what? I eyed the cupcake she'd set down, the marzipan "B" listing to the side. Well, hopefully when they did callbacks, they wouldn't be looking for a 'Rodie' instead of a Brodie. "I'm an accountant."

Blank stares.

Yeah. They really hadn't been paying attention. Figured. "I'm kidding," I told them. "I run an internet business called Katy's Short Cakes. I create custom cupcakes and ship them all over the country." I automatically pulled out a business card and offered it to the closest person.

The woman plucked it from my hand and glanced at it, then added it to her clipboard. "You're adorable, Katy. And sassy. We like that. So why don't you tell us about yourself?"

"Well," I drawled. "I'm here with my brother, Brodie. I'm pretty sure he's twice as sassy as me."

As if realizing for the first time that I'd mentioned him, the woman looked up from the notes on her clipboard. "There's a brother?" A knowing gleam caught in her eye and she reached over and took a bite of cupcake. She then snapped her fingers and circled her hand in the air. "Someone go find the brother."

"There's a brother," I agreed. "You're eating his 'B'. I'm here for him."

"You don't want to be on TV, Katy?"

I shrugged. "I'm more interested in launching my business. It sounds like it'd be fun enough, though." A sinking feeling began to form in the pit of my stomach. If I got cast and Brodie didn't, he'd kill me.

"How athletic are you?"

"Um." I thought for a moment. "I can carry three dozen cupcakes without breaking a sweat?"

There were titters around the cupcake box.

The casting director smiled, icing in her teeth. I automatically licked my own, hoping she'd pick up the hint. "Do you have a passport, Katy?"

I thought for a moment, then nodded. "I do. Brodie does, too."

"That's perfect," the woman said, marking something down on her clipboard. She glanced up again and yelled. "Did someone find the brother yet?"

A long, uncomfortable moment passed and I fidgeted on the stool. No one was asking more questions, but the audition tape was still rolling. Maybe this was a good sign. The fact that they were hunting down Brodie meant that they liked him, right?

Sure enough, my brother appeared a few minutes later, his blond faux-hawk noticeable next to the bald assistant that pushed him forward to stand next to me. Brodie looked excited, and I quietly crossed my fingers.

The assistant maneuvered Brodie to stand next to me.

He immediately gave me a noogie, ripping at my blonde hair with his knuckles.

I screeched and wriggled out of his arms. "You jerk!"

"Katy," Brodie said in a warning tone, the smile still on his face. "I'm just playing around."

"Then you don't mind if I kick you in the nuts when I play around?" I grumped, touching my hair. Noogies were fine and dandy—well, at least less obnoxious—when we were at home but here? In front of cameras? I was going to kill him.

Luckily, everyone laughed. "You guys are cute," the clipboard-carrier said.

Brodie automatically threw an arm around my shoulders, grinning a mega-watt smile for the cameras and dragging me back against him. "I see you all met my little sis, Katy?"

"Matching outfits," someone whispered. "They look perfect. Casting still needs a brother and sister duo, remember?"

"I know," the woman with the clipboard said smugly. Then louder, "So Brodie, you're the older brother?"

"Yes, ma'am," he said in a cheerful voice. "Katy came with me this morning to show support. She knows how badly I want to be on *Endurance Island*. We're close. Very close."

I snorted.

While Brodie and I were the typical bickering siblings, it was true about *Endurance Island*. As soon as we'd heard casting was coming to town, Brodie hadn't been able to shut up about it. This was his chance, he'd told me over and over again. Lots of reality TV stars used the show to get their foot in the door in Hollywood, and if this led him to a career in modeling or TV, he was all for it. I had my own doubts, since most of the people in reality TV shows weren't exactly killing it in show-business, but Brodie wouldn't be dissuaded.

"And you guys are local?"

"Yes, ma'am. We're from Broken Arrow, Oklahoma."

"Ever travel much?"

Brodie glanced down at me. "We had a family trip to Cancun once. Katy got so sunburned she looked like a tomato."

"He's lying," I chimed in, poking him in the gut. "I wasn't that red. And he's also neglecting to tell you about how he spent a week in London last summer, but I guess that doesn't count as 'travel' since he never made it out of the pubs."

There were a few laughs, and Brodie's arm tightened around my shoulders to an almost painful degree. Automatically, I reached over and pinched his side, like I always did when he tried to be the bossy big brother.

"Katy doesn't really want to be on *Endurance Island*," he blurted. "She's just here for me."

I pinched him again, wishing he would shut up. Where was my brother's suaveness now that the cameras were rolling? He was coming across like a tool.

"We're sorry," Clipboard Woman said. "But we've already got a couple of blond Southerners for *Endurance Island*. Casting's full."

Disappointment swept through me. Poor Brodie. He'd be heartbroken. I felt all the tension leave the arm looped over my shoulder.

"But," the woman said. "We're looking for teams for *The World Races*, and the brother-sister duo we had selected fell through at the last minute. We're currently one team short."

"*The World Races?*" Brodie asked.

"Teams?" I squeaked.

"Yes," Clipboard Woman said with enthusiasm. "We'd like for you both to come to Hollywood for a second round of casting. If you make it on the show, you'll be gone for a few weeks as you travel from location to location. It's a bit of a different dynamic than with *Endurance Island*, but it gives you a chance to see the world. What do you think?"

"A few weeks?" I echoed, my mind racing. I had orders I was waiting to fill. There was a wedding—my biggest order yet—scheduled two weeks from today and I planned on spending every moment baking and then driving the cupcakes down to Dallas before icing them to ensure that they'd be perfect. I couldn't leave for several weeks.

Brodie obviously knew where my mind was going, because his arm tightened around my shoulder again. "I'm sure I could get the time off of work."

I bit back a sarcastic remark. Of course he could. Brodie was a waiter.

"If you make it on the show, you'll automatically be paid a salary of twenty thousand dollars per team. The winning couple wins a quarter of a million dollars."

My brain froze. Wait. We got *paid* to be on TV? Twenty thousand dollars—my share would be ten grand. Ten grand would let me buy a state of the art website and some key advertising. That would make up for the bank loan I hadn't been able to get to truly launch my business.

"Shall I mark you down as interested?" Clipboard asked. "We think the two of you would be perfect. You've both got that Southern charm, you look adorable in matching outfits, and we love the brother-sister angle."

"We're in," Brodie said automatically.

"Twenty thousand dollars?" I blurted, unable to help myself.

Clipboard chuckled. "That's right."

"Sounds good to me," I told her. "When do we go to Hollywood?"

"Next weekend, if you're free."

"Oh, we're free," Brodie told her, squeezing my shoulder so tight I was pretty sure I'd have bruises. "We're definitely free."

Chapter Two

"Have to admit, I didn't see any serious competition in the other teams. Get to know them? No thanks. I'll let Tesla do that. She's the people person. I'm just the guitar." —Liam Brogan, Day 1 of The World Races

Six weeks later

MY STOMACH WAS CHURNING.

The sun was beating down overhead, my yellow shirt was blinding me, the backpack on my shoulders weighed a ton, and I was pretty sure I was going to throw up as one of the off-camera assistants pointed us toward the starting line.

"Here we go," Brodie said with excitement, shaking my arm. "This is it. Are you ready?"

"I'm going to barf if you keep shaking me," I muttered.

"You should have eaten something," Brodie said, not an ounce of sympathy in him. He put a hand to his eyes, shielding the sunlight, and watched for the other teams to arrive. "Think we're the fittest ones in the race?"

"Don't know, don't care," I told him. "We get paid the same if we come in second or dead last, except if we come in dead last, we get a three-week vacation in Acapulco." Apparently as you were kicked off of the race, you were sent to a private beach house in Acapulco so no spoilers would leak onto the internet. As soon as I'd heard that? My motivation to compete had pretty much disappeared. Money and the chance to lounge on the beach for weeks? Who wanted to sleep in airports when I could sleep in freaking Acapulco?

He shot me a nasty look, as if reading my thoughts. "Katy, you'd better race like you've never raced before, or so help me—"

I raised a hand. "I will. Just don't expect me to be excited right now, okay? The only thing I'm going to be racing for is some Pepto."

He was right, though; I should have eaten something that day. Of course, I hadn't counted on being quite so nervous.

We'd arrived for the casting call last night and had been sequestered in the hotel rooms given to us. No contact with the outside world for the next three weeks, according to our non-disclosure agreements. No cellphones, no email, nothing. I'd had to temporarily put my business on hiatus, and it rankled a bit, but I just thought of that twenty grand. I'd make it up to the customers I'd disappointed somehow.

As soon as we'd woken up that morning, we'd been dragged into a whirlwind of preparations for the show. A casting assistant had been assigned to us and had gone over our bags one more time, removing every-thing that might interfere with 'the experience.' No sunglasses. No hats unless approved first by the network. No clothing except the mandatory gear they'd given us. One backpack apiece. No food or drink, nothing that would set off airport security, and for me, no bright lipsticks. They'd even gone so far as to assign me a hairstyle—the two dorky pigtails I'd worn for the initial casting call. They wanted to create a 'look,' they'd told us. We were characters on a show, and characters needed a memorable look. It was in the contracts, and I'd had no choice but to comply. My look, unfortu-nately, seemed to be backwoods cowgirl.

That was probably my fault. Stupid pigtails at the audition.

Our clothing was not so bad. The show had an athletic sponsor, and so everything we wore was branded with the same logo, right down to my sports bra and panties. Each team was assigned several shirts with the name written across the back, and a color for their team. Brodie and I were yellow, and I had black leggings with a yellow racing stripe, a yellow t-shirt with KATY written in big letters across the back, a matching hoodie, and a puffy yellow jacket for colder climates.

Once we'd been patted down, we were dragged to pre-show interviews. The network itself took at least an hour's worth of interview footage with me, one with me and Brodie together, and then we'd been rushed around to a few different radio and TV press junkets for use in the future.

And then we were dashed into a sedan and drove to where we currently stood—a football stadium. Not just any stadium, but the Cowboys Stadium. Row after row of seating loomed over us as we walked out onto the field, cameramen circling us.

We stopped in the end zone, like we'd been instructed, and waited for the other teams to slowly trickle out. We were the first ones on the field, which would give us a prime opportunity to gawk at the other teams as they arrived. Nearby, cameramen tested their equipment while others filmed us for intro shots. In the distance, the host sat in a director's chair getting his makeup touched up.

I already wanted to collapse from nerves. Who knew that a game would be so stressful?

Brodie nudged my arm again. "Look. Here comes the first team."

I couldn't help but look, since Brodie was trying to drive his elbow into my upper arm. We'd marathon-watched the two previous seasons of *The World Races* to try and figure out the kinds of people they were going to cast as our opponents. Like casting had mentioned, they definitely had a type of character they liked to cast: newlyweds, guy best friends, girl best friends (which they wanted to hook up with the guy best friends, naturally), a dating couple, siblings, a child-parent relationship, a gay couple, a D-list celebrity couple of some kind, and then a 'comic relief' couple. Sometimes the comic relief was a pair of rednecks. Sometimes they were nerds. They always did terrible in the challenges, since they weren't picked for athleticism.

Sometimes the team dynamics overlapped. The comic relief could be siblings, and then that would leave room for another couple or another celebrity or something. I was told from a gushy assistant that the producers liked to mix things up a little, but they stuck to stereotypes overall. We were creating a 'story,' she reminded me.

Like I was going to be able to forget? Characters. Story. Everyone in casting mentioned it every five minutes.

"Girl besties," Brodie murmured at my side. "Or lesbians. They look pretty strong."

"Way to be a creep, Brodie. Now *you* sound like casting." But I admit, I tried to figure out their stereotype, too. They *did* look strong. I didn't recognize them, which meant they weren't the celebrities, so they had to be the female best friends team. One wore a shirt that said 'Summer' and the other said 'Polly.'

They stood at a marked spot a fair distance from us, and the next team came out.

"Here's someone else. They're obviously mother and son," Brodie told me, nudging me and staring at a couple walking in behind the two female athletes. 'Wendi' and 'Rick' were easy to pick out, I decided. Wendi had gray hair and a matronly figure, and Rick, well, Rick was a skinny kid with long hair in his face, big glasses, and skinny jeans. The entire effect was supposed to make him look trendy, but it just made him look incredibly awkward instead.

More teams flooded out of the entrance, pair by pair. We saw Hal and Stefan, dressed in flaming pink shirts, holding hands as they walked in. Cute. I liked them already. Then there was a pair of blondes with enormous hair and loud voices that talked with their hands—Steffi and Cristi. Myrna and Fred were the elderly couple, though they looked pretty fit despite the white hair. There were a pair of alpha males named Joel and Derron that went into a military stance as soon as they arrived, which made Brodie frown. My brother didn't like competition, and that pair looked like they'd be tough to beat.

I was relieved to see a man and a woman with matching mullets, cowboy boots, tight Wranglers, and kelly green team shirts. Kissy and Rusty. Thank god. The comic relief wasn't us.

"Hey, isn't that Dean Woodall?" Brodie leaned in to my ear. "The Olympian?"

I perked up. I'd seen him on TV before. "You think so?"

"Yeah. Not happy about that. They sure did cast a lot of athletic people this year."

"I think he's retired," I told Brodie. I remembered him from *Endurance Island* last year. I'd been addicted to the TV, fascinated by the romance that played out between him and a fellow contestant. Sure enough, Abby was at Dean's side, dressed in a purple shirt to match his. Her curly hair was pulled into a loose ponytail on top of her head and when they came into line, Dean's arm went around her waist. Double cute. They were clearly the newlyweds *and* the celebrities.

Or so I thought.

"Holy shit."

I tore my gaze away from Dean and Abby to glance at my brother, Brodie. "What now?"

"The celebrities," Brodie breathed, staring down the field. "Holy shit, they got *Finding Threnody*."

"Huh?" The name sounded vaguely familiar, but I was more of a country girl. I was short and couldn't see around Brodie, since he'd moved and was now standing directly in front of me and blocking my view. "Who's *Finding Threnody*? It's a band?"

"They're huge," he told me. "Don't you know the song 'Dark Stars?' 'Worm in the Apple?'"

Um, okay. "Doesn't sound like my kind of thing. I don't like rock." When he paced in front of me again, I pinched his arm. "Stand still, damn it. You're not a freaking window."

Brodie sighed and moved back a step, giving me my view. Of course, it wasn't an unobstructed view, because the camera crew was hovering around them as they sauntered down the field, toward the starting line. It was clear that they were designated to be stars of the show. That was fine with me. I studied them. Both were wearing black as their team color, and the woman had hair that was dyed black with bright red ends. Her nose was pierced and she had small tattoos along her neck and sleeving her arms. The man had lip piercings, eyebrow piercings, and his arms were just as heavily tatted as hers. The man frowned at the group, while the woman gave us all an arch smile.

Their t-shirts read LIAM and TESLA.

Of course. Total rock star names. I could feel myself giving a mental eye roll as the woman sauntered up to the starting line and stuck her hip out, revealing jeans covered in chains and zippers. Naturally. "I can tell you right now I'll be glad when they're gone," I told Brodie. I'd taken an instant dislike to the two rockers. Maybe it was their attitudes, or the way the cameras crawled all around them, but they didn't seem to have the fun sort of spirit that the others brought. Hell, even Dean and Abby—who I'd thought were the celebrities this round—had seemed genuinely excited to be here.

Those two? Just acted a bit like they were slumming it to be around the rest of us. Which got on my nerves. Contrary to what everyone thinks about country girls, I'm not the most friendly and open type. I may have my hair in pigtails and wear jean shorts, but that's as far as the stereotype goes. You've got to prove yourself to me before I like you. And right now? Liam and Tesla were on my 'do not like' list until proven otherwise.

I glanced around, but no one else was coming out of the stadium. I quietly counted teams as the cameras did another pan of us lined up on the starting line, scoping each other out. Ten teams. Ten men, ten women. I wouldn't be the fastest woman, I guessed, judging by the competition, but I wouldn't be the slowest, either, so that was fine with me. And Brodie was fit. Our odds were decent.

"*Makeup*! It's hot as piss out here and my forehead is shining. Where's the goddamn makeup artist?"

All eyes immediately turned in the direction of the angry voice. My jaw dropped a little as I saw Chip Brubaker, the normally smiling host of this show and *Endurance Island*. As I watched him stalk down the field, he grabbed a powder puff out of a woman's hand and dabbed at his forehead. "When I say makeup, you come running. Understand?" he yelled again.

I leaned in and told Brodie, "Guess his smiles are just for the camera." I saw Abby roll her eyes at the host's antics.

Chip finished patting down his face, examined it in the mirror held up for him, and then strode past the scurrying assistants. Someone pointed for him to stand on an X marked on the grass, and he did. As soon as he stepped there, it was like a light switch was flipped. His face lit up in a friendly smile and he grinned at us as if we were his new best friends. Cameramen immediately circled, filming.

"Welcome to *The World Races*! I'm your host, Chip Brubaker, and you're about to undertake an incredible journey around the globe." He spread his arms in a magnificent gesture. "You'll travel to exotic locations and foreign countries, competing against each other for a quarter of a million dollar prize."

We cheered and clapped appropriately at that. Brodie was getting excited. He bounced on his feet in place, which was just making me anxious. I clutched the straps of my heavy backpack and concentrated on Chip as he rattled off the rules of the game. Blah blah find a clue, perform a challenge to win a *World Games* disk. Each teammate had to compete to win an individual disk and then there was a team disk. Once you had all three disks, you could advance to the finish line for that round. It was the same as it was every year.

"This time on *The World Races*," Chip said, and then gave an ominous pause. "We're switching the rules up on you a bit. The team that conquers the first country on our map? Wins an Ace in the Hole." He held up a big, obviously fake looking Ace of Spades that was larger than a sheet of paper. "This ace will allow that team to save one other team at any point in the game."

"Why would we want to do that?" I hissed at Brodie under my breath. "I thought the object was to get rid of everyone else?"

He shrugged and gave me a 'shut up' look.

"You can use this ace to your advantage and save a team you're allied with," Chip said. "Or not. The choice is yours. There will only be two aces in the entire game."

The cameras suddenly swiveled again, startling me. All but one began to film our reactions as Chip raised his hand in the air.

"Are you ready to begin *The World Races*?" Chip bellowed. "At the far end of this stadium, you'll find that the opposite end zone is covered with hundreds of footballs. Ten of these footballs are numbered, and the number you get pertains to your airline seat. Only teams one, two and three will be on the first flight out. Good luck! May the best team win!"

Nervous butterflies began to sprout in my stomach.

Chip lowered his arm. "GO!"

We ran.

BRODIE WAS THE FIRST ONE AT THE MASSIVE FIELD OF FOOTBALLS, AND I wanted to cheer my brother on. I stumbled early, twisting my ankle, and yelped in surprise. I recovered quickly and limped over to the footballs, the last one to arrive. Ignoring the cameras that hovered like vultures, I stared at the others as they pushed forward. People were tossing their packs aside and grabbing footballs like they were covered in gold.

Okay, clearly I'd missed out on the memo that told us we had to act like insane people.

I picked my way forward and kicked aside a football, looking for a number.

"Hurry it up, Katy!" Brodie bellowed at me. "Flip them and flip them fast!"

I sighed and shrugged off my backpack, tossing it aside and then diving into the fray. People were shoving and pushing like wild animals. I charged into the fray, grabbing the first football and flipping it over. Nada. I tossed it back down to the ground and headed for the next. And when that one was blank, the next. And the next.

"I got six," someone called. Another team yelled out their number—nine—and were less excited. No one wanted a high number.

I grimly picked up football after football, looking for a number amidst the chaos. I'd probably flipped about twenty footballs and dodged the other pushy contestants (and rolling balls) when I noticed one sitting alone at the back of the field, clearly overlooked. I could see a hint of white behind the football stand and a clench in my stomach told me that this was a numbered ball. Perfect!

As soon as I began to run for it, the rocker guy did too. Frowning, I picked up the pace, running faster. He didn't slow down. That son of a bitch had seen it and was going to race me for it.

We both dove for it at the same time. I landed on the ball, triumph rolling through me.

He landed on top of me.

The air blew out of my lungs. I groaned, wheezing, even as the ball popped out from under me and launched into the air a foot.

It bounced once. The rocker rolled off of me and neatly plucked it from the ground.

I remained on the ground, struggling to breathe.

He moved to stand over me and offered a hand down, ball tucked under his arm.

I slapped it away, my chest burning with the need for air.

He looked down at me a moment longer, shrugged, then flipped the football in his hand. "I got number two," he called out. Somewhere in the distance, I heard his partner squeal with delight.

Damn it! That jerk had just stolen second place from me. I clutched my ribs and groaned, forcing myself to my feet. A camera hovered nearby, no doubt catching my black scowl as I staggered to the next football and began to flip.

The field was clearing out as teams departed. Brodie trotted up to me, a football in hand. "I can't believe he stole number two from you. You should have fought him."

I rubbed my ribs. "Thanks for asking, Brodie. I'm fine."

He raked a hand through his hair, clearly frustrated. "Sorry, Katy. You ok? Seriously? Want me to get a medic or something?"

"No. I just need to suck it up. My pride smarts more than anything." I nodded at the football under his arm. "What's that one?

"I found number ten," he told me, disgruntled. "Keep flipping and maybe we can find something better."

I rubbed my ribs one more time. "'Kay."

More teams departed around us, and after about five minutes, I looked up and realized that the team that had found the number nine was handing in their football to Chip Brubaker. That left just us on the field. We were stuck with number ten. Brodie straightened and tossed aside the football he'd just picked up, as if coming to the same conclusion.

The race had just started, and we were already last.

Chapter Three

"Some of these people are stronger than they look. That short blonde with the pigtails? She looks all sweet and innocent, but she's scrappy as hell. The brother's kind of a jackass, though. I hope they go home soon." —Liam Brogan, Greenland Leg of The World Races

To my surprise, when we got to the airport and purchased our tickets, we found all the other teams seated at the terminal, still waiting and looking not too happy about it.

"Good," Brodie said under his breath. "We're caught up."

We couldn't really be caught up if nothing had happened yet. Something wasn't quite right. I watched as Brodie bee-lined for Tesla and Liam, and then proceeded to greet and smile at everyone else. He jumped right into the throng of people, clearly forgetting about his little sister, who wasn't quite as extroverted as him.

I hung on the fringes of the group, then glanced around, deciding to get answers on my own. Another person was hanging back from the boisterous group—Abby. Dean's wife and the woman from *Endurance Island*. Luckily for me, she was the only person I was even halfway interested in chatting with. I headed toward her. "Hey. What happened? Why's everyone still here?"

She smiled over at me and waved a hand at the empty flight attendant stand in front of the rows of seats. "Air Iceland doesn't fly out until the morning, and we all hit Reykjavik at the same time. From there, the charter flights are staggered, but it looks like we're starting this race all grouped together." She shrugged and stuck out her hand. "It'll give us a good chance to get to know each other. I'm Abby."

"I know," I said with a grin. "I saw you on *Endurance Island* last year."

She groaned. "You probably saw way too much of me, then. I swear, I'm never going to live that down." She thumbed a gesture at her spouse a short distance away. "That's Dean, though I guess that was easy to figure out."

"I do. I'm Katy." I pointed at my brother, who was shaking hands with the black-dressed duo. "That's my brother, Brodie."

"Ah, the brother-sister team." She nodded, as if this answered some things for her.

"That's us."

She glanced over at me. "Not sure why we're sharing names. We're practically tattooed with them." She gestured at the bold ABBY written across the chest of her shirt. "They think viewers won't remember who's who unless they brand us."

I chuckled at that. Abby didn't seem dazzled by all of this, and I liked that about her. "We can at least try and be normal about it." I studied her. "I'm kind of surprised to see you and Dean here. I thought after watching *Endurance Island* that you guys were done with this sort of thing."

She sighed, as if suffering. "I thought so, too. But we do strange things for love." Her gaze warmed and she watched Dean's back with affection. "It's not so bad, though. At least in this, no one can backstab us out of the game." As a cameraman circled close, she grimaced. "Though I can't say I missed that aspect of things much."

I didn't blame her. It was getting a little weird for me, too. I carefully stepped aside as a cameraman zoomed past and headed for Liam, Brodie and Tesla. I guessed they were more exciting than we were. "You're old hat at this sort of thing. Any advice for me?"

Abby tilted her head, thinking. After a moment, she gave a calculating grin and leaned in. "Make good TV."

"Good TV?"

"Yep," she said, and flipped one of my perky pigtails. I flushed at that— she must have guessed that it hadn't been my hairdo of choice. "Make good

TV," she repeated again. "Dean doesn't believe me, but I know I'm right. You make good TV and the producers will tweak things to go in your favor so you last longer. Not all of the challenges are random."

Interesting. As we stood there, I heard Brodie burst out into a wild laugh, and it was joined by Tesla's flirty one. I glanced over at them and they seemed to be having a grand old time. Well, except for Liam, who was ignoring my brother as Brodie proceeded to make a fool of himself all over Tesla. Liam stared out the window onto the tarmac, his fingers drumming a beat on the bag across his lap, as if he were writing a song.

"Looks like your brother's already decided he wants to make good TV," Abby commented. "Unless he's wrangling for an alliance with them."

I snorted. "He's more likely trying to get her phone number." Though I did frown a little in Brodie's direction as Tesla flipped her red and black hair and giggled at whatever my brother was saying. We were *not* about to ally with those two. Not when the guitar-playing jerk had knocked me to the ground and stolen my number. Forget that. I glanced back at Abby. "I don't want to ally with them."

"Well," she told me in a low voice. "You look harmless and you're not hamming it up for the camera, so you're on my good side. We could always have a private alliance just between us two. Help each other out if we get the chance and all." She raised a pinky in my direction.

I locked mine with hers and grinned. "Now you're talking. Us wall-flowers can stick together."

She laughed. "I knew there was a reason I liked you."

ABBY AND I ENDED UP CHATTING FOR HOURS OFF TO ONE SIDE AS THE others played social butterflies—including her husband, Dean. She didn't seem to mind that, though. She was relaxed and comfortable in her own skin, and it showed. Dean didn't ignore Abby the way Brodie did me, though. He flirted with her, teased her, brought her snacks, and pulled her into his lap when the seating area got full. She would give me tolerant looks, as if she were enduring this for his sake, but there was a constant smile on her face and a glow to her that bespoke happiness.

Me, I was content to people-watch and chat with Abby. People came up and slowly introduced themselves, but I let Brodie be the chatty, friendly one. That was what he was good at. The others were nice enough, though, and I chatted with all of them while we waited for our flight. The strong girl team? I learned Summer and Polly were Olympic beach volleyball players. The strong guy team, Joel and Derron, were vets from Afghanistan. Hal and Stefan were the other guy team, both TV weathermen and married to each other.

And after Brodie had gotten to know everyone, he zoomed right back to Tesla's side. She seemed to take all his attention with a pleasant smile, and I couldn't tell if she was just tolerating Brodie, or if she was genuinely interested in him.

Her bandmate was sitting right there, so it was awkward for me to watch Brodie hit on her right in front of him. Were Tesla and Liam in a relationship? I guessed not, but I had no way of knowing. He glanced over at Tesla and Brodie occasionally, but seemed bored by them.

Actually, he seemed bored by pretty much everything—cameras, teams, airport, you name it. He ignored everyone. He just put a pair of earbuds in, listened to music, and stared out the window. I thought I was kind of unfriendly, but out of all the racers, he was the only one that hadn't come by to say hello.

And I certainly wasn't about to go over and get friendly with him.

"Flight 1222 to Reykjavik, now boarding," an airline attendant said in a smooth voice, interrupting the hum of voices.

I yawned, remaining in my seat as everyone else leapt to their feet. I had never understood the rush to get onto the plane. After all, seats were assigned. It wasn't like shoving to the front of the line changed your priority. So I sat and waited for the crowd to disperse and for Brodie to reappear.

After a few minutes, the sea of legs cleared and I noticed only two people still sat, waiting for the congested crowd to disperse. Me, and Liam. I ignored him, getting to my feet and shrugging back on my heavy backpack.

Brodie returned to my side in a cheery mood. "Isn't this awesome? We're on our way to our first destination!"

"It's pretty exciting." I studied my brother as we got to the back of the line. Tesla had moved to Liam's side and was nudging him with one of her metal-covered boots. "You didn't make an alliance with them, did you?"

"Tesla and I talked about it," Brodie told me. "They're in second place, so it'd be smart."

"Brodie Short," I hissed at him. "Did you or did you not see that guitar-playing asshole knock me to the ground and steal second place from me?"

"I'm sure it was a mistake," Brodie said easily. My brother had zero killer instinct. "And Tesla told me that Liam was pretty remorseful about it."

"So remorseful he didn't even bother to come over and apologize? Oh, I'm sure he's just dripping with regret," I snapped back to him.

"He can hear you," Brodie told me in a low voice.

I glanced over and saw both Tesla and Liam staring in my direction. Tesla seemed to be amused, but Liam was impossible to read. For some reason, that just made me more irritated. "I know they're listening," I said, in an even louder voice. "And in case they didn't catch it all, I said, *the guitar-playing asshole knocked me to the ground and stole second place.*"

I was so loud everyone turned and stared. The look Liam shot my way could have withered foliage. And cameras swung in my direction.

Brodie shushed me again.

I elbowed him. "Why are you taking their side? I'm your partner!"

"You're my sister," Brodie said, and reached out to rub a noogie in my blonde pigtails.

I yelped and backed away from him.

"You're also holding up the line," Tesla called from the back.

I danced away from Brodie's grasp and we pushed forward with our passports and tickets.

The plane was a big one, though because of the rules of the game, we couldn't fly anything but coach. Since we had last-minute bookings, we ended up with whatever seats were available—which meant the ones that no one else wanted. Single seats spread all over the plane, and middle seats.

Brodie and I were split apart. Brodie was somewhere in the back, and I was a middle seat towards the middle of the plane. I stuffed my enormous backpack into one of the overhead compartments and sat in my seat, twitching nervously at the sight of the two empty seats next to me. Maybe neither one would be filled and I could relax on the flight. It was going to be a long one—over ten hours in the air.

An elderly man came and sat in the aisle seat, squashing my hopes of having my small row to myself. I closed my eyes and rested my head on the headrest of my seat while waiting for the plane to take off as people milled around us, pushing bags into overhead bins and getting comfortable.

Just as I started to get comfortable, the man to my left got up to let someone else in. I blinked awake, and looked up in horror at Liam's unsmiling face.

He pointed at the empty window seat next to me. "That's the guitar-playing asshole's seat."

I ground my teeth and said nothing. Instead, I simply got out of the row and gestured for him to enter. He did, and I could immediately tell that it was going to be an issue. For one, Liam was tall. His arms and legs barely fit into the small, squeezed seat, and he practically oozed into my middle seat. Nostrils flaring with irritation, I ignored it. He didn't want to sit next to me, either, after all.

I sat back down in my seat with a thump and buckled in.

Next to me, Liam stretched, and his elbow practically jostled me in the side. To my left, the elderly man slid his shoes off, then proceeded to unbutton his pants. After they were undone, he gave a sigh of pleasure and leaned back, as if to go to sleep.

And the damn plane hadn't even taken off yet.

It was going to be a long, long flight.

ONCE WE LANDED IN KEFLAVIK AIRPORT, THE AIRPORT WAS A MESS OF running, shoving people. Brightly-colored shirts paired up as soon as they got off the plane and ran through the terminal, heading for the charter flight that would take us to Greenland. Brodie and I had to wait as the Rednecks and the Rockers got on the first flight out, thanks to their footballs.

We were stuck in the back of the pack with Myrna and Fred, the elderly couple who'd had the misfortune to get the other high number. They were nice enough, but conversation was kind of awkward, and Brodie wasn't his normal super-chatty self. I knew why—he didn't see them as someone worth allying with. He didn't think they were strong. And I wasn't the social one on our team, so it was a long wait.

Eventually, our chartered flight arrived, and we took the tiny airplane to Kulusuk in Greenland. As soon as we landed, Brodie shoved my backpack in my hands and we dashed down the stairs, pushing ahead of Myrna and Fred. I tried not to feel bad—it was a race, after all. We'd gotten our coats out while the flight was going, and had zipped up in anticipation of the cold weather.

The airport was ridiculously small, the tarmac covered with snow. The terminal itself seemed about the size of a one-room gymnasium. Directly behind it, steep mountains rose. From the other side, the icy water of the bay rippled.

Standing in front of the terminal was a man in an enormous fur-lined parka, holding a flag emblazoned with The World Races logo and standing on a *World Games* mat. Camera crews swarmed the area, filming as we tromped down the steps of the airplane and crossed the snowy tarmac. It was bitterly cold, the wintry breeze biting through the layers of clothing that I wore.

"Come on, Katy," Brodie encouraged, racing ahead of me despite the snow and ice on the tarmac. I followed at a slower pace, holding onto my enormous backpack. I wasn't as big as Brodie, and it was a hefty load for someone of my stature to carry. Not that my brother noticed—he dashed to the race station ahead of me and then shot me impatient looks until I caught up.

As soon as I stepped onto the mat, the man in the coat held out a disk. "Welcome to Kulusuk," he said, his accent thick. He smiled, his weathered face friendly, and I smiled back.

Brodie snatched the disk from him and raced to the side so he could study it, turning away.

I gave the man an embarrassed look, thanked him, and then followed Brodie. We'd have to have a talk about manners after this leg was done. There was playing a game, and then there was just flat-out rude.

Brodie was reading the writing on the back of the disk without me. I peered over his shoulder, but couldn't see anything, so I poked my brother in the side. "Hello, partner over here?"

He glanced at me, then finished reading the disk and handed it to me reluctantly. The front was the logo of The World Races, a bright grid in the shape of a globe and the name of the show. I flipped it over and read it aloud. "Go to the sled rentals in Kulusuk—"

Brodie jogged in place, clearly ready to get going. "Are you done? Come on. You can read it on the way there."

I ignored him and kept reading. "—You'll receive a map and a dog team. From there, drive your dog sled out to the marked location on the map. Individual challenges will follow." I squinted up at the snow-covered mountains nearby. "A dog sled, huh? Should be interesting."

"Should be fun," Brodie said, with a huge grin on his face. "Come on!"

We didn't see a taxi waiting for us, so we hiked into town. It wasn't far from the airport, though the ground was rocky and covered with snow. The village spread out before us like something from a movie, and I was fascinated. This was really damn cool.

"Come on, Katy," Brodie yelled back at me, trotting a good distance ahead. "This is a race!"

I gritted my teeth. Okay. Brodie kind of sucked as a partner. He acted like I was a liability instead of his sister. I knew my brother was competitive, but this was getting annoying. "I'm coming," I yelled back at him.

When we found the dog sled place, we didn't see any other teams. Oh no. That was a bad sign. There were only two sleds left, which meant Myrna and Fred were the only ones behind us. I tried not to worry as an attendant led us to our dogsled and began to explain how to sit on it and how to drive, and how to control the dogs. He'd be riding with us, he explained, but both Brodie and I would have to drive the sled for a distance.

I sat on the sled first, while Brodie volunteered to drive us out of town.

"How far are we behind the other teams?" Brodie asked immediately.

"Bout a half hour," the man told us. "Some of them had trouble with their dogs."

I tried not to look excited at that. Brodie didn't even try. "Hold on," he called out, getting in the musher's spot on the sled as I clung to the blankets piled onto me. "We're going to try and make up some time." He turned to face the dogs. "MUSH!"

The sled leapt to life and I clung to my seat, praying Brodie wouldn't get us killed.

WE PASSED TWO TEAMS ON THE WAY TO THE NEXT LOCATION.

One had stopped to look at their map, and the other was struggling with the sled itself. Brodie whooped and hollered at the sight, drawing their attention with his loud cheers. I cringed again at my brother's thoughtlessness. The way he was acting was totally going to bite us in the ass if he wasn't careful.

We switched out drivers at the halfway point, and I clung to the sled as the dogs leapt to action. The other teams were now behind us—following us, Brodie told me—but it didn't matter as long as they were behind. I mushed the hell out of the dogs, leaning in to the sled to give us as much advantage as possible. The cold wind whipped at my face, chapping it underneath the goggles the race had given us, but I didn't care. We were catching up!

In the distance, I spotted a splash of color—The World Races flag. I drove toward it, then began to apply the brakes on my sled, slowing the dogs down. As we approached, I saw an encampment. Ten igloos were set up in a line, and cameramen dotted the area. I saw another flag and mat, and then two areas that had been roped off for challenges.

We were here, and we weren't in last place. Things were looking up. "This must be where we're doing the individual challenges," I shouted into the wind, leaning forward.

"Brake," Brodie called, pumping his arm with excitement. "Brake! I see the flag!"

The sled stopped, and we leapt off, handing control over to our guide. As we struggled to put our backpacks on, we sprinted for the check-in point. Waiting under The World Races flag was an Inuit man dressed in traditional clothing, and he looked a heck of a lot warmer than we were. He held our next *World Games* disk out for us.

Brodie automatically snatched it and began to read, and I was left to try and peek around my brother's shoulder once more.

"Two challenges," he read aloud even as I tugged his arm out of my way. "Both are traditional Thule tasks. One team member must show their strength on the water, and the other must demonstrate strength in the belly. Choose your task and good luck."

The Inuit man moved to one side and gestured at the sign he was standing in front of. Two arrows pointed in opposite directions, a crossroads of sorts. One bright green arrow said 'Thule Meal' and the other said 'Thule Craft.'

Brodie peered at the water in the distance. "Thule Craft looks like a kayak of some kind."

I took the disk from him, studying it. "And the other one's clearly a gross food challenge. Which one do you want to do?"

He turned and looked behind us. "I see two more teams on the horizon. Whatever we do, we need to do it sooner rather than later."

"All the others ahead of us must be here," I told him. "So they might still be doing the other challenges. We have a chance to catch up." In the distance, I could see a long wall of snow that had been packed high, preventing anyone from looking around it. A cameraman hovered nearby, obviously filming something.

"We need to decide." Brodie said impatiently. "Can you eat?"

"I guess so," I told him, steeling myself. "Though if I have to eat fish guts, I'm going to kick your ass when we get home."

He grinned and ruffled my hair. "I'll kayak, then. This thing says to return here once we've completed both tasks and gotten our tokens, so we'll meet back here when we're done. Sound good?"

I nodded, tucking the disk under my arm. "Good luck!"

Brodie dashed off towards the distant shore, his yellow coat bright against the sea of white snow. He followed a marked path and disappeared out of sight a moment later.

Time for me to do my challenge, too. Ugh. I was not looking forward to chowing down on whatever horrors they could come up with. I glanced at the sign, and followed the arrows that said 'Thule Meal.' There was a path dug into the snow, and I raced forward, clutching the disk in hand.

Sure enough, the marked path led behind that thick snow wall I'd seen earlier. I could hear some odd sounds as I approached, my cameraman dogging on my heels as I headed toward the task. When I turned the corner at the wall, the sounds of retching hit my ears just as a horrible, overwhelming fishy smell hit my nose.

Oh…gross.

There was a table marked with a flag, and I headed there. An Inuit woman nodded her head at me and handed me another disk. I flipped it over, reading the instructions. *Choose a banquet table. You will be dining on an Inuit delicacy that has been popular for thousands of years, dating back to the days when the Thule lived in Greenland—a dish called mukluk. Mukluk is whale blubber still attached to the skin. Sometimes it is eaten raw, sometimes cooked. You will have a chance to sample both cooked and uncooked versions.*

My stomach heaved a little at the thought.

Select your table and begin eating. You must clean both bowls before the judge will hand you your challenge disk. If you need to get sick, a bucket has been provided under your table.

Oh dear. I clutched the disk to my chest, scanning the competition area. Sure enough, ten folding tables had been set up in the snow, covered with a red tablecloth edged with traditional designs. On the center of each table, two bowls had been heaped high with…stuff.

Five of the tables had someone seated in front of them, eating slowly. The sixth table had someone bent over their bucket, clearly puking.

I counted heads. Six people at the challenge. Three teams behind us. That meant…everyone was still here. Holy shit, we'd caught up. It was probably planned that way by the race organizers for additional drama, but I didn't care. We weren't dead last.

I headed for the closest open table—next to the puker—and sat down at the folding chair there. A napkin had been left on the table and I folded it in my lap. There was a water bottle at my feet, in case I wanted a drink.

I pulled the first bowl close to me and took a look at it.

It was…not good. The mukluk had been carved into chunks, and each chunk was two different colors—dark on top, and white on the bottom. I guessed the white was the fat, since it was shiny and glistened. I swallowed hard. This must have been the raw food, right? I leaned in and sniffed the bowl, while the person next to me got sick again. I glanced over, frowning, just as the puker sat up and leaned back in his chair.

It was Liam, the rocker.

Ha! I tried not to smile at his misery, since I was probably going to be in the same state pretty soon, but it was clear that Liam couldn't hold down his mukluk. Both bowls in front of him were less than halfway gone, and he'd probably gotten there a lot earlier than everyone else. His complexion was tinged an unpleasant green.

He looked over at me, and must have noticed me studying him, because he scowled darkly in my direction.

So I grinned. And popped the first piece of mukluk into my mouth just to fuck with him.

Immediately, I regretted that choice. Mukluk was awful. The taste was something like super fatty, slimy sushi, and it had a texture like gristle. It was cold on my tongue, and it smelled worse than anything. I shivered and forced myself to swallow the piece, then reached for a piece of the cooked mukluk. It wasn't nearly as bad, though still pretty foul.

I alternated pieces, gagging between each one. Every few minutes, to my side, Liam would make a quiet heaving noise and then proceed to grab his bucket, which only made my stomach turn a bit more. I began to hum to myself to drown him out, grabbing pieces of mukluk and eating as fast as I could.

There was a lot of damn mukluk in the bowl. Soon, my entire mouth tasted like fish, and all I could smell was the scent of slightly-turned mukluk. I held my nose for a few pieces, and then decided to just suck it up and cram a piece of cooked mukluk in with the raw and chew fast. The taste was still awful, but it helped masked the slimy gristle-texture, and so I kept pairing and swigging with water.

It wasn't a fast process. Even as I ate, I saw one of the girls on the end get up, stagger toward the judge, and was handed her token. Abby. She'd finished the challenge first.

She headed off into the snow, likely to meet up with her partner Dean. That was okay, I told myself. Everyone else was still here. I crammed more mukluk into my mouth, eating as fast as I could. It was pretty awful, but I'd had worse at culinary school when we had to taste our own experimental dishes. I could hear someone else get sick nearby, and it made my stomach roil uncomfortably, but I ignored it and kept eating. I crammed my mouth full of mukluk and glanced down the tables at my competition.

Liam had his head down on his table, clearly trying to compose himself. He hadn't eaten another bite in several minutes. Others picked at their food, gagging at the taste or the texture. I continued to sandwich mine between the less slimy pieces and drank lots of water, glancing at the people that had just sat down. I was doing all right.

I grabbed the last piece at the bottom of my bowl and choked it down, ignoring the fish smell and the way it felt in my mouth. Almost done. I stared up at the clear blue sky overhead as I chewed, willing myself not to barf and ruin this. Gristle and fat squished between my teeth as I chewed.

And chewed.

And chewed.

Then, I reached into the bowl for the next piece...and there was no more. I was done. I jumped to my feet, flipped the bowls over, and trotted over to the judge.

He handed me my disk, and I gave him a nod of thanks, then ran down the path.

I started out jogging, but as soon as I did, my stomach gave a sick little gurgle, and I had to slow down. Sure enough, my mouth filled with saliva, and I paused on the side of the snowy trail to puke my guts out.

Mukluk splashed all over my shoes and the snow, and I grimaced, moaning at how awful I felt. I had to keep going, I told myself. We were in second place right now. I couldn't let anyone else pass me. Dragging myself forward, I headed down the marked path, following the trail.

Over a crest, I saw a finish line ahead. Each race always had a mini finish line set up, complete with waving flags and a tape that you could break through. The tape was still unbroken.

Two people milled by the tape, waiting for their partners. One was Abby, clutching her stomach...and the other was Brodie. Holy shit, where was

Dean?

Brodie gave a whoop of delight and a jump when he saw me, racing for me. "Come on, Katy! We're in first place!" He grabbed me and began to drag me forward, toward the tape. My stomach roiled in protest.

I staggered with him across the finish line, and we landed in front of Chip Brubaker, who stood below a colorful *World Games* flag. "Brodie and Katy," he said with a beaming smile. "Congratulations on being the first team for the Greenland leg of the race!"

"We did it," Brodie yelled, and grabbed me and spun me around. "You did fuckin' awesome, Katy!"

My stomach gurgled again. "Put me down, Brodie," I whispered. He did, and I sank to the ground, resting my cheek in the snow. Blessed, blessed snow. I was pretty sure I was going to puke again.

Overhead, I heard Chip talking to Brodie. "Here is your prize for winning the Greenland leg—an Ace. You can use this Ace to save another team at any time in the game."

"Great," Brodie said enthusiastically.

"Pepto," I moaned, clutching my stomach. "My kingdom for Pepto."

Brodie came to my side and thumped me on the back, hard. "We did awesome, Katy! I totally smoked everyone in the kayak race."

I gave him a weak thumbs up, still sitting on the ground.

A moment later, Dean and Abby trotted up to take second place. Abby looked as green as I felt, and collapsed next to me in the snow a moment later.

"You puke?" She asked breathlessly.

I held up two fingers. "Twice."

She nodded. "Me too."

Taking a cue from us, our partners sat nearby. One of the cameramen pointed us off to the side, indicating that we should get out of his shot, so we all sat on a nearby snow bank, drinking bottled water to settle our stomachs and watching other teams arrive. The girl Olympians were third, and not too far behind Abby and Dean. Over the next hour, the other teams crossed the finish line, pair by pair.

Last to arrive? Tesla and Liam. I felt a twinge of pity for Liam, who looked a bit like death warmed over. He was sweaty and pale, and clearly had not done well in his challenge. Tesla looked unhappy with her partner, annoyance stamped over her pretty features. Her arms were crossed over her chest as they came to the finish line.

"Tesla and Liam, you are the team that has finished last," Chip said in a dramatic voice. "Unless someone wishes to use their ace to save you, you will be eliminated from The World Races."

I snorted. Not likely.

To my horror, Brodie stood up, brandishing the sealed envelope that had been marked as our prize. "I'll use the Ace."

Chapter Four

"That douchebag just fucked me, all because he wanted to sleep with my partner. What? No cussing? Fine. That jerk just dicked over his sister and me. What? I can't say dicked on camera either? Come on." —Liam Brogan, Ireland Leg of The World Races

"**W**HAT THE FUCK, BRODIE?" I CALLED, STAGGERING TO MY FEET.
Chip plucked the Ace from Brodie's hand, brandishing it triumphantly. "And we have our first Ace of the game in use! Yellow team is going to use it to save the black team! That makes this round a non-elimination round!"

My jaw dropped. "Wait, don't we have to vote on this?" But no one was listening to me, it seemed.

Tesla gave a small cry of happiness and jumped on Brodie, kissing his cheek and bouncing all over him as she squealed her thanks. I rolled my eyes at that, and eyed Liam, who was bent over, hands on his knees, as if he were about to hurl again.

I didn't blame him. I kind of felt like puking at this moment myself, and it had nothing to do with a bellyful of mukluk. What the hell was Brodie doing?

"But this Ace," Chip boomed, and held the envelope aloft, "has a twist!"

And he tore the top off the envelope.

I groaned. Of course there was a damn twist. Nothing was ever simple in this damn game. My stomach gave an uncomfortable anxious lurch (but it might have been the mukluk).

I was going to kill Brodie for doing this to us.

Chip pulled out the bright green card inside the ace packet with a flourish and read it aloud. "Since the teams are all safe on this leg, the next leg will be double elimination. In addition, since Yellow Team saved the Black Team, there will be a mix-up of those two teams. You will swap partners."

I stared at Chip, aghast.

Liam straightened, frowning.

Tesla gave a happy giggle, and Brodie just hugged her again.

"Swap…partners?" I said slowly, then looked over at Tesla and my brother. "So I'm with Tesla?" I asked, deliberately misunderstanding.

Chip shook his head. "Since the teams were initially boy-girl, we'll keep them boy-girl. You're now with Liam, and Brodie is now with Tesla."

"Seriously?" I stared at my new partner in horror. Liam had the grim expression of someone who'd just been told he needed a root canal.

"Gee, that's a bummer," Brodie said, in a voice that didn't sound bummed at all.

I turned and gave him a scathing look. "You? Do not talk to me. At all. Ever again. I'm here on this race because of you, and you just screwed me over."

Brodie gave Tesla a look that said I was being tiresome, which just infuriated me all the more. "Quit being so dramatic, Katy," he told me. "Liam's a nice guy."

"Yeah, and I'm a nice girl who had to shovel raw whale blubber into her mouth so we could get first place! Except now I've lost my partner and I'm paired up with the dude that pushed me to the ground and can't eat whale blubber to save his life! So you'll forgive me if I'm throwing a bit of a fit here."

My new rock-star partner said nothing at my ranting, but that didn't surprise me. Heck, the guy never said anything around me.

"So which one of us is in last place, then? Huh?" I gestured at the four of us standing in front of Chip. "Who's yellow and who's black?"

"We'll draw straws," Chip announced, seemingly unruffled by my rage.

An assistant rushed forward to hand him the straws, and he mixed them up in his hand and then held both of them out to us, the bottoms carefully masked. "Whichever one is tipped with black means that they will be black team...and last place. Yellow will remain in the lead."

He held the straws out to Tesla. She glanced at me. I waved a hand at Liam. "Let him do it. Doesn't matter what I say around here anyway."

Liam pulled a straw.

It was black-tipped.

I ignored Brodie's whoop of delight and shook my head. "Someone point me to my tent, because I'm done for the day."

"Igloo," Chip corrected.

I could have cheerfully pushed everyone into the icy waters of the bay in that moment.

IT WAS COLD IN THE IGLOO. NOT A SURPRISE, CONSIDERING WE WERE IN Greenland, in a shelter made of ice. I'd more or less sulked in there for the entire afternoon. Abby had come by to try and cheer me up, but I could tell she thought I'd gotten a shit deal, too. "If Dean and I get an Ace, we'll use it to save you, I promise," she told me. "And if we have a chance to sell your brother down a river, we'll totally do it. Dean thinks he did an awful thing today."

"He did," I agreed. Hearing it from another person made me feel a bit better, at least.

"Just hang in there," Abby had told me. "You've got to move up two places in the next round or else you'll get eliminated."

Two places might as well have been impossible, since I was with Liam the Loser. But I kept that to myself and told her I'd do my best.

My brother Brodie had swung by at some point to try and explain himself, too. "It's nothing to do with you, Katy," he told me in a patient voice, after I'd thrown snow in his face. "You know I want a TV career out of this. I have to make big moves in this game to get on the producers' radar, and I'll do whatever it takes."

I'd said nothing. Abby's earlier advice of *make good TV* rang in my ears. Hell, I hadn't even shared that with Brodie and he'd already known what to do. I felt a little less angry at him after hearing him say that. He had been totally honest with me about what he wanted out of this. He wanted a career. Me, I wanted a check for twenty grand to kick-start my business and a vacation in Acapulco at the Loser Lodge.

But even as I told myself that, it felt untrue. I might have wanted to come into this race for the consolation prize, but now that I was here? The competitive spirit was catching up to me and I was in it to win it.

So I laid in the sleeping bag provided by The World Races people, huddled in the icy darkness, and hated everyone. Well, except Abby. I hated my brother most of all for selling me out so he could make good TV.

And I hated that I was stuck at the back of the pack. The only thing good about me probably getting kicked off next was that Liam wouldn't be getting the prize money either. Then again, I'd be stuck at the Loser Lodge with him for the next three weeks, so that didn't sound like fun either. I was screwed either way.

A shadow moved across the entrance of the igloo, and I stifled a groan of irritation as I heard the rustle of Liam's thick parka as he came into the igloo. This team switch was awful—not only had my brother sold me out, but I had to bunk with Liam the Girl Shover.

I said nothing as I heard him rustling around in his bunk. It got quiet, and I assumed he was laying down to sleep. Long moments passed, and neither of us said anything. I stared up at the darkness, practically vibrating with resentment.

"I tripped," he said, in a voice that was so low I almost didn't catch it.

"Huh?" I turned to look in his direction.

"I tripped and fell on top of you. I wasn't trying to. I just tripped." His voice was low and even, the words so slow to emerge that they were almost hesitant. "I didn't push you."

Oh. Some of my rage deflated. I thought about the scene with the footballs. It had been pretty chaotic. Horrifically chaotic, even. I could see someone tripping in that mess. And I remembered him offering me a hand after the fact. "You still stole my football," I told him.

"You dropped it."

"You could have given it back."

"I could have, but it's a game."

That wasn't the answer I wanted to hear. I rolled over and tried to go to sleep, but I was too angry and cold to do more than stare into the darkness.

The next morning, I woke up and began to shove my gear back into my backpack. We had twelve hour rest periods between race legs, and the time was dependent on when we finished the last leg. Since black team was in the back, I had at least an extra hour before I had to get going.

Which was fine, because I was pretty wrecked physically, due to sleeping in an igloo. I was also wrecked mentally, due to my brother, the selfish jerk. The only good thing about being so wrecked was that I was pretty sure my new partner was, too. He looked like he had a mukluk hangover, and his shaggy black hair hung in his face.

Tesla, meanwhile, looked fresh as a spring rose as she giggled and cooed and hung on my brother as they paraded to the starting mat. That ratfink. I narrowed my eyes as the cameras moved in close to Brodie and Tesla to film their take-off. One of the Inuit appeared and handed them their next disk.

I watched as Tesla grabbed the disk before Brodie could and flipped it over to read. This time? Brodie was forced to peer over *her* shoulder. Glad to see someone was turning the tables on my brother, at least. They glanced at each other and immediately shrugged on their packs and headed back toward Kulusuk, the small town on the shoreline that held the airport. Made sense, considering that was the only real town I'd seen so far. My eyes narrowed as Tesla twined her fingers with my brother's and they held hands as they raced off. I glanced over at my teammate, but he was looking anywhere except at me. That was fine. I was pretty cranky as it was.

After what seemed like eternity, Liam and I were the only team left. I huddled in my black jacket—better than yellow, at least—and headed toward the starting mat as the cameras zoomed in close. When the Inuit guide offered the disk to us, Liam gestured that I should take it.

I did, grudgingly, and flipped it over.

"Your next clue is at Blarney Castle in Ireland. The charter planes will take you back to Reykjavik, Iceland, and from there you may select your flight to Ireland. One hundred dollars has been provided for food, drink, and necessities." The hundred dollar bill was inside an envelope fitted to the back of the disk. "Have this disk—along with the others you receive— when you cross the finish line." I held it out to Liam to read.

He declined with a wave of his hand, glancing at the distant horizon. "I suppose we should head back to the airport, then. I'm guessing we're going to be on the last charter flight again."

"I'd say that's an accurate guess," I replied sourly. I shrugged on my backpack. "Might as well get it over with, then."

One trip to Acapulco, coming right up.

* * *

IT WASN'T SURPRISING TO ME THAT WHEN WE ARRIVED AT THE AIRPORT in Reykjavik, all the other teams were still there. A travel agent had suggested that we fly in to Cork, the next flight to leave, and sure enough, all the other teams were waiting at the terminal.

They didn't look happy to see me and Liam, either. I supposed that if we hadn't caught the same flight, they would have been assured that we were one of the teams sure to go. This way, it was a toss-up all over again. I had a hunch that the producers were deliberately shoving all of us together just to see how the two new teams—mine and Brodie's—reacted to each other.

Too bad for them. I was still in a bad mood, so I took my water bottle and headed to a seat away from all the others, not feeling particularly social at the moment. I didn't care about getting to know the others or 'hanging out' with them, since they didn't seem to want to get to know me, either. No one had made any effort but Abby, and she was cuddled up next to Dean, her eyes closed as if trying to take a nap before the plane got here.

Brodie was sitting in the center of the group with Tesla at his side, looking for all the world as if she'd always been his partner. His arm was loosely around the back of her chair, and she leaned into him, laughing at everything he said. I rolled my eyes and ignored them. Sitting down, I pulled my legs up into my chair and rested my arms on my knees.

Liam glanced at me, and set his backpack down next to me. Then, he went to chat with Tesla, likely to talk strategy or to bitch about his partner. I didn't care. This wasn't fun anymore. If we were the first ones kicked off? I'd be just fine with that. I'd gone from being genuinely excited about being in first place and thinking we had a shot at the money to feeling abandoned.

"Oh, don't worry about her." Brodie's voice rose above the crowd, and I could hear it from where I sat. "She's just in one of her Cranky Katy moods. She'll get over it soon enough."

The teams around him tittered. I narrowed my eyes as a camera zoomed in on my brother, who didn't seem to give a shit that I was miserable.

"Maybe she's cranky because her brother abandoned her to hook up with a hot girl." The voice was deep and smooth and held just a hint of reproach. "I imagine that anyone would be in a bad mood if that happened to them. She got sold out by her partner."

I looked up in surprise. Liam's back was to me, so I couldn't see his expression. But that voice had been his. Was he defending me?

The crowd went quiet. Tesla wriggled in her seat, as if uncomfortable, and Brodie scowled at Liam.

I glanced away, pretending not to notice that Liam abandoned their little crowd and came to sit next to me in the empty seat. He didn't look over, just grabbed his pack, put his headphones on, and began to drum a beat on his backpack, acting as if nothing in the world bothered him.

Me, I was full of confused thoughts. I'd been nothing but nasty to the guy and he'd defended me. Meanwhile, my brother, who was supposed to have my back? Had been calling me by the childhood nickname that he knew drove me crazy—Cranky Katy. Brodie and I argued—that was just how siblings were—but on TV? It was kind of embarrassing.

And yet Liam hadn't sat around and laughed at Brodie's words. He hadn't joined in the little party that was trying to make me feel bad for being unhappy. He'd chided Brodie to his face and then turned and left.

At least *someone* had my back.

"BLARNEY CASTLE, JUST UP AHEAD," I TOLD LIAM, FOLDING UP THE MAP I'd been reading. I was in the back seat of the small car with the cameraman, given the task of navigating while he'd drove, since Liam was better with a stick shift than me.

We'd more or less reached an uneasy truce since getting off the flight at Cork. While we weren't exactly friendly with each other, we'd fallen into a working relationship of a sort. We were polite and efficient as we'd gotten into the car rented for us, bought a map, and found our way to the next location. Liam was a rather quiet sort, so I didn't know what he was thinking.

Not that it mattered, I supposed, since it was still looking as if we'd be the first ones kicked off of the race anyhow. We'd had the bad luck to have seats in the very back of the airplane since we'd arrived last at the ticket counter, and Liam wasn't the type to shove his way to the front of the plane in a hurry to get off. He'd simply sat in his seat and waited for his turn, and I'd followed his lead. By the time we'd gotten off the plane and found the rental cars marked for the racers, we were the last ones to leave the airport.

"There," I said quickly, pointing as we drove over a tiny bridge. "Parking is in that direction." The castle was a fair distance away, the tower of it on the horizon. "Looks like we hike it from here."

"Looks like," he agreed, and then gestured at the line of identical silver hatchbacks already in the parking lot. "All the others are already here."

"Not surprising," I said. We'd known we were in last place and nothing had happened to change that.

We parked our vehicle and grabbed our backpacks out of the trunk. To my surprise, he grabbed my pack and swung it onto his back next to his own, doubling up.

I gave him an odd look. "I can carry my own bag."

"I know," he said easily. "But it's a long walk to the castle and we can make up time if I carry it."

I hesitated. "I'm not helpless."

Those dark eyes lit on my face. "Never said you were."

Okay, then. I nodded and we sprinted up the winding path toward the castle.

Ireland was really, really green. I'd expected that, but I was still surprised at how brilliantly pretty the grounds of the castle were. Abundant plant-life was everywhere, and flowers were blooming—a wild contrast from the cold snow of Greenland. As we arrived at the front of the castle, The World Races mat and flag came into view. A man in a black jacket and a short green kilt with white socks was there to greet us. He held out a disk as we approached.

Liam gestured that I should take it, so I did, and flipped it over. "Blarney Castle is known for two things—its remarkable gardens and the Blarney Stone," I read. "As a team, your task is to plant an appropriate item in each of the four main gardens of the Blarney Castle gardens. Only plant in the marked sections. Once you have planted all four items in the correct spots, a gardener will give you your next task." I flipped over the disk to make sure I hadn't missed anything else, then looked up at my partner. "Ten bucks says that someone has to kiss the Blarney Stone while we're here."

"I'm not taking that bet," he told me, and his mouth curled on one side in a hint of a smile. He really did look like a rock star just then, especially with the lip piercing.

I found myself smiling back, and I tucked the disk under my arm. "Well, let's find these gardens, shall we?"

We followed the marked path, and there was a spot with another *World Games* flag flying overhead. There were rows of potted plants lined up, guarded by a pair of gardeners in the same green kilts that our greeter had worn. We set down our backpacks next to the pile of the others, and

I tucked the disk into mine, then we each grabbed a potted plant to start the task.

I stared down at my pot. Mine looked…well, like weed. I giggled and showed it to Liam.

"Pretty sure that's illegal in most states," he murmured to me as we walked to the nearest garden. His was a plain fern of some kind. "Hope there's not an Irish cop around to watch us plant that."

There were signs all over the extensive grounds, and from what I could tell, there were four main gardens—the Fern Gardens, the Poison Gardens, the Irish Garden, and the Bog Garden.

"No smoke garden," I joked. "Maybe we should plant yours first. It's obviously the one that goes in the Fern Gardens."

We headed for the Fern Gardens and found a pair of shovels, the marked area, and two other teams still digging away at their marked plots. I got excited at the sight of that, especially when I realized that one team had no clue what they were doing, since they were planting their cannabis in the Fern Garden.

I set my pot of, well, pot down next to Liam's fern and grabbed a shovel. "Come on," I told him in a low voice. "We can catch up right here." I pushed ahead and began to shovel dirt. It was soft and loose, not hard packed, and already wet. This wouldn't be hard to dig at all. I tossed the shovel full of dirt to the side and stuck my shovel in again.

"I should be the one digging," Liam told me.

"Why's that?" I asked, even as I hopped on the edge of my shovel to dig it into the ground even deeper.

"Because I'm…bigger than you."

"You were going to say 'because you're a guy,' weren't you?"

He said nothing.

As if sensing an argument, a cameraman zoomed in on us working.

"Admit it," I told him. "You think I'm weak because I'm a girl and that's why you're being all weird."

"I never said you were weak or girly. You're just…short."

I tossed the shovel-full of dirt on Liam's buckle-covered, expensive boots.

He snorted. "Fair enough. I deserved that."

"You did," I said in a cheerful voice. "And you can dig the next one. Now, hand me your plant."

"Yes, ma'am," he told me, and he sounded almost amused at my bossiness.

We planted our first two quickly, electing the Poison Garden for the cannabis, and then heading back for the last two. We planted something that looked like a water lily in the bog garden, and the last plant, I had no idea what it was, but we just guessed at that point, and then flagged over a gardener.

Apparently we'd guessed right, because the gardener immediately handed over a disk. "Congratulations."

Whooping with excitement, we quickly flipped over the disk and read it, heads bent. My hand brushed over Liam's as we flipped, but I didn't have time to focus on that. We read the next clue together.

"*Make your way to the Blarney Stone,*" the disk read. "*One team member will need to volunteer for the kiss, and receive the gift of gab.*"

He glanced over at me, and I noticed how close our faces were for the first time. "Well, you called it."

"I did," I told him, unable to stop looking at his mouth, so close to my own. "I figured they'd use every opportunity to make someone kiss in this game." Abby's comment about making good TV was permanently stuck in my head. I began to get flustered as I thought about kissing him. He was tall, and, okay, if I admitted it to myself, good looking. Sure, he had tattoos and piercings, but he was pretty hot if I was paying attention to that sort of thing.

Which I wasn't. Theoretically.

"Do you know much about the Blarney Stone?" he asked me.

"Just that it involves kissing. Maybe you have to stand on it and kiss someone for this gift of gab thing," I told him, and felt my body get all flushed again. Was I going to have to kiss him for the next clue? Why did that make me feel all weird and kind of excited instead of reluctant and unhappy?

"Only one of us is mentioned, though," he said thoughtfully. "What if we have to kiss a stranger?"

"Oh," I breathed. I hadn't considered that. I elbowed him in a playful manner. "Well, you're the one that could use the gift of gab, if you ask me."

He stared at me, eyes narrowing. "Fine. I'll do it." Then, he turned away, clearly angry.

Guess I'd ruined our easygoing mood. *Way to go, Katy,* I told myself. We grabbed our bags—though he insisted on carrying mine—and followed the signs back to the castle itself.

I guess when I'd pictured the whole Blarney Stone thing, I thought it would be a big rock in a field that everyone went to and kissed. To my surprise, the Blarney Stone was just a stone set in the middle of one of the castle walls, nothing particularly special about it. I watched as one of guys from another team—Derron—laid on his back and grasped a pair of ropes attached to the wall. Two men held his legs as Derron lowered himself backward and kissed the stone while upside down. As soon as he was done, someone reached down with a scrub brush and cleaned the wall.

Okay, that was…not what I had been picturing. I looked at Liam sheepishly. "I guess I was wrong about the Blarney Stone."

"Guess so," he said in a bland voice, and I frowned. I'd hurt his feelings with my comment about the gift of gab. Now *I* was the bad guy.

He set down his backpack against the wall and got into line behind another team. I studied him, then noticed a camera hovering nearby.

Make good TV, Abby had warned me. *They'll fix stuff in your direction to keep you on.*

And the silent treatment between us? *Not* really good TV. Plus, it bothered me that Liam and I had come to a sort of understanding earlier, and we had almost had…fun.

Except I'd gone and blown things by making a comment about how quiet he was. So I needed to fix things, and I needed to make good TV. Somehow.

I considered this as I waited with our bags. The other person finished smooching the rock, and then it was Liam's turn. They carefully lowered him backward to the stone and he kissed it, then came back up a moment later. He got to his feet in an easy, fluid motion, and someone handed him a disk. Instead of reading it, he immediately headed for me so we could read it together.

He was like night and day from Brodie, really. And for the first time, I really, really wanted to make this work. And make good TV. And I kept thinking about how I'd misinterpreted the whole Blarney Stone thing, and how I'd been a bit disappointed when I realized that we wouldn't be kissing after all. And that was a little weirdly disappointing. I mean, wouldn't a kiss make great TV? I thought so.

He came to my side and held his hand out for his backpack.

I threw my arms around his neck and planted my mouth on his.

It was impulsive and a little crazy. Okay, a lot crazy. But I didn't care. I kissed him, pressing my lips against his and feeling the bite of metal at the edges of his mouth. For some reason, that was a bit erotic, and it distracted me.

It was, however, not half as erotic as when his tongue snaked out and brushed against my lower lip.

I was so startled by that, I almost stopped kissing him. Instead, I made a small noise of surprise in my throat, and my mouth softened. His tongue dipped into my mouth, and I felt a tongue stud brush against my own smooth tongue. And oh god, that was…really good.

"Guess he's sharin' his gift o' gab," someone called out merrily behind us, accent thick.

"Sharin' somethin'," someone else commented.

I broke apart from Liam, my face flushing. "Um…good job," I told him, brushing my fingers along the edges of my lips thoughtfully.

He stared down at me, as if trying to figure me out. After a long moment, he said nothing and simply handed me the disk.

I took it in trembling hands and flipped it over to read. "Drive your way," I began, but I noticed he was leaning in close, and I could practically feel his breath on my skin. My voice was squeaky and weird, and I had to clear my throat and start again. "Drive your way to Trinity College in Dublin. Head to the College Library and you will receive your next task there."

"Shall we go, then?" Liam's voice was low, and just a bit husky.

"Sure." I didn't know what else to say, and there was the weirdest blush on my cheeks. "Sure," I repeated, and didn't protest when he grabbed my backpack again.

The drive to Trinity College took a few hours, and they were weird hours. Neither myself nor Liam were in a chatty mood. We'd gone back to our efficient sort of quiet, speaking only when directions needed to be given or to speculate about the race.

I didn't know what to say, so I didn't blame him for being silent. We'd gone from hating each other last night in the igloo to practically making out atop Blarney Castle this morning. He probably thought I was nuts.

Hell, I wasn't sure that I wasn't nuts.

I did keep playing with my lip as he drove, though, thinking of the feel of the metal in his mouth against mine. His lips had been soft in contrast to that. The lip ring on his lower lip had pressed into my skin, and I'd felt that tongue stud graze against my tongue in a way that had made me dazed. I'd known that he'd had it, but I just hadn't thought about it when it came to kissing.

And now I couldn't stop thinking about it.

"Almost there," Liam told me in his quiet voice, breaking my reverie. His dark gaze locked on my face via the rearview mirror.

I put my hand down, realizing with a slight flush that he'd caught me playing with my mouth. "Great."

"I see two other cars," he told me as he pulled into parking.

"Maybe we'll see Tesla and Brodie," I told him. And then a horrible thought occurred to me. What if Liam and Tesla were an item? Oh god, and I'd kissed him on national TV. No wonder he'd stiffened up like that. No wonder he was acting weird now.

But...I was also pretty sure he'd kissed me back. It was mystifying.

We grabbed our bags, and he carried mine again, despite my protests. With our gear in hand, we hiked across the campus, following The World Races signs toward the library. Several red-brick structures surrounded us, and as we headed to one massive building, I wasn't sure that it was the right place. It seemed too large to be a library.

Of course, as soon as we opened the doors, I changed my mind.

The breath escaped me. Holy cow, that was a lot of books. I stared in fascination as I walked in, surprised at just how many books were in this building. Row after row after row of bookshelves lined up as far as the eye could see, neatly cordoned off by red velvet ropes. Each aisle had a bust of someone old or famous at the end, and when I looked up, I could see that there was a second floor of even more books.

"Wow," I said.

"I hope you don't have to find a particular book," Liam told me in a quiet voice, staring around us. He looked equally impressed.

"Oh god, I hope not, too. I'm a baker, not a librarian," I told him.

"A baker, huh?" He seemed amused by that. "I'd have guessed camp counselor with the pigtails."

I rolled my eyes. "The pigtails were a casting decision."

He chuckled. "They're cute."

Cute? Was he flirting with me? I cast him a look, but he was pointing down the long alley of bookshelves. "I see our guy."

I followed his gaze and sure enough, there was The World Races flag.

We picked up the pace, stepped onto the mat, and retrieved our next disk.

"This challenge is mine since you did the last one," I told Liam, and began to read the disk. "The Trinity College Library is home to the famous Book of Kells, one of the most ornately decorated manuscripts ever found. Using the materials provided to you, you will recreate the page that the book is currently open to. A judge will decide if your copy is worthy. When you are approved, you will receive directions to the finish line for this leg of the race."

"You good at painting?" Liam asked, glancing down at me. I could have sworn there was a hint of an amused sparkle in those dark eyes.

I rolled up my sleeves, grinning. "Dude, I frost cupcakes on a regular basis. I am ace at painting. Just watch me."

"Don't get cocky," he told me, but there was a teasing note in his voice.

I simply grinned and headed for the roped off area. There were three other contestants there, and as I watched, Steffi from the purple team handed her page to the judge, who laid it down on the table, scrutinized it with a magnifying glass, and then shook his head. "No."

Okay, so this wouldn't be easy. I headed to the table set up for me and peered down at the materials, taking a quick assessment of things. Paints in small pots were neatly lined up on the far end of the table, along with multiple brushes. A long piece of thick, weird paper had been laid out on the table, and as I leaned over it, I saw that a drawing had already been done on the paper. It was crazy ornate, too, with a jillion lines and swirls moving back and forth, all in black and white. Obviously our job was to color it to match the Book of Kells. I studied it for a moment, and then looked around for the book.

Off in the distance, there was a roped off section. I watched as Summer got in line again, headed straight to the glass-case covered book, stared at it for a long while, her lips moving, and then raced back to her table to return to her page. So this was coloring and memorization. There had to be a smart way to do this. I stared down at the paper a moment longer. It reminded me of paint by numbers. All right then, I'd treat it like that. I raced to get in line to view the book, and when the contestant in front of me was done, I moved up to the podium.

And stared. The book was gorgeous. Illuminated by a soft light, the book was opened to a page of one of the Apostles, his head crowned by a golden glow. He held up a hand and cupped an object in it, and his robes were a heavy blue. I studied the colors for a moment, then decided to tackle it one color at a time. I'd start with gold. Crown, I told myself, then looked for other bits of gold. Sandals, sparkles in the sky, and the border. Repeating this to myself, I ran back to my page and dipped a paint brush, then blobbed the appropriate pieces.

Each object in the picture had been broken into several different sections—no doubt to try and throw us off, so I dabbed a bit of the appropriate paint color in each section, then set my brush down and returned to the painting. I'd do blue next, and then work my way through all the colors, so I'd know I was right. It'd take some time in advance, but it'd pay off when I only had to do it once. Even now, I watched another person—Myrna—call over the judge, only to be told 'no' right away. This challenge was about accuracy.

So I returned to the book and looked for blue. Then red. Then green. Then black. Then the smaller, less numerous colors. I took my time, carefully dotting each color on my page. Sometimes I had to return once or twice to the book, unsure of the block I was looking at, so I just skipped that and checked it the next time I went. By the time I had most of my picture blocked out, the three teams that had started at the challenge were still there, and the last two had arrived.

I wasn't flustered, though. I had this. I leaned over my table and began to carefully paint in the boxes I had marked, taking my time with each one. I had careful, steady hands, thanks to my practice icing and decorating delicate cupcakes and wedding cakes. I was fast, and I was steady, and I was totally rocking this challenge. When my back began to cramp up from leaning, I got up and headed to the book again, filling in the last few blanks.

At last, my picture was done. I carefully lifted it from the frame, holding it so it wouldn't smear, and shot a triumphant look at Liam. He stood with the other teammates, looking cool and casual, but as I glanced over at him, I saw him give me a subtle thumbs-up.

I brought it to the judging stand and laid it flat to be judged. The judge pulled out his magnifying glass and began to pore over my finished painting. He took so long to study it that I was sure he was going to find fault, and my stomach dropped. Had I missed something? Had I dripped into the wrong box? I watched him, holding my breath.

He straightened, looked at me, and then nodded. "Good job." And he held out my disk.

I bounced with excitement and hugged him. "Thank you! Thank you!" I grabbed the disk and dashed to Liam, and on impulse, hugged him too.

Liam seemed surprised by that, but after a moment, he hugged me back. The other teams clapped politely, but I could tell they were nervous that we had already finished.

"Let's go outside and read this," Liam told me, whispering in my ear.

We grabbed our bags and headed outside, and I flipped over the clue. "Make your way to the Shelbourne Dublin. Bring all disks with you so you may cross the finish line." I looked up at Liam. "The Shelbourne Dublin? It sounds like a hotel."

"I know where that is," Liam told me. "I've stayed there before."

"You have?"

He nodded, slinging my backpack over his shoulder. "On tour. Come on."

We made it to the Shelbourne Dublin a short time later, though we had to stop and ask for directions twice. I nearly chewed my nails off in anxiety as Liam navigated the streets of Ireland, but he didn't get lost once and listened intently to my directions.

In the front of the large building, I could see The World Races flag and the cameramen milling about. No teams waited outside—I didn't blame them. Why hang out on the street when you can take a break in the nice comfy hotel? And I was suddenly exhausted. We parked the car, and then Liam and I were racing for the finish line. The tape had been broken already, which meant we weren't first, but we didn't care.

We bounded past the finish and waited for Chip to announce our place.

"Black team," Chip said in a grave voice. "You are team....number five."

I gave a happy squeal of excitement, even though I'd known we were at least five, considering we'd left five teams back at the last challenge. And to my surprise, Liam reached down and grabbed me into a hug, lifting me into the air.

And I laughed. Today? We were safe.

Chapter Five

"I have to say…I'm not exactly unhappy to have Katy as a partner. She's a tough one, despite the pigtails. I think the others underestimate just how strong she is because she looks so small and cute. And she kisses like a fiend." —Liam Brogan, Paris Leg of The World Races

EVERYONE LINGERED IN THE LOBBY OF THE HOTEL. IT WASN'T THAT we particularly wanted to hang around. All the racers were exhausted from the constant flight-hopping and then heading straight to the challenges, not to mention the constant nerves when you thought you were in last place. I was wiped, Liam was wiped, everyone was wiped. And yet, we were all still in the lobby.

No one had the money for a hotel room.

Rooms were just a bit over two hundred a night, and we'd been given twenty dollars for the Greenland leg, and a hundred for the Ireland leg. Considering that we liked eating, we had to save some money for food and drink. Even two teams pooling their money together couldn't afford one room, as the price we'd been quoted was over two hundred and twenty a night. No one was quite willing—yet—to fork over most of their money to split one double room between six people. No one wanted to be that third couple that didn't get to sleep on a bed.

So we hung out in the lobby, our two bucket chairs scooted close together, and watched the others come in for the race. Brodie and Tesla had come in fourth, one spot ahead of us. They now sat in the bar of the hotel, eating dinner and flirting. It was like my brother hadn't even noticed I was there.

I glanced over at Liam to see if he was feeling the sting of Tesla's lack of attention, but he didn't seem to be bothered.

In fact, he was leaning in to my chair. He whispered, "Kissy and Rusty came in ninth, so they're out."

I couldn't say I was surprised to hear that, since the Rednecks hadn't proven themselves to be particularly good with the challenges. I was, however, surprised by the shiver that rocked through me at his breath against my ear. I squirmed in my chair and counted heads of the other contestants, loitering in the lobby. "Who does that leave?"

"Just Myrna and Fred, I think." Liam glanced around the room and nodded. "Yep. Just them."

"The two easiest teams," I mused. "It's going to get a lot harder after this. Who do you think will go next?"

He considered the others, then leaned in close to me again to whisper his response. "Depends on the kind of challenge. If it's a water challenge, I say Wendi and Rick, because Wendi's not athletic and Rick doesn't have the musculature."

The mother and son team. I could see that.

"If it's something athletic…maybe Steffi and Cristi. They don't run as fast as the others."

"And if it's an eating challenge?" I asked lightly.

"Then we'll win," he said. "If you do it, anyhow. If it's me, be prepared for the Loser Lodge."

"Sensitive stomach?"

He gave a small laugh. "Would you believe me if I said that my failure at that challenge had more to do with memories of a bad sushi experience than anything else?"

I chuckled. "I believe it. I don't think I can ever eat fish again after that challenge. And it wasn't even fish. It just smelled like it."

"It was a nightmare."

"I'm shocked—you're not a big fan of the raw, blubbery insides of marine wildlife?"

"Don't remind me," he said, clutching at his stomach as if in pain. "I'm still getting acid reflux flashbacks."

I laughed again, just as someone thumped into the chair next to me. It was Abby, with Dean hovering over her shoulder.

Liam immediately went quiet, glancing over at me.

Abby leaned in, a twinkle in her eye, and whispered, "How much money do you have?"

"Why?" I asked warily, glancing over at my partner. His face was a mask of indifference. Gone was the easy smile he'd worn, and I felt like our hard-won truce had just disappeared into smoke. Which kind of sucked.

"Because," Abby said, and then leaned in, glancing around at the crowded lobby. Her voice lowered. "Dean worked his magic and got us a discount on a room that was vacated."

I sucked in a breath, staring up in wonder at Dean. He winked at me, all cocky and pleased with himself. "I pulled a few strings, might have signed a few autographs, things like that."

Oh, that was right. Dean was a big shot Olympian swimmer. Five medals or something like that. I looked over at Liam in excitement. "You're famous too—maybe you can squeeze us a discount?"

His mouth twitched and he shook his head. "Tesla, maybe. Everyone recognizes her. Me, I'm just the guitarist. Without her at my side, I'm anonymous."

Abby waved a hand impatiently. "We don't need another discount. They're willing to give us the room for half price as long as we're out by seven am."

I glanced at my watch. We had a twelve hour rest break between the time we'd arrived and the time we received our next clue. "We got here at five," I told her.

"We got here at three thirty," Abby said. "So that's perfect."

"And that means we only have to pay about a hundred and ten or so... fifty five apiece if we split it between two teams."

I looked over at Liam.

He shrugged.

"Hot showers," Abby cajoled. "Pillows. Someplace to sleep that's not an airport floor."

It was so incredibly tempting. I bit my lip, and then stole a glance at

Liam again. "What do you want to do?" It would be half of our money, but we'd also be well rested and well showered. It was worth it to me, but this was a partnership, and that partnership meant that we'd have to agree.

Something Brodie and I had sucked at.

Liam noticed my hesitation. "It'll mean watching our money for meals for a bit."

I nodded.

"I have half of the money from when Tesla and I got split," he told me. "Six dollars and fifty cents."

"I have nothing other than what they gave us for this leg of the race," I said cheerfully. "Brodie sucks with money." My brother and I had argued over some high priced protein bars at the general store in Kulusuk, but Brodie had insisted, and we'd spent every dime. Liam apparently had saved his cash better than we had.

"Looks like he's still determined to spend all of his team's money," Dean pointed out. "They're having a few beers in the bar. That's gonna cost them."

I was hungry too, but I'd gladly give up dinner for a nice bed and a hot shower. I looked at Liam again.

"I'm in if you are," he told me.

I could have kissed him—again—in that moment. "Totally in."

"Great," Abby said with excitement. "Dean's going to get the room." She glanced up at her partner, who leaned down and kissed her forehead, then headed off to the counter. She turned back to look at me and Liam. "We don't want the others to know we're sharing a room or they'll probably crash it and try to squeeze some pillows or floor space. I'll find out what room we have, and then I'll take the elevator to the top floor. Wait five minutes, and then meet me there, and we'll go to the room together."

"Sounds good," I told her, and when she stuck her pinky out, I linked mine through hers.

It was good to have friends on this race.

FIFTEEN MINUTES LATER, I FLOPPED DOWN ON ONE OF THE QUEEN BEDS in the hotel room and groaned with pleasure. "Oh my god, a mattress. I've died and gone to heaven."

Next to me, Liam sat on the edge of the bed and dropped his pack to the ground. He didn't flop backward like I had, just sat and looked at me.

Which made me feel weird and selfish, like I was hogging all of the bed.

So I sat up and curled my legs under me.

On the other bed, Abby slid her shoes off and wiggled her feet as Dean sprawled onto the bed behind her. "This was the best use of money ever. I'm so glad we did this."

"I'm so glad you invited us," I told her. My stomach growled, and I winced. I had a protein bar in my bag, but it wasn't sounding super appetizing at the moment.

Liam glanced at me again, then turned to Dean and Abby. "I don't suppose you guys want to go halves on dinner? We can get a pizza for pretty cheap if we don't mind picking it up."

"Pizza sounds great to me," Abby said, rubbing her stomach. She glanced over at Dean. "Paper rock scissors for who has to go get it?"

He laughed and leaned in to kiss Abby. "Tell you what. I'll get it and you owe me."

"Mmm, deal," she told him with a teasing grin.

Dean got back to his feet and put some money in his pocket, then glanced at Liam. "You want to come with?"

"Sure, man. Give the girls a few minutes to relax without us." He looked over at me again, that hesitant almost-smile on his face, and then they disappeared. The door shut a moment later, and silence fell. It was just me and Abby in the room, basking in the fact that we didn't have to go anywhere for at least several more hours.

The silence didn't last long, though. Abby rolled onto her side on the bed and gazed over at me. "Sooooo, how's the new partner? What's it like being paired up with a rock god?"

I sat up, crossed my legs, and thought. I felt like I could trust Abby. It was like having one of my best friends here on the race with me. And I didn't think she'd dick us over. "He's…not what I expected."

"He seems different than your brother," Abby said bluntly. "And I mean that in a good way. I think you lucked out."

I gave her a wry look. "Brodie's my brother, but yeah, he tends to think of Brodie first and Katy second."

"Why do you let him get away with that? I'd have beat him with my backpack if he'd treated me the way he treated you."

I shrugged. "I don't know. I guess because he was honest about what he wanted out of this? He wants a career. Me, I just want the consolation prize money."

She snorted. "I told myself that until I made the merge on *Endurance Island*. Trust me, when you get closer to that big prize? You want that money."

She had a point. I had to admit that when I saw everyone racing, it made my blood get fired up and my competitive spirit kick in. Still, I didn't know if I could deliberately push ahead of Brodie, not when I'd be just as happy with the last place check. It seemed selfish somehow. Even though Brodie hadn't been awesome to me on the race, the race would end and he'd still be my brother long after these people were out of my life. So I said nothing.

"Well, at any rate, I'm glad we're allied with you and not Brodie. He doesn't seem the loyal type," she said with a yawn. "You want the first shower? I'll wait until Dean gets back and we can share ours."

A shower sounded incredible. I pulled myself up from the bed and grabbed my backpack. "I promise not to use all the hot water."

"Good." She waved me away, yawning and laying back on her bed.

By the time the guys got back with pizza, I had showered and changed into new clothes, and was combing out my wet hair. We tore into the pizza, divvying it up four ways. I only ate two of my slices, being the smallest of the group, and nudged my extra slice over to Liam. He was a tall guy and would probably need the fuel.

He took it with a wink at me, and then devoured it.

Dean patted his stomach and glanced at the bathroom. "Shower free?"

"All yours," I told him, uncapping my bottle of water and taking another drink.

"Wait for me," Abby said, getting to her feet. "I thought we'd share."

"Just like old times," Dean said with a grin, and smacked Abby on the butt as she sauntered past him. They disappeared into the bathroom and I was left alone with Liam.

I glanced over at him as he wiped his hands with the napkin, and then looked over at me.

"So," he said, then paused.

"So," I said back.

He seemed more at ease now that it was just the two of us, and now that I wasn't glowering at him every moment. Instead, he simply studied my face, as if considering me. After a moment, he stuck his hand out. "I think we got off on the wrong foot on this race. Hi, I'm Liam."

I laughed and took his hand. "Hi, I'm Katy."

"And what brings you on The World Races, Katy?"

"Well," I said, crossing my legs and getting comfortable on the bed. "I actually didn't want to be on the show. I got talked into it because Brodie needed a partner. And I want the money to invest in my business."

"Business?" He looked impressed. "What kind of business?"

"I have a custom cakes and cupcakes business," I said proudly. "Katy's Short Cakes."

He nodded, as if it somehow fit me, and then he crossed his legs on the bed until he was sitting, facing me. "So you're a baker?"

"I am." It felt weirdly intimate to be facing each other on the bed like this. It was...direct. And personal. There was no hiding or averting eyes with this. We were one on one, face to face.

"And the pigtails? Are you a children's baker or something?" There was a hint of a smile on his mouth.

I groaned and ruffled a hand through my loose, wet blonde hair. "The pigtails were decided by casting, not by me. I think they picked it because I'm short."

"And because you're cute," he agreed. "It makes you look perky."

For some reason, I blushed at that. So he thought I was cute? Or just perky? Perky didn't necessarily mean attractive. Squirrels were perky. "So, what about you?"

"What about me?" His dark eyes studied my face.

"What made you come on The World Races?"

His mouth twisted a bit. "The label."

I frowned at him. "The label?"

"Yeah. Tesla wanted to go on the show. Thought it'd be a good opportunity since our next record drops in the fall, when this airs. We had a large lead time." He shrugged. "The label wanted one of the band members to go with her. I was picked."

"So you and Tesla aren't," I gestured with my hand. "You know."

His eyes widened. "Oh, god no. She's just a bandmate. You know, the whole *Finding Threnody* thing." And he looked at me like I should know exactly what he was talking about.

I winced. "Is it bad if this is the part that I say that I've never heard of you?"

He stared.

"I listen to country music," I said lamely. "Sorry. I'm sure your band is good."

He continued to stare.

"I'll buy your CD when I get home," I told him. "I promise."

He shook his head a little, as if to clear it, then laughed. "So you really don't know who we are?"

"Well," I told him. I thought for a moment, trying to determine the best way to say it without hurting his feelings, and then gave up. "Not a clue. Brodie's a fan, though."

Liam chuckled and shook his head. "Well, that explains why you weren't very friendly to me."

"Are a lot of girls friendly to you because you're in a rock band?"

"Yes," he said simply.

I snorted. "They might be until you push them down reaching for their football."

He scowled. "It was an accident."

"How do I know that?" I asked innocently, putting a teasing lilt in my voice. "Maybe you thought it was a mosh pit."

That slow, almost reluctant smile spread across his lean face again. "Now I know you're fucking with me."

"Just a little."

He laughed. "I suppose I deserved that."

I studied him as he smiled. I'd initially thought Liam tall, grungy, and a little scary. The piercings were new territory for me, as were the tattoos. He even had them on his neck. But the smile he extended my way was genuine, and for a moment, he looked like any other guy my age that just happened to be covered in black tattoos, multiple facial piercings, and was the lead guitarist in a supposedly big deal rock band.

"So..." he rubbed his chin. "I suppose there's a special irony in this considering that neither you nor I wanted to be on the race."

"We could always sabotage the next leg of the race and win ourselves an extended stay in Acapulco," I told him, keeping my voice innocent.

"Is that what you want to do?"

I considered it. I really, really did. But we were still in the race, and we were doing rather well, if I admitted it to myself. And Liam wasn't a bad partner, as long as we didn't run into any more mukluk or eating challenges on the race. "Part of me wants to bail out on the race, but a bigger part of me wants to see how far we can go."

He nodded. "Me too." That dark, intense gaze focused on me again. "So why did you kiss me at the Blarney Stone?"

Oh. Wow, okay, that was super direct. I thought about my answer for a moment, then shrugged. "I wanted to?"

"You did?"

"Well." I ran a finger across the blanket. "Abby told me that if we made good TV, we stood a better chance of staying in the race. That the producers would rig things to ensure that we'd do better. So, I kissed you." I gave another shrug, trying to make it seem casual even though I was feeling rather nervous. "Good TV."

Liam watched me for so long without saying anything that I began to wonder if it was a mistake to tell him. After a long moment, he said, "So it was just for TV?"

I couldn't tell if that was a good thing or a bad thing. "Maybe?"

He considered this. Then, he leaned in. "You want to keep making good TV, then?"

"What do you mean?"

Liam gave me a wicked smile. "I mean we make sure that they keep us around as long as possible by making some really good TV."

And just like that, heat flushed through my body.

THAT NIGHT, IN THE HOTEL ROOM, ABBY AND DEAN TOOK ONE BED, AND Liam and I took the other. We slept clothed, of course, but the bed was small enough that I couldn't move without bumping into his arm, or leg. At one point, I woke up to find his arm around my waist, and a tingle of anticipation moved through me.

But then he shifted and his arm moved away again. I bit my lip, thinking. Just a fluke, then? Of course it was. So why had I been so thrilled at the simple touch?

Paris, France

"THERE'S THE PALAIS GARNIER," I TOLD MY PARTNER, POINTING AT THE majestic building in the distance. "We're in the right place."

"Come on, then," he said, and grabbed my hand in his, pulling me down the busy streets of Paris.

That weird feeling fluttered in my stomach when his hand grasped mine. That goofy flutter had pretty much been my constant companion on this leg of the race. The Liam that had been my silent companion at the beginning of the team-up? Gone.

Instead, I found myself with a Liam that I didn't quite know what to do with. A Liam that was attentive, asked for my opinion on directions and flights, and liked to lean in and whisper into my ear when we were sitting close together. Unlike Brodie, Liam was proving to be a partner that stuck by my side, bought me drinks when he thought I might be thirsty, and generally made me feel valued.

He'd also taken to holding my hand.

It had thrown me off at first; we'd been at the airport, waiting for our flight into Paris when he'd simply reached over and taken my hand in his. I hadn't missed the fact that Abby's eyebrows had shot up to her hairline, or the fact that the cameras had zoomed in and then proceeded to hover for the next hour in the hopes that we'd do something exciting or flirty.

We were just making good TV. Sort of. Our flirting had definitely escalated to a different level, and it was a level I hadn't quite been prepared for. Not that I was complaining. I'd started it, after all, with my impulsive kiss.

Except now that I'd started it? I was having a hard time distinguishing real from fake. The hand holding mine felt real. It was for the camera, I kept telling myself. But I couldn't quite relax and accept that. Maybe I wasn't as good as pretending as I thought I was.

Maybe I'd really wanted to kiss Liam. Which was weird. He wasn't my type. He was silent, and tatted, and pierced, and famous. I was just small town Katy, who went to culinary school and wanted nothing more out of life than to make fancy cupcakes. We weren't in the same league. We weren't the same type. I normally went for big, muscular cowboys with boots and a tan. Liam was tall, lean, with dark hair and not much of a tan at all. But his eyes were dark and intense, and I found my gaze constantly going back to those fascinating piercings.

As if he could hear my thoughts, Liam stopped and dragged me close, his mouth hovering near my ear. I immediately froze, my breath catching in my throat. "To your left," he whispered. "Standing by the corner. It's the Olympians. Do you see the flag anywhere?"

I glanced around and pretended to be studying the Paris streets. My gaze focused on a green and blue blurb at the far end of the Palais. The World Races logo. "I see it."

"Summer and Polly don't see us yet," he murmured, tugging me close. "Good thing we're in black and not a bright color."

He looped his arm around my shoulders and we pretended to be a couple, loitering with the crowd as we headed toward the Palais Garnier. The streets of Paris were incredibly busy, and buses whizzed past on a regular basis. The buildings around us were tall, adding to the vague feel of claustrophobia that I felt, sandwiched in between them. The Olympians wandered past, ultra-noticeable in their bright green, and appeared to be looking for the flag. They hadn't spotted it yet. As soon as they headed in the wrong direction, I squeezed Liam's hand and signaled that the coast was clear. We sprinted for the mat.

A man in a tuxedo, red cape, and white mask stood under The World Races flag, and held the customary disk out to us. We grabbed it with a quick *thank you* and then dashed away a good distance, making sure we weren't nearby if Summer and Polly spotted us.

We huddled together and I flipped the disc, reading the back. "Welcome to the Palais Garnier, the site that inspired Gaston Leroux's famous work, *The Phantom of the Opera*. Today, you will choose between two tasks inspired by the novel—'Chandeliers' or 'Performance.'"

I looked up at Liam, and shrugged, then kept reading. "If you choose 'Chandeliers,' you must work on one of the famous chandeliers in the interior of the Grand Foyer. Each chandelier has multiple lights that are burnt out. You must insert the correct light bulbs into the appropriate slots. Each time you do so, this will also cause another light to turn off. You must figure out the puzzle and determine how to turn on all lights. Once you do, you will receive your next task. If you choose 'Performance,' you must learn a simple *pas de deux* from the famous ballet, *Sleeping Beauty*. You must perform the *pas de deux* to the approval of a preschool ballet teacher. If you do so, you will receive your next task."

"Interesting choices. Dancing or electrician work."

I looked up at Liam, considering. "The chandelier might be easier to do. It's just replacing bulbs and figuring out which ones turn off what."

"Yes, but we're here to make good TV, remember?" And he smiled at me, his lips stretching around those fascinating piercings. "And what makes better TV?"

I felt my mouth move into a grin. "Performance, of course. You any good at dancing?"

"Shitty."

I laughed. "Me too."

"Then this should definitely be interesting." He took my hand again and tugged me towards the Palais entrance. "Come on. Performance it is."

We headed in, and my breath locked in my throat. The building was beautiful, all delicate Corinthian columns and straight lines leading up to the flat roof that was topped by golden angel statues. Once inside, it was equally breathtaking. The ceiling was ornately decorated, the stairs winding through the main foyer. I held my breath—I didn't think I'd ever been in a place so elegant.

We descended the staircase and entered the auditorium of the opera house. The place was massive, our footsteps echoing in the room. The stage was lit, and several dancers stood in a line, waiting for us. Off to one side, I could see a couple—Hal and Stefan—practicing moves in front of a frowning tutor. They were both wearing black leotards.

One of the ballet dancers stepped forward as we took the stairs to the stage, her stiff tutu bobbing with every exaggerated move. "Please pick a tutor to show you the steps to the *pas de deux*." She gestured at the row of dancers behind her.

I glanced at Liam, but he shrugged. "Just pick someone."

I did, and the woman stepped forward with tiny, precise steps, her feet arching with every mincing motion. Her mouth was tucked into a tight line, as if she weren't thrilled to be chosen. She gestured to the far end of the stage, and we followed her.

She gave a little sniff at our clothing. "You both must change into the proper attire."

I glanced over at the other team and noticed their clothing again. "Oh. Um, where do we get the clothing?"

She rolled her eyes as if that was the most ridiculous question ever. "The dressing room, of course."

"Of course," Liam murmured.

At our teacher's huffy instructions, we headed to the back of the opera house and followed colored flags to the dressing rooms. There were two—one for men and one for women—so we separated. I found a small room full of dark tights, leotards, and pink ballet slippers that were made of soft leather. I checked the inside of the shoe—no wooden block for going *en pointe*. Thank god for that. We'd hurt ourselves if we tried to do that, and we still had a race to run.

I dressed quickly and slid the shoes on, then raced back out.

I ran into Liam in the hall…and was unable to smother my giggle. He was scowling, the piercings flashing as he caught sight of me. He tugged at the stretchy material of his ballet outfit, the legs and leotard skin tight and outlining his, uh, equipment.

"Before you say anything about my junk," he growled, "It's sticking out because it's an athletic belt."

"It's not all a belt," I said in a delicate voice, trying not to laugh at his expression.

He snorted. "Come on, let's just get this over with."

We returned to the dancer and she began to show us the series of moves that had been designed for the competition. This would not be a traditional *pas de deux*, she informed us in an icy voice, as we were not talented enough and novices. A traditional *pas de deux* would be far too hard for us. So they had coordinated several easier moves for us to learn for our dance. There were five parts—the entree, in which we would enter the stage. The *grand adage*, in which Liam would partner me. Then we would each have a small solo, and then the *coda*, which would bring the dance to a close. There was one lift in which Liam would have to grab me and hoist me into the air.

The teacher showed us the moves, and I caught a few of the other dancers tittering as we clumsily tried each step. Still, after several minutes, we had figured out the basic steps and the order they went in. I wasn't the best with rhythm, but I was good at memorizing. I stole a few peeks at Hal and Stefan. Surely we had to be better than them. The dancers were giggling at the other team's attempts to practice non-stop. We could do this.

Just then, Liam put his hands on my waist.

I shrieked and squirmed out of his grasp, much to the surprise of my partner, and the dismay of the teacher.

"What are you doing?" The teacher looked as if I'd just insulted her.

"Ticklish," I gasped, putting my hands on my sides.

Liam chuckled and wiggled his fingers at me. "Can you hold it in for this challenge?"

"I'll try." I exhaled, trying to compose myself, and then assumed the dance position I'd been shown.

When his hands went on my waist again, I laughed once more, but held, my lips twitching. I could do this. I could. I—

Liam's fingers brushed over my sides in what had to be a deliberate tickle. I squealed and darted away again.

The dancer rolled her eyes, but Liam actually laughed. Laughed aloud. Like I'd just done the funniest thing ever. And that warm, hearty laugh? Made my insides go all gooey with warmth. Liam had an aloof sort of attractiveness to him normally, but when he laughed? I quivered. All over.

It was going to be really hard to concentrate now.

"He's going to have to put his hands on you," the dancer said in a displeased voice. "You need to concentrate."

I nodded and forced myself to loosen up, giving Liam a mock-warning look. This time, when he put his hands on my waist, I felt his thumbs caress my sides, as if he couldn't help but give me little additional touches.

And instead of getting ticklish, I was instantly aroused.

Oh, damn. I blinked rapidly, forcing myself to pay attention to the dance moves and the cameraman that hovered nearby, taping everything. I could feel my nipples getting hard and prayed they weren't sticking out against my leotard enough that the camera would catch it. Our ballet dancer made us go over the waist move, over and over again, until we could do it without me breaking down in a fit of giggles or getting all flustered.

This challenge was taking a long time, but I didn't care. We were making good TV like Liam had said...and he was touching me. And I couldn't quite bring myself to suggest that we go and screw some light bulbs instead.

"Now to practice the lift," the dancer informed us. "The female partner must get into the modified *arabesque* I showed you."

I grimaced and raised my arm into the air, raising my leg as high as I could. I ignored the amused snorts of the other ballet dancers, knowing my form was terrible.

"Now," the teacher said. "The man should place his hand on her thigh to begin the lift."

I felt Liam's hand curve along the inside of my thigh, and I jerked in surprise at how his fingers had felt, skimming along my flesh. A hot pulse of desire raced through me, and I felt my face flush.

"Keep form," the dancer snapped.

"Sorry." I pressed my lips together and lifted my leg in the air again, wobbly.

"Ready?" Liam asked. At my nod, his hands slid to the inside of my thighs again and I shuddered, feeling the heat rock through me again. Okay, I shouldn't have been turned on during a challenge, but I was.

Because Liam's hands were strong, and they were between my thighs. How could I not get all hot and bothered from that?

"Keep your body stiff," the dancer snapped at me as Liam lifted me with a little grunt, about a foot into the air, and then dropped me back down again. Our goal was to have him lift me from his right side and move me to his left in an extended hop while I held my form. Judging from the ballet dancer's near-sneer, it wasn't a real move at all, but we'd probably pull something if we tried a real *pas de deux*. Heck, we weren't exactly good with this one.

She made us practice the lift. Over and over, I'd hold form as Liam's hands slid against my inner thighs. And I quivered each time.

"Close enough," our teacher told us. "You can perform once the stage is free."

IT TOOK US THREE TRIES TO GET THROUGH THE DANCE. ON THE FIRST try, the ballerina judging us stopped me halfway through and informed me that my posture was horrendous. We had to go to the back of the stage and wait as Hal and Stefan attempted to dance their routine again. They were stopped by the ballerina as soon as the music started, since Stefan's timing was off.

On our second try, Liam flubbed the lift and I didn't help by giggling when he touched me.

The third time, though? We nailed it. As we finished the Coda, we held our positions, waiting for the ballerina's verdict. She scrutinized us, then gave a sharp nod and held out the disk for our clue.

I gave a happy cry of delight, and turned and leapt into Liam's arms. He grabbed me and twirled me around, and my legs automatically went around his waist as I clung to him, cheering. When we slowed, I was reminded of the fact that we were both wearing skimpy ballet leotards that allowed you to feel every curve of your partner's body, and he was wearing a belt that gave him a massive bulge.

A bulge that I slid down as my feet landed on the floor.

We stared at each other for an electric moment longer, and then Liam recovered his senses and took the disk the ballerina held out to us.

Everyone stared and waited for us to leave the stage, so I grabbed Liam's hand and dragged him off to the side. "Come on. Let's go."

He gave himself a little mental shake. "We need to change clothes and get out of here."

"We could stay in the ballet clothes," I told him thoughtfully. "Buy ourselves a few minutes and just head straight to the next task."

"Hell no," Liam told me, and grabbed his bulge.

I laughed at that. "Point taken."

He held the clue disk out, flipped it over, and then smiled at me.

Damn, that smile. I gave myself a little shake, then started to read the instructions in a low whisper.

Time to concentrate on the game once more.

As we left the Palais Garnier behind, we passed by two teams working on the chandeliers, and had left Hal and Stefan still at the dance challenge. That meant we had a decent lead on the others, though we were pretty sure we weren't in first place.

The disk instructed us to head to a French patisserie, and we ran into Abby and Dean there. Liam and Abby decided to take the first challenge, since it involved bicycling through the streets of France. Unless I had a map? I was bad with directions, so we'd elected to have Liam participate for our team.

He and Abby worked together to deliver baskets of fresh baguettes to six different locations in Paris while on bicycles. Dean and I sat at the corner of the bakery and split a hot, fresh loaf of bread ourselves, speculating as to what the next challenge would be. We agreed to run it together, since we knew we were ahead of at least three other teams.

The next challenge sent us into *l'Ossuaire Municipal*—the French catacombs. We headed down the dank steps into the shadowy cavern, and a chill raced through me. Inside, the walls were covered with hundreds of years of graffiti, and some of the rooms seemed to be nothing but skulls.

Our task was to find the hidden message that would give us our next clue. Dean took one portion of a wall while I took the next, and we worked our way through wall after wall, looking for a message.

My heart nearly stopped when I saw along the bottom of one wall, written in English, "*Make your way to the Italian ruin of Pompeii at the base of Vesuvius and look for the Games flag.*"

Yes! Hiding my excitement, I quickly read the phrase over again, memorizing it so I could repeat it back.

Summer from the Olympian team moved to my side, scanning the wall. "Find anything yet?"

I blinked in the low light, considered, and then shook my head. "Nope." I headed further down the wall and pretended to keep scanning. I sucked in a breath when Summer crouched at the base of the wall I was standing in front of, gave it a cursory look, then sighed and flounced over to a row of lined up skulls, peering at them as if they'd have the clue.

She hadn't seen the phrase.

Biting my lip, I pretended to keep looking, and moved closer to Dean. I tapped him on the shoulder when I passed by and gave him a meaningful look. When Summer headed further into the tunnels, I leaned over to Dean. "I found it."

"Really?" His eyes widened and he jerked around. "Where?"

"Base of the wall nearby," I whispered. I gestured at it furtively, making sure that Summer didn't see my hand motions. "We need to fly to Pompeii."

Dean left my side and pretended to continue searching the wall, knelt, read the clue, and then wandered away, still pretending to look for the answer. He circled back to me a moment later, an excited look on his face. "That's it," he breathed, grinning. "Flying straight through to the next leg without a rest? Damn."

"I know. We need to tell the others."

He leaned past me and gazed to where Summer was. "She find it yet?"

I shook my head. "She'll suspect something's up if we leave together, though."

"I'll leave," he told me. "After a few minutes, come up and we'll all head to the airport together."

I nodded and pretended to examine the wall he'd been staring at while he sneaked out. Slowly, I counted to sixty as Summer moved past again, then shook her head and headed further into the long, dark tunnels.

I pretended to keep searching the walls until she disappeared down a tunnel curve and was no longer in sight. As soon as she was gone, I raced up the stairs and headed back out to where Liam was waiting. Abby and Dean were still there, practically bouncing with excitement.

"So should we head straight to the airport? Or do you think there's another part of the clue that we missed? That almost seems too easy," Dean commented, shrugging on his backpack.

"I didn't see anything else on the wall," I told him, then glanced at Liam. "I guess we'll know for sure if we head to the airport and the other teams are there."

"Good point," Liam told me. He leaned and whispered so only I could hear him. "And good eyes."

"Thanks," I said as he handed me my backpack, and wondered why that small bit of praise made me so freaking flustered. It wasn't like he'd told me that I looked hot, or he'd been as aroused as I'd been when he'd grabbed my inner thighs.

He'd simply told me I had good eyes. Good lord, I needed to get over this crush I was forming.

WHEN WE ARRIVED AT THE AIRPORT, WE PURCHASED TICKETS TO Naples, the closest airport to Pompeii, and I purchased a travel guidebook. There was a three-hour wait on the flight, which meant the other teams might have time to catch up to us.

Sure enough, we arrived at our gate, and there was Joel and Derron, the war heroes, and Brodie and Tesla. Brodie and Tesla were cuddled by the gate, wrapped around each other like they'd been a couple for years. As I watched, my brother leaned over and gave Tesla a long, tongue-filled kiss.

Ew.

I shot a look at my partner, and he was eying Tesla and Brodie with the same mixture of disbelief and disgust. Abby and Dean went to go find something to eat, and Liam and I found a quiet corner of the terminal and sat down with our travel guide. There were plenty of chairs, but I wanted to stretch out my legs, and I was getting used to sprawling on the airport floor to get comfortable, so I sat down against a nearby wall and stretched my legs out in front of me. Liam sat next to me on the ground, his shoulder pressing against mine.

"They're kind of ridiculous, aren't they?" I told him, and nodded at Tesla and Brodie, who were still making out and hadn't acknowledged our presence.

"That's Tesla for you," Liam said, his voice wry. He glanced at me. "I can't believe you thought I was with her."

I shrugged, and thought of his hands on my inner thighs again, then shivered.

"Cold?" He looped an arm over my shoulder and pulled me close.

I'd been about to protest that I wasn't all that cold, but his arm against me felt really, really good. Comforting. Warm. Heavy and delicious. So I snuggled a bit closer and pulled out the travel guide so we could review it while we waited for the flight.

And put it away again when a cameraman was suddenly in our faces. "Katy, why don't you tell us what place you think you're at right now?"

I mentally groaned. We were sometimes dive-bombed by the cameramen who wanted us to do insta-interviews. The more footage they had, the more they could create a compelling story, I supposed. And an insta-interview usually meant that you had to get away from your partner and go quietly speak one-on-one with the camera. I'd never had one shove into my face and start interviewing me like this. Maybe it was because I was cuddled against Liam.

Good TV and all.

Damn, Liam was really good at this pretending stuff. Might as well make good TV myself. I put my hand on Liam's thigh and glanced at him, appearing to consider things. My nails scratched at his leg through his jeans, idly rubbing. "Well, there are three other teams here besides us, so we're definitely in the middle of the pack. I think that's a good thing." I squinted up at the camera. "Though I wouldn't mind if the other teams missed the flight. It sounds mean to say that, but I have to keep reminding myself that this is a race."

Liam's arm over my shoulder tightened, and I felt the muscles in his leg tense as I continued to scratch him. Then, I felt his fingers play along the edge of my shirt sleeve, brushing against my exposed skin. It sent tingles through my body.

"How do you feel about Brodie and Tesla's partnership? They seem to be dominating."

I glanced over at my brother, who was still sucking face with his partner, oblivious to the cameraman that filmed them a few short feet away. "Um, Brodie and Tesla are interesting, I guess. I was really hurt when he abandoned me, at first. But I think Liam and I are making a pretty good team." I looked up at my tall partner, whose shaggy hair was halfway in his face, covering one of his eyebrow piercings.

Liam smiled at me, that finger still teasing along my arm. "I think so."

"You two seem to be getting friendly," the cameraman prompted.

To my horror, my face turned bright red. I could feel the flush moving up my cheeks, heating them. Liam chuckled and tugged me against him, tucking my head onto his shoulder. "She's not going to answer that right now. She's too tired."

I gave the camera a yawn and snuggled closer to Liam, who made a surprisingly delicious person to rest against, and closed my eyes. I felt his fingers begin to play with one of my blonde pigtails, and I smiled to myself. Eventually, the cameraman moved on and we were left alone again.

"The coast is clear," Liam murmured. "You can wake up now."

I could. But I was suddenly exhausted and Liam was so good to lean against. I yawned again and turned my face into his neck. "Do I have to?"

I felt his laugh more than I heard it. "Nah," he said. "Take a nap. We can plot our race domination on the plane." His fingers continued to play with my ponytail, almost idly. "I'll stay awake."

And even though it wasn't fair and I should have stayed up to keep him company, he was warm and snuggly and I was so incredibly tired. Liam smelled wonderful, his neck barely brushing against my nose. I drifted off to sleep.

Chapter Six

"Can I put in a request that we have more legs like the Paris one? More partner on partner action?" —Liam Brogan, Paris Leg of The World Races

WHEN WE ARRIVED AT THE AIRPORT IN NAPLES, IT WAS LATE AT night. We took a cab out to Pompeii, and even though it was dark, we bought tiny flashlights at one of the airport stores with the last of our money and hunted up and down along the roped off tourist areas until we found The World Races mat.

To my surprise, it wasn't a local waiting for us, but Chip Brubaker and a camera crew. Brodie and Tesla were already there, sitting off to one side, and so were Dean and Abby. Liam and I arrived in third place, and we were promptly handed our next clue.

The clue indicated that our team task would start once Pompeii opened at seven in the morning. Until then, there was nothing to do but wait.

The nice thing about this leg, though, was that we were given two hundred dollars, which we carefully pocketed. We'd been almost broke up to this point, every dollar carefully spent on food and taxis. Two hundred dollars would be a total luxury.

With nothing else to do and hours to go before daylight, we sat down with the teams to wait for the others to arrive. There was an open spot between Dean/Abby and Brodie/Tesla, but Liam's hand tugged mine, indicating we should sit a short distance away, and so we did. We kept a flashlight out, pulled out our guide book, and began to plot.

"It's a team challenge," I told Liam as we re-read the clue. We could choose 'Apollo' or 'Jupiter' according to the clue, which didn't tell us too much. "The guidebook mentions a Temple of Apollo, and a Temple of Jupiter. That has to be it."

"Maybe we have to visit one of the temples?" Liam suggested.

Made sense. "I think there's a floor plan in this thing. We could figure out which one is simpler and go to that one—"

A shoe scuffed to my side, and then Brodie was squatting next to me. "Hey, sis."

Liam leaned in front of me protectively, glaring at my brother. "Buzz off."

I closed the guidebook and gave Brodie a suspicious look. "I see you remembered that I exist?"

"Nice to see you too." Brodie smirked. "So I guess you're still mad at me?"

"You'd guess right. You ditched me, and you've been ignoring me to play tonsil hockey with the rock star. Like I'm supposed to be grateful that you're paying attention to me now?" I shifted, moving a little closer to Liam. "You made it quite clear that you're not in this for family, and that's just fine with me."

"Look, I said I was sorry, Katy."

"Actually, you didn't—"

"How was I supposed to know the Ace would split us up?"

"Why did you use it to save another team anyhow?" I looked over at Liam. "Sorry. No offense."

"It's okay," he told me, but his face was tight with dislike as he watched my brother.

"Cause it was Tesla Spooner," Brodie told me. "Fucking hottest rock chick ever."

"So you sold me out because you wanted to make out with a rock chick?"

"Well, yeah." And he grinned boyishly.

I wanted to kick him in the nuts. "You suck, Brodie."

"I'm sorry you're still mad, Katy. I just wanted to see if you two wanted to work with me and Tesla for the rest of the race. We can still make it to the end with both of our teams, you know. I think it'd be a good thing."

I stared at my brother. "Are you serious? You ditched me and now you want my help? Our help?"

He shrugged his shoulders. "Makes sense to me. Now instead of just me and you, it's two teams. We can work off of each other and push to the end." His gaze moved to our guidebook. "And we can share information."

"Or," I said in a sarcastic voice, "we could share our information and you could use it to hose me again. Nice try, Brodie."

"Fine. If you're going to hold a grudge, I can't stop you." Brodie gave me a sad look that I didn't buy for a minute. "Can we borrow your guidebook for a few, at least?"

"No," Liam said. "Get your own."

"We didn't have the money on the last leg," Brodie said, talking to me and ignoring Liam. "It'd be really helpful if you could let us just see it for a few minutes—"

"No," I said this time. "There's plenty of time before seven am. Go get your own guidebook."

"But you've got one right here—"

"And we said no," Liam reminded him. "You've been a dick to your sister the whole time. You shouldn't be surprised that she doesn't want to help you."

"Fine. You don't want to help me?" Brodie reached over and plucked the guidebook out of Liam's hands, getting to his feet. "Then I'll just take it—"

Instantly, Liam was on his feet, going after Brodie, and grasped the guidebook. "That's not yours."

Brodie put a hand on Liam's jaw, planting it and trying to shove him aside to keep the guide from him. The two men began to scuffle, and I screamed as they started to get a bit violent. What the hell was happening? "Stop it, Brodie," I yelled, leaping to my feet.

"Liam, quit it," Tesla bellowed off to the side.

"Hey, buzz off," I called at her, even as the men's struggles got more aggressive.

A ripping sound cut through the air.

Suddenly, Chip was there, pulling Brodie off, and Dean stepped in, blocking Liam. "What's going on here?" The host asked. Cameras hovered all around, catching every humiliating moment for TV.

"This asshole stole what wasn't his," Liam said, waving what was now one half of a tourism guide to Italy. "And I'm tired of him walking all over my partner. Katy's been nothing but nice about this whole shit deal and her brother thinks he can just do whatever he wants."

My jaw dropped a little to hear Liam defend me like that—against my own brother. It was…really nice.

Chip frowned at the two men. He looked at Brodie. "Is it true that you stole from this team?"

Brodie gave a sigh of disgust and tossed the ripped half of the stolen guide onto the ground. "I didn't realize they were going to be such pussies about it."

"I'm sorry, but stealing is against the rules. Yellow team, you will have to take a two-hour penalty for rules violation at seven am, when the facilities open."

The look Brodie shot my way was withering. "Seriously?"

"I'm afraid so."

"Too bad," Liam said in a bland voice, then scooped up the discarded half of the guide.

"Careful," Chip said. "I can give you a penalty too."

Liam returned to my side and said nothing else. I could practically feel the tension vibrating off of him. I put an arm around his waist and steered him away from the tense little group. "Come on. Let's just go sit down."

The crowd dispersed, and a cameraman came to our side, filming as Liam and I sat down off to the side again. I barely noticed that another team came up to the mat, looking confused as everyone scattered. Summer and Polly. I looked at Liam, noticing that his lip was swollen on one side. My fingers brushed over it. "You okay?"

He ran his tongue over his lip, and it slid against my fingertips, which just made my entire body flare up. "Yeah. Your brother elbowed me in the face."

My eyes narrowed. "He's such an ass. You want me to say something?"

"Nah. They'll kick him from the game."

"And you don't want that?"

"Not if it'll make Tesla run screaming to the label about what I did." After a moment, he grinned. "Pretty sure I elbowed him in the gut, though."

I smiled back, and let my hand drop back into my lap.

To my surprise, he picked up my hand and kissed my fingertips, right where his tongue had brushed against them. "He doesn't know what he missed out on when he lost you as a partner."

Warmth flooded through me. I tried to think of what to say, but my gaze was fascinated by his mouth on my fingertips.

A large hand clapped me on the back, startling me. "You guys ok?" Dean leaned over us. "That was some messy shit, huh?"

I nodded and pulled my hand back toward me, hoping Dean and the others hadn't noticed that electric moment between Liam and I. "We're fine. Thanks, Dean."

He nodded. "You let me and Abby know if you need anything."

As Dean left, I squeezed in next to Liam and tucked my legs close. Like at the airport, I pulled my body close to his and snuggled in as we waited for dawn. Neither one of us spoke, and it seemed like a bad move to pull our guide out right away again.

"I'm sorry," I whispered to Liam.

His fingers reached out and brushed along my jawline in a tender caress. "I'm not."

WENDI AND RICK, THE MOTHER AND SON TEAM, WERE THE LAST TO arrive in Pompeii. They showed up some time around four in the morning, while I was trying to sleep, and the sounds of Wendi's high pitched bawling woke me up. We were a little sad to see them go because they were genuinely nice, but teams had to leave. That was just how the game worked. As long as it wasn't us, I didn't much care.

When six am rolled around, the remaining teams started to head back to the entrance designated for the competition. Liam and I waited a bit, then consulted our guide again.

Two major temples inside Pompeii—Jupiter and Apollo. We studied the floor plans, then decided that we'd head to the Temple of Jupiter, despite it being just a bit further into the city than the Temple of Apollo, since everyone would probably head to Apollo first. Then, we joined the others.

At seven, the teams flooded into Pompeii. The ruins were magnificent— from the cobbled streets to the graffiti-covered and frescoed buildings around us. I wanted to stop and look at the fascinating city, but we didn't have time. It was a race, after all.

The first temple we passed was the temple of Apollo, and we could see the challenge areas set up. Immediately, four teams broke off and headed for it. Abby and Dean hesitated and looked at us, and we headed on to the next temple. They followed us, since we'd agreed to work together on this leg of the race as well.

Each station was set up with dozens of white broken pieces, all supposed to resemble marble but felt like plastic. Our goal was to create a replica of each temple as it stood once upon a time, and a judge would swing by with our next clue. Except we had a mountain of pieces, and they all looked the same.

More puzzles. Ugh. I picked up one block, studied it, and gave Liam a helpless look. "I don't even know where to begin."

He took the piece from me, studied it, and then handed it back. "I wonder if the other temple's any easier."

I flipped to my diagram of the Temple of Apollo. The Temple of Jupiter had one single row of columns. The Temple of Apollo had many, many rows of various sized columns. "Not according to this."

"Nothing to do but get started, then," Liam said, and sighed.

I echoed the sentiment and gave a heavy sigh of my own.

BY THE TIME THE ITALY LEG WAS OVER, I NEVER WANTED TO SEE anything Roman ever again. It was easily the longest day of my life. We'd ran around on only hours of sleep, and as the day wore on, the weather became oppressively muggy and too warm.

The temple build took hours to do. Abby and Dean and Liam and I worked together, consulting the chart in our guidebook, the current ruins, and good old fashioned hunches. We tried, failed, tried again, and failed once more. When Abby and Dean finished theirs, Abby immediately ran over to me and whispered what was wrong with our model. We fixed it minutes later and received our clue, just as Brodie and Tesla ran up, their penalty completed.

For once, the penalty would end up being in their favor, because all they had to do was look at our models and pattern theirs after ours. Damn it. I felt the strongest urge to kick mine over, but I didn't know if that would make us have to restart.

The next clue was for an individual task. "I'll take this one," I told Liam. "You did all the heavy lifting of the temple pieces. Sit down and rest a few."

He nodded and collapsed in the shade of one of the buildings. His brow was beaded with sweat and he pulled out a bottle of water, looking rather winded. I didn't blame him—he and Dean had worked like animals on the last challenge while Abby and I stood around and pointed out directions.

My task was a simple one—theoretically. It was a visual scavenger hunt. I had to go to one villa, pick up a scroll, go to the next villa, pick up a feather pen, and the next villa had a shopping list of 'items' I had to find in the paintings and frescoes. Then, I needed to visit sixteen different marked villas in the ruins and note where each object was found. Then, I had to run to a judge and show him my list. If I had everything marked correctly, we could move on to the next task.

It seemed almost too easy. Of course, I hadn't realized why the producers had wanted to do this particular challenge until I arrived at the first villa and saw the cameraman set up in front of the mural, ready to film reactions.

The murals in Pompeii? Were dirty. Hugely dirty. There were murals of a woman receiving oral in a bathhouse, murals of a threesome, murals of gods with penises longer than an arm. You name it? The Pompeiians had made a beautiful mural of it. I giggled and blushed my way through each one, ran into Abby about halfway through, and we compared notes.

She pointed at the house with the mural of the well-hung god. "I called that one 'Dean.'"

I died laughing. I almost joked that I hadn't found one to call Liam, but my mind flashed back to the mural of the woman in the bathhouse receiving oral from the guy kneeling in front of her, and my face flamed bright red.

My partner and I hadn't done much more than hold hands. I couldn't be thinking such dirty things about him.

Unfortunately, I thought them anyhow.

We snickered our way through the last house and then ran back to the judge with our answers, laughing the entire time.

Once we had the next clue, it was our turn to rest and the boys took over. Abby and I sat in the shade of a building and drank bottles of now-warm water as the boys performed a grape stomping challenge that would somehow end up as wine. By that time, Brodie and Tesla had caught back up with us, and Brodie climbed in to his grape bucket next to Liam.

I was thrilled for Abby when she and Dean finished first with the grapes and received their clue token. She gave me an excited look, then they ran off to find the pit stop. I tried not to feel impatient as Liam stomped grapes in a slow, methodical motion even as Brodie was stomping so fast and so hard that he looked like he was dancing a jig. He was determined to beat us to the next task. My brother wanted this so bad he could taste it. So bad that he was willing to fight with my partner over a guidebook that might give an advantage.

Guilt flickered through me. Was it such a terrible thing if Brodie wanted this badly enough to play dirty? Was I a bad sister for not helping him out? He'd never pretended that he didn't want anything except to be a star.

And me, I was playing at a fake relationship with my partner to get more TV time. It made me feel a little dirty just to think about. I mean, here I was fantasizing about Liam and he was just making sure we were interesting on TV. That seemed wrong.

"Done," Liam shouted, holding up his wine amphora, now full of foot-stomped grape juice. The judge nodded and handed him a disk, and I jerked to my feet. I hauled our backpacks even as Liam hopped on one foot, trying to shove a sock back onto his grape-stained foot. "Read it," he breathed to me as he worked on putting on his shoes.

I read it silently, noticing Tesla hovering a bit too close nearby.

Make your way to the finish line for this leg of the race. Chip's waiting where you met him.

I hugged the disk to my chest and grinned at Liam. Finally, a freaking break. A finish line meant a twelve hour rest period between this leg of the race and the next one, and I couldn't wait to sleep and take a hot shower. Preferably both.

Ten minutes later, we crossed the finish line, hand in hand, and stopped in front of Chip Brubaker.

He gave us a brilliant white smile, his face heavily caked with makeup that was looking streaky thanks to the sweat on his brow. "Katy and Liam, you are the second team to arrive. Congratulations!"

I gave a weak cheer and flung my arms around Liam's waist, too tired and hot to do more than that.

"You have twelve hours between now and the next task. I suggest you find a place to get some rest," Chip told us.

We nodded and walked off the mat, away from the cameras. As soon as we did, all the tension seemed to leave my body, and I felt exhausted. I wiped at my own sweaty brow, wishing that my backpack wasn't quite so heavy.

As if reading my mind, Liam tugged at my backpack and pulled it off my shoulders. "Let me get that for you."

"You don't have to," I protested. "We don't need to be anywhere fast."

"Yeah, but you're small and you look wiped."

I *was* small—barely five foot. But it wasn't fair to him. I protested again.

He shook his head. "You and Abby had to run all over the city for your task. Did you see how tired she was? I wouldn't be surprised if she and Dean left to find a private hotel room."

"Can we do that? Do we have the money?"

"Won't hurt to check, will it?" He slung my backpack over his shoulder. "Come on."

He took my hand and we headed into the city around the ruins.

It didn't take long to find a few hotels. The first two we tried were pricier than we wanted to spend, but the third one had a room for about the right price—eighty dollars for a night. We decided we could give up that much money, paid, and headed up the stairs to our room.

I blinked at the sight of the small, clean hotel bedroom. It was nice enough. There was a large window overlooking the city, a nightstand, a bathroom...and a single bed.

Again.

Liam didn't notice my hesitation. He set down the bags, moved over to the air conditioner, and turned it on. Then, he sat down on the edge of the bed and began to pull off his shoes, grimacing at his purple-stained feet. "Okay with you if I use the shower first?"

I nodded. He was definitely dirtier than I was.

Liam grinned and stripped off his shirt, displaying his bare chest. I tried not to look, but couldn't help myself. When it had been Abby, Dean, and both of us in the room? He'd been careful to stay fully clothed. Now that it was just me, though? All bets seemed to be off. I watched him as he undressed. His back was decorated with several random, smaller tattoos, and one pectoral seemed to be covered in a giant spider-web tattoo. After a moment, he undid the fly of his jeans and dropped them to the ground, standing in only his boxers. When he turned, I saw his back was sculpted enough that he actually had back dimples just above his rather tight ass.

Oh. Damn. I lay back on the bed and grabbed one of the pillows, closing my eyes and pretending to sleep. I didn't move a muscle until I heard the bathroom door shut and the water turn on. After that, I relaxed, flipping onto my back and staring up at the ceiling of the small hotel room.

Was Liam this casual with Tesla? Did he strip down to his boxers in front of any chick? Or was it just because of our special situation?

And why was I paying so much attention to it?

I shook my head, annoyed with myself. The guy probably had no idea I was so ultra-focused on everything he did.

An arm slid around my waist, a warm body spooning against my back. I gave a small sigh and snuggled in closer, enjoying the feel of the person wrapped around me. His body was big and long compared to mine, entangling with my limbs, and the arm around my waist felt heavenly. And as my bottom shifted, I heard a barely audible male groan.

My eyes flew open. I stared around me, disoriented. Hotel room. Okay. Unfamiliar hotel room. Through the window, I could see the skies were pink with dusk, the curtains fluttering as the air conditioner blasted. I lay on a comfortable bed, and a man had his arm around my waist. I glanced down and saw the familiar black lines of Liam's tattoos.

We were spooning in the only bed.

It was my fault, I told myself, squeezing my eyes closed. I'd sprawled on the bed and grabbed at pillows while he showered. I must have fallen asleep, and when he'd gotten out, instead of waking me up, he'd crawled into bed next to me to catch a few hours of sleep. Totally plausible. Logical. No problem.

Except for that tiny groan that had made my pulse race and my nipples harden. They were hard even now, aching points of awareness as my backside pressed against him.

Okay, maybe he'd been asleep and hadn't realized that he'd groaned aloud. Maybe he didn't realize that my bottom was pressed up against his groin, and I could feel his cock growing hard. Guys got boners when they slept, right? Right. No problem. I'd just sneak away, hop into the shower, and make enough noise that would wake him up and we'd go back to our normal companionship.

After all, there were no cameras around right now. There was zero benefit to kissing me. None. Zilch.

I rolled onto my back, slowly, and opened an eye, daring a look at Liam.

He was awake. His hair was nearly dry, he'd shaved, and the look in his eyes was sleepy, but he was awake.

Heat flushed through my body all over again, and I lay there, frozen in place, my heart thumping in my chest. He was inches away from my face, his arm still around my waist.

He'd groaned while *awake*.

My nipples were so incredibly hard at the realization. We were in bed together. Alone. For the first time since we'd started this crazy journey, we were alone.

And suddenly, I wanted to kiss him again. I reached out, hesitant, and brushed my fingers along the planes of his jaw. He gave another soft, low groan, but didn't move. His eyes watched me with intensity as I stroked my fingers along his skin, then brushed them against the ring on the side of his lip, the mark that Brodie's elbow had left on his mouth, and then just traced his lips because they were there.

He nipped at my fingers as I did.

I whimpered then, feeling heat pool between my legs. I leaned in closer, until my forehead pressed against his, and my gaze went to his mouth. I hesitated for a moment, then changed the angle, slanting my face so I'd meet with his mouth in a light, teasing kiss.

"Katy," he whispered, my name a mere breath on his lips. And that made me shiver all over again.

I brushed my lips against his once more, then ran my tongue along his lower lip, exploring it. His mouth parted under mine, and I sucked on his lower lip, gently, tasting him. He groaned against me, and his tongue brushed against my lips, a silent entreaty. I angled my mouth against his again, and met his tongue with mine. Suddenly, the kisses changed in intensity from a slow exploration to a wild hunger. The kiss grew deep, and I felt Liam's arm tighten around my waist, dragging me closer to him in the bed. My nipples brushed against his chest and I gasped, even as his tongue thrust into my mouth.

And then I forgot about everything but that kiss. Because holy hell, the man could kiss. His tongue stud flicked against my mouth, at once foreign and titillating as his tongue stroked over mine. The kiss deepened again, his tongue stroking deep into my mouth, even as his thigh moved over my leg, twining my body with his. I dragged a hand to his hair, wanting to twist my fingers in those dark locks, and gasped when he used his tongue stud to flick against my tongue again. I whimpered when the kiss grew deep once more, as his hips rolled against mine in a suggestive manner that left nothing to the imagination, and felt my own body move in response.

He groaned and his hand slid from my side up to my breast, cupping it.

I felt his thumb brush over the hard, aching peak and my cry of pleasure was swallowed into his kiss. I pushed against his hand, need ratcheting upward as our kisses grew more intense.

And then my stomach growled. Loud.

I broke the kiss in horror, my eyes flying open.

Liam chuckled. "Hungry?"

"I...I guess." But he was still giving me that sleepy, delicious look that made me want to fling my arms back around him, roll him onto his back and then straddle those hips that had rocked so deliciously against mine a second ago.

"Your stomach probably has more sense than us," he said in a low voice. "We should eat a big meal and sleep it off before continuing on the race."

"You're probably right," I said, my voice sounding far more normal than I felt. "How long was I asleep?"

"About two hours," he told me, and rolled away to sit on the edge of the bed. "You want to take a shower? We can head out afterward."

"Okay," I said breathlessly, but didn't move. My body was still thinking about that deep, wicked kiss, the way his mouth had moved against mine, the way his hips had ground against my own. That strange and wonderful tongue piercing. His big hand on my breast.

But Liam put on his earbuds and dragged his backpack over to his lap, and began to tap out a song. It was as if I wasn't there all over again. And that made me feel...weird. Like I was just a convenient stand-in for Tesla.

Frowning, I slid off the bed and grabbed my own backpack, heading to the shower.

THE SHOWER DID A LOT TO RESTORE MY MOOD. BY THE TIME I EMERGED from it, fresh scrubbed and in a clean set of clothes, I felt almost human again.

Liam sat up when I emerged from the bathroom, my wet hair twisted into a sleek knot on top of my head. "Shall we go out to dinner?"

I smiled, still feeling a little out of sorts after our kiss. "I guess we can't visit Italy and not eat some food before we go, right?"

"Exactly right."

We left our backpacks in the room but kept our necessities—money, passports, room key—with us. I was disappointed to see there was a cameraman waiting in the hall when we left our room, but I supposed that was his job. I ignored it and headed down the hall with Liam, both of us trying to act like we weren't being tailed.

We exchanged a bit more of our money and then walked the city streets, trying to find a place to eat that wouldn't be too pricey. One place smelled absolutely heavenly, but the prices on the street chalkboard were more than I'd wanted to spend.

Liam stopped in front of the restaurant, as if reading my mind. "We could split the food and only spend half the money."

"Now you're talking," I told him, and we headed inside.

As we sat down at one of the tables, I smiled over at Liam and put my napkin in my lap…and froze. This was…

He noticed the weird look on my face and laughed. "This feels like a date, doesn't it?"

I nodded. "You feel it, too?"

"Can't help it," he told me as the waiter approached. He glanced over his shoulder, where the cameraman hovered, still filming. "That kind of kills the mood, though."

That it did.

Our waiter didn't speak a lick of English, but between him and a helpful person at another table, we managed to communicate that we wanted to order one plate and share it. We didn't know what to order, so the waiter suggested in rapid-fire Italian that we get the special of the day. And it wasn't Italian food without wine, so our helper at the next table ordered us two glasses, despite our protests. We looked like a nice young couple, he told us, which made me giggle nervously.

Liam just reached out and took my hand from across the table.

My eyes widened. "What are you doing?"

"He's buying us wine," Liam told me with a grin. "The least we can do is look like a happy couple." When I began to protest, he lifted my hand to his mouth, kissed the back, and murmured, "Good TV, remember?"

"Blackmailer," I said, but I laughed.

He winked at me, and then rubbed his thumb across my knuckles.

A prickle of awareness moved over my skin and I pulled my hand away just as the waiter brought us our wine. I sipped it, then made an exclamation of surprise. "Wow, this is really good."

Liam tasted his, and then agreed. "Doesn't taste a bit like that stuff I stomped earlier today."

I laughed again. "At least you didn't have to stare at giant penises."

He snorted. "I am sure I could have handled that challenge just fine."

I tilted my head. "You're used to handling giant penises?"

He wagged his eyebrows at me, that piercing moving back and forth. "I handle one in particular every day."

"I...walked right into that one, didn't I?"

"You did."

I chuckled and shook my head. "I take full responsibility, then."

"You did well today," he said, his voice growing serious. "Extremely well. I think Brodie messed up in switching partners."

A glow of pleasure spread through me. "Oh?"

He nodded. "Tesla's aggressive, but she also high maintenance. If she gets tired, he's going to hear about it. If she's hungry, she needs fine dining. I was tired of her on day one." His mouth curled into one of those secretive smiles. "But I can't say that to her or she'll complain to the label."

"Well, Brodie seems to like her just fine," I said. "He was quick to ditch his little sister as soon as a hot rock star showed up."

"He's an idiot," Liam said. "You're one of the reasons we've been doing so well on our challenges. You're smart and you work hard and you never complain. Like I said, I think I lucked out."

His praise was making me glow. "You're just saying that because you kissed me earlier."

"Actually," he said slowly, drawing the word out. "If you want to get technical, you kissed me. Twice now."

I stared at him. Oh. I guess I had. Twice now. "Um." I had no idea what to say to that.

"I'm just teasing you, Katy," he said. "I wasn't exactly fighting to get away either time."

"No, you weren't, were you?" I regained a bit of my confidence at that. "Nor were you fighting to get away when I woke up and you were sprawled all over me."

He just grinned. "Can I help it if you were hogging the only bed in the room?" He shrugged his big shoulders. "Besides, you were so small and cuddly looking, I couldn't help myself."

I felt myself get warm again, and knew I was blushing. I sipped my wine, thankful that the waiter arrived with a large plate of pasta and set it down in front of Liam. It smelled delicious.

He raised an eyebrow at me. "I guess this is all mine."

"Screw that," I told him, and pulled my chair to the side of the table so I could better access the plate. "You're sharing or I'm throwing the next challenge and we're through."

"Well, I don't want that," Liam murmured, and the look he gave me was hot with need. It was the same look he'd given me when we were curled around each other on the bed, and my pulse fluttered wildly in response.

We had two sets of forks, but the food was so pretty that I didn't know where to start. I hovered my fork uncertainly. It looked like an angel hair pasta covered with some sort of chunky, vegetable red sauce, and fresh mussels lined the bowl, artfully cracked open.

Liam got a wicked look in his eyes as he saw me hesitate. He inclined his head at the cameraman hovering in the distance, ever filming. "Want to make some good TV?"

"I'm not sure I like that look in your eyes," I teased. Did I want to make good TV? Did I ever.

He stabbed his fork into the food, and began to swirl it in the rich noodles and sauce. Then, when he'd crafted a forkful, he held it out to me to eat.

He was going to feed me.

"You sneak," I whispered, and leaned in, mouth open and lips parted. I watched his gaze drop there, and felt my body flush with his attention again. Then, he pushed the fork into my mouth carefully.

I pulled away, chewing as the flavors burst on my tongue. It was delicious, and I gave a little moan of delight. The forkful had been messy, though, and a bit of sauce lingered on my cheek. I reached up with my napkin, and Liam stopped me. Instead, he leaned in and lightly ran his tongue over my cheek, tasting the sauce.

"Delicious," he told me a second later in that husky voice.

And every note in my body sang.

"Turnabout's fair play," I told him, and tugged the plate toward me. I swirled a few noodles onto my fork and then lifted it for him to take. And when Liam leaned in to eat off of my fork? I had to admit that it was pretty erotic.

After the initial sharing, our hunger took over and we ate like normal people. Liam refused to eat the mussels, and I knew he was thinking of mukluk. I laughed and ate them all, since I had a cast-iron stomach. They were delicious, too, fresh from the Mediterranean. All of the food was incredible, and so was the wine. We even splurged on a dessert, because how could we not?

Eventually, though, our meal was done, our wine drank. My eyes were beginning to droop with exhaustion, and Liam glanced at a clock. "If we head back to the hotel soon, we can probably get another six hours of sleep before we have to head out to the starting line."

I gave him a sleepy smile. "That sounds good to me."

His gaze focused on my face. "I can sleep on the floor, if it really does make you uncomfortable to share the bed with me."

I shook my head. "I wouldn't do that to you, Liam. You know that." After a moment, I added, "And it doesn't make me uncomfortable. I kind of like it."

He smiled.

We paid for the food and headed back out into the warm night. When Liam reached for my hand, I automatically took his and we strolled, hand in hand, back to the hotel. By the time we got back to our room, we were so tired that we didn't do more than take our shoes off and crawl under the covers. He pulled me against him and we spooned again, but this time, all we did was sleep.

There'd be time enough for more flirting in the morning. For now? We needed to rest up so we could be on our A game.

Chapter Seven

"You know, when the label made me come on this race, I didn't think beyond the fact that I was going to have to cater to Tesla for the next few weeks. I didn't expect to get partners flipped, and I didn't expect to meet anyone like Katy. She's, well, she's pretty incredible. I'm fascinated by her and I find myself wanting to spend every waking moment just watching her. How she moves, how she thinks. I've got it bad, don't I? I'm going on like a freaking sap." —Liam Brogan, *Egypt Leg of The World Races*

SOMEWHERE AROUND THREE IN THE MORNING, ITALY TIME, WE WOKE up and headed back out to the flag site in front of Pompeii. A man in a white toga waited for us, and when we arrived at the starting line, he promptly handed us our next disk.

I took it, flipped it over, and began to read. "Make your way to the Pyramids at Giza in Egypt and look for the next flag station. You have one hundred dollars for this leg of the race." I looked at Liam. "We're rich."

He laughed, rubbing his eyes. We were both still worn out from our interrupted sleep, but trying desperately to wake up. "We are. A hundred dollars might buy us another hotel room for the next stop."

"Nice," I said, tucking the disk under my arm and trying not to blush too much. "It'll be good to get a real night's sleep."

Yeah, because I was totally not thinking about sleep at the moment. I was thinking about how it'd felt to wake up that morning with Liam curled around me again, both of us under the covers and fully dressed. His arm had been around me again, and my legs had been tangled with his. Instead of facing away from him, though, I'd woken up and found my head was on his chest as if he were my pillow.

And it had been awesome.

There hadn't been time to kiss or make out this morning, though. It had been all race, all the time. A little disappointing, but we needed to keep our heads in the game if we wanted to beat Brodie and Tesla.

We headed away from the starting line, and as we did, Liam spoke. "We can head straight to the airport, or we can see if there's a nearby travel agency and book tickets ahead of time. Grab some breakfast, too."

"That sounds good," I said with a yawn. "I could use some coffee."

The race had called taxis for us, and we instructed ours to head to the nearest travel agency. We found an all-night one and headed in. At the sight of a computer in the main area, Liam glanced over at me. "Why don't I order tickets and you look up information online? See what we can find out about the pyramids. Visiting hours and stuff like that."

"Sure." I headed over to the computer. There was a placard in front of it that said "*Uso Gratuito*" and "Free Use" underneath in English, and a smaller sentence underneath in Italian that I couldn't make out, but was probably "No porn" or something. I sat down and began to web search for the Great Pyramids and travel. There were a million links, of course, so I clicked on the first one and began to read.

As I did, I peeked over the computer monitor and looked at Liam. His back was facing me, his shaggy black hair messier than usual, given that we'd just woken up. I felt warm just watching him, and knew I was harboring a serious crush at the moment. We were just making good TV, after all, so there was no need for me to get all crazy obsessed over him, but I was heading in that direction.

He was just so freaking cute. Cute with a hint of dangerous. I was an idiot to get all goofy over a rock boy, but I couldn't help myself.

I had an idea and opened another web browser, and did a search for *Finding Threnody*. A jillion web hits came up, and I pulled up their

Wikipedia page. Tesla's picture was splashed everywhere, and she stood in the forefront of every photo while the three dark-haired guys stood in the background. Liam was there, but it wasn't a good picture. I frowned and scanned the text instead. There was a list of hits, and three platinum albums mentioned. They had sold six point five million albums to date, which was really impressive in the digital age, and over nine million downloads of their biggest hit, *Worm in the Apple*.

I headed to their webpage next, and sure enough, Tesla's picture was sprawled all over the page with Liam and two other guys standing in the background. Jeez. Camera hog much? For some reason, I was irritated on his behalf. Didn't he deserve the limelight just as much as Tesla did? I clicked on 'bios' next. Tesla's was half a page long. Under 'Liam Brogan' there was only a small paragraph.

Liam Brogan started to play guitar at the age of seven. He joined his first metal band at the advanced age of twelve. When he was seventeen, he dropped out of high school to focus on music full time and lied about his age to audition for lead guitar for Finding Threnody. His dedication impressed the band, especially Tesla Spooner, and he was invited to join. He and Tesla dated for a short time, but broke up when they realized it was going to come between them and the ability to make great music. They remain friends and their breakup inspired the song Dark Stars.

I stared at that small paragraph in horror. Liam had dated Tesla. Shit. Why had I ever thought he'd be interested in me? Silly little Katy Short, with her cutesy blonde pigtails and dorky cupcake business. I was nothing compared to the kinds of girls he was interested in, if he'd dated wild, exotic Tesla with her tattoos and stripey-colored hair. Feeling sick to my stomach, I clicked over to 'videos' and began to play the first one, turning the speakers down so no one could hear but me.

The entire thing was ridiculously dramatic, done in black and white. The only thing in color, of course, was Tesla, with her vivid hair and bright red lips. She clutched the microphone as if she was dying and sang soulfully, her eyelashes fluttering with each word. Every so often, it would cut back to the band, and then just as quickly flash away again, which drove me absolutely nuts. It was like they didn't even count, and Tesla was the only one they were interested in.

At least, until the guitar solo. Suddenly, Liam was front and center in the video, blasting into color. He held the guitar low against his hips, braced there, and his fingers danced along the strings in a familiar movement that I recognized—when his hands were moving along the backpack, he wasn't drumming. He was strumming a song. I watched in fascination as the video Liam closed his eyes as if in ecstasy, fingers moving along the neck of the guitar at a rapid pace I couldn't even fathom, as the wild notes of the song climbed higher and higher. He looked so incredibly in to the music that it felt intimate just to be watching him—

"That doesn't look like the Great Pyramid." Liam's amused voice interrupted my train of thought.

Horrified at being caught, I quickly clicked off of the webpage, only to expose the web browser search I'd done for *Finding Threnody*. I clicked off of that too, face burning, and returned to the Pyramids of Giza page. "I, uh, was just looking at…stuff."

"Uh huh," he said, but he sounded amused.

I was going to die of embarrassment right about now. I stared at the computer screen, unable to look my partner in the face.

Liam pushed a piece of paper in front of my nose. "Travel itinerary. We have a flight in about two and a half hours, which leaves us just enough time to get to the airport. And we should get there tonight."

"Tonight?" I took the itinerary from him and studied it, glad that it gave me the chance to avoid eye contact. "Wow, long flight."

"Yeah. Plenty of time to catch up on sleep." He paused for a moment, then added, "Or watch more *Finding Threnody* videos."

My face burned. "You suck."

"Apparently you don't think so." There was affection in his voice, and it made my stomach feel all quivery all over again.

As we got back into the taxi, I wondered what Liam thought of me. Had I gone from partner to fangirl in the blink of an eye? That was distressing to think about, but I couldn't take it back. The only thing I could do was continue on and act like nothing was wrong.

Meanwhile, it was starting to feel like everything was out of control.

Egypt

"I want to quit," I proclaimed loudly into the darkness. "I'm serious. I can't do this."

"Looks like we finally found something that Katy can't do," Liam murmured into my ear, but his hand squeezed mine. "You'll be okay."

"I'm not so sure about that," I said, dropping to a low crouch and trying not to hyperventilate.

When we'd first heard that we were heading to the Pyramids at Giza, I was excited. *Really* excited. If I could think of places in the world that would be exciting to visit? The pyramids were high on the list. It'd be such a fun experience to go inside and see what it was like. When we'd seen the outside of the pyramids, I'd been ridiculously stoked, practically dancing up to The World Races flag where a man gave us our next clue.

Visit each of the burial chambers in the three pyramids and find a clue. String all the clues together to determine your next task.

Simple enough. And not only were we going to visit the interior of one pyramid, we were going to visit all three. Fun!

Or so I'd thought.

We'd lucked into first place somehow—our stop at the travel agency had put us on a flight ahead of the others. We'd somehow managed to score the last seats on the plane. We'd arrived in Cairo late at night and even though the cab driver had insisted that the pyramids would be closed for tourists for the evening, we headed out anyhow.

Sure enough, the flag had been there, and the task. The World Races had made special arrangements with the tourism board and the pyramids were open just for us. Which meant we could go ahead and start the next task.

Except it was really, really dark. And I hadn't counted on claustrophobia. Nor had I counted on the fact that when we entered the Great Pyramid, the first passageway was narrow and steep. We'd had to bend over—even at my short height—to go up the steep steps. All around us were tons and tons of rock, and the inside of the pyramid was oppressively hot, and dark despite the anchor lights along the halls.

Then it hit me. I was fine for the first few steps, following behind Liam. But when I looked up into the darkness and saw nothing but the continually rising, narrow shaft? My breathing became shallow and I began to sweat, hard.

Just when I couldn't stand it any longer, the interior passage opened up, and I breathed a sigh of relief. We continued on into the King's Chamber, and studied the walls. We found a small group of tiny figurines in the center of the sarcophagus with a word marked on them—'the.'

"This must be the clue," I told Liam, and counted the figurines. "There's five others left, which means someone got eliminated last round."

"Great. We can head back out and go to the next chamber." Liam didn't look bothered at all. Meanwhile, I was all sweaty and flustered and breathing hard as if I'd ran miles instead of simply walked up a passageway.

Heading back down the passageway was hard, but not as hard when I knew we were almost out. The queen's chamber wasn't as bad, but I was still grateful when we found the next clue. Another figurine, this one labeled with the word "Take."

"At least we're done here," I panted. "I hate this pyramid."

"Just one more chamber, actually," Liam corrected. He looked at a brochure he'd gotten in the city. "There's a third chamber heading down. The subterranean chamber. We should probably check it just to be sure."

"It said burial chambers," I protested. "Not all chambers."

"Yeah, but if we miss a clue, we'll have to come back, and we're already here. Come on."

We'd arrived at the subterranean chamber stairway, and that was when I had my meltdown. It descended into the darkness at a steep angle, and as I watched Liam fold himself in half to try and get his tall body down there, I took a few steps into the shaft, and then began to tremble. The walls felt like they were closing in on me. It was hot, and dark, and cramped, and…I freaked out. I sat down in the tunnel, unable to go further. Panic was hammering through me, making my pulse pound and my heart race. I couldn't breathe.

"I can't do this," I told him, and to my horror, I felt tears prick behind my eyes. Oh jeez, I was going to start crying like a baby.

"Yes, you can, Katy. It's not so bad. I'll go in front of you, see?"

I shook my head. "I want to quit. I'm serious. I can't do this."

He grasped my hand in his. "Looks like we finally found something Katy can't do. You'll be okay."

I took huge gulps of too-warm air, my eyes squeezed shut as I tried to calm myself. I clung to his hand and we sat there in the middle of that cramped passage as I had my freak-out.

Liam didn't push me, though. He just sat and held my hand, waiting for me to get better.

"I'm sorry," I said, and hated when that it came out so incredibly wimpy.

"Hey, it's okay," Liam told me in a soft voice. "I couldn't do the mukluk.

You can't do this. I totally get that. Unfortunately, though, we both have to go down to each chamber."

I sucked in a deep breath, nodding. "I'm sorry. I'll try."

His hand slid along my leg, rubbing it to comfort me. We were wearing shorts for this leg of the race, and his hand felt comforting despite the oppressive heat of the tunnels. It was night—they should have been cooler, but it was disgusting inside, and that wasn't helping my panic. "I'm here with you, Katy. You'll be all right."

"I bet Tesla wouldn't be scared of this," I said in a miserable voice. "You got stuck with the wrong partner."

"Nah, Tesla wouldn't be scared of this," he agreed. "But she's scared of animals."

"Animals?"

His hand continued to rub my leg soothingly. "Yeah. She freaked out with the dog sled. Big time. She thinks animals are full of diseases."

I gave a mildly hysterical little giggle at that, trying to picture sexy, sultry Tesla flipping out over a few huskies. "I hope there's a freaking camel race for this leg, then."

He laughed at that. "You know what? Me too."

We sat there for a moment longer, and then Liam's fingers stroked my hand comfortingly. "You know, we have plenty of time before the next team arrives. Do you want to try and scoot down the tunnel on your backside? That might make you feel better."

I squeezed my eyes shut, picturing that horrible stifling blackness and having to descend into it. "I...I don't know."

"How about I hold your hand, and you keep your eyes closed. You can keep one hand on me, one on the railing, and just kind of scoot down at your own pace." His voice was a low, soothing hum. "We'll take all the time you need."

I sucked in a deep breath, trying not to imagine the walls pressing in around me. If I kept my eyes closed, it was better, but only a little. Panic still threatened to overwhelm me.

"Come on," Liam coaxed in that soft voice. "I moved down a step. Can you move down a step toward me?"

My eyes tightly shut, I reached out and found the railing again, and slid down a bit, toward his voice.

"That's it," Liam told me, encouraging me onward. "Take your time. We can do this."

And a few seconds later, I gave another half-assed shuffle downward.

"Good job, Katy." His voice was warm and full of pleasure that I was trying.

"You probably think I'm the world's biggest idiot," I told him, doing another blind little slide down to the next step.

"Actually, no. I find you pretty damn sexy."

My eyes flew open at that, but then I saw the yawning black behind him and gave a frightened meep, squeezing them shut tight again. "You're distracting me!"

"Is it working?" He chuckled, the sound low and delicious, and gave my hand another encouraging tug. I followed him down another shuffled step.

"Maybe a little."

"You're doing great. Just hold on to me."

"This...this isn't freaking you out?"

"Me? Nah. A bowl of mukluk freaks me out. Going on stage freaks me out. Holding the hand of a pretty girl that I like kissing? That's not freaky at all."

"There you go, trying to distract me again," I said breathlessly, even as I slid down another step or two. "You don't like going on stage?"

"Hate it," he said in an easy voice, and tugged my hand to encourage me along. "Some people love performing. That's their favorite part of the gig. I hate it. I'd much rather sit in a studio and write songs all day long, but the rest of the band likes to tour." He gave a soft chuckle. "The label likes that, too. Imagine that."

"You should tell them you don't like touring," I said, sliding down another step. "It doesn't seem right that you have to tour if you hate it."

"I do. I have the worst kind of stage fright. That's why I'm perfectly happy to let Tesla get in front of everyone and make a spectacle of herself. It means all I have to do is sit in the back and play guitar. Another step. Come on."

I slid down a bit more. "You looked like you were having fun in your video."

"Of course. And another step. There you go. Videos are shot in a studio. And they're shot over and over again until they get just the right look for what they want. No one's going to be excited if they see the guitarist looking like a deer caught in headlights at the sight of a crowd."

I slid down again, and stifled another giggle. "I can't picture that."

"It's not pretty," he said, and his voice was wry. "So I noticed you're avoiding the subject."

"Subject?"

"I called you pretty and sexy and told you I like to kiss you, and all you want to ask about is how scared being on stage makes me. Come on, another step. There you go. I kind of think you're avoiding the subject, Katy."

"Nah," I said nervously. "I…kind of thought you liked kissing me because it made good TV."

"You were the one that said you wanted to make good TV. I was just going along with it because it got me some alone time with you."

I felt that prickle of awareness on my body, of his hand holding mine, even as I slid a bit further down the stairs. "Oh."

He chuckled. "That's all you have to say?" I heard his feet hit something and then he gave my hand a small shake. "You can open your eyes now. We made it to the chamber."

I slid down just a bit more, and then squeezed one eye open. Sure enough, the narrow passageway had opened up to a much larger stone chamber that was lit with electric lights strung up along the walls. The room wasn't all that interesting, except for another narrow crawl-hole in the far end of the room and a railing around the center of the chamber that protected a deeper hole.

I breathed a sigh of relief. This room was not all that scary, and I found my anxiety slipping away again. "I guess we should search for the next clue, huh?"

"In a minute," Liam said, and tugged on my hands, helping me to my feet. When I was standing, though, he didn't let go of my hands. He continued to hold them and stared down at me. "You're still avoiding the question."

"The question?" I asked, a little flustered at his intense gaze.

His hand released mine, and he reached up to tug on one of my pigtails. "I want to know if all of this chemistry between us is just for TV."

Just like that, the breath escaped my lungs again. I gazed up at him. "Not on my side," I admitted.

"Good. Mine neither." His hand cupped the back of my head and he bent down to press a light, grazing kiss on my mouth. "You want to know what's keeping me going right now?"

His lips remained so close to mine that it was making desire surge through my body, blocking out any thoughts of fear or the race. "What?"

"The thought that at the end of this leg?" His mouth slicked over mine again, his tongue flicking against the parted seam of my mouth. "That we have enough money for another hotel room." Again, that stealthy, sweet kiss that was more of a tease than anything. "And that maybe we don't have to go anywhere or do anything for a nice, long twelve hours." Again, that flick of tongue. "And we get to spend that twelve hours in bed. Together."

Each stroke of his tongue felt like it was moving directly to my clit. I gave a small moan of response, my hands releasing his to cling to the front of his shirt.

"But maybe I'm the only one that wants that?" he asked in a low, sultry whisper. "Because you're not saying anything."

I shuddered, barely suppressing the moan rising in my throat. "No, I want that too." The thought of sliding into bed with this gorgeous man and exploring each other for twelve glorious hours? It sounded like heaven. I thought of his body curled around mine in our chaste bed in Italy. It had been delicious…and it had been torture. Torture because I wanted the real thing. Liam naked, in bed with me, his skin sliding over mine, his tongue doing that erotic dance along my mouth like it was right now.

And so I decided to show him just how much I wanted it. I dragged his mouth to mine in a hard kiss, my tongue sweeping into his mouth. My leg rose and curled around his, dragging our hips together.

He groaned and his hands planted on my ass, curving my body against his larger one until I was pressed against him, and our mouths met and meshed over and over again. It didn't matter that we were at the bottom of a pyramid, or that it was hot and muggy inside, or we were in the middle of a race. All I knew at this moment was that this delicious man wanted to sleep with me.

And I wanted him, too. I couldn't wait for tonight.

The kiss broke off after a moment, leaving us both gasping. I could feel Liam growing hard against my thigh, and my nipples felt like they were about to come through my shirt, they were so tight.

"Well," he said raggedly, and then slicked another kiss over my mouth, as if he couldn't leave me alone. "I guess we should look for that clue."

"I guess so," I said, and nipped at his jaw again, not moving from his arms.

He chuckled and gave my ass a firm squeeze with his hands—such strong hands—and slid me back down to the ground. "Come on."

"Gotcha," I said breathlessly. We gave the room a cursory look, though there wasn't all that much to see.

There was, however, a black hole carved into the shadowy wall. Another tunnel, small and cramped and barely wide enough to crawl into.

Liam glanced over at me. "I don't suppose you want to go in there and check?"

"How about no?"

He grinned and dropped to his knees in front of it. "Somehow, I thought you'd say that."

"I'll make it worth your while," I said in a flirty voice. "Later tonight."

He looked back at me and grinned. "Now you're talking." Then he dropped to his elbows, and began to shimmy into the hole.

I shuddered and looked away, unable to watch him climbing even deeper into this hellhole pyramid. Rubbing my arms, I glanced around the chamber...

And just barely caught a green light flashing. Frowning, I headed over to that light, and noticed that there was a small camera mounted in the wall next to one of the lights.

Well, damn. So much for not caring about making good TV. We'd just made some pretty awesome TV with our impromptu make out session.

And somehow, I couldn't find it in me to be upset. I was looking forward to more kisses far too much.

By the time we'd visited all three pyramids, the sun was coming up and we had eight different figurines. Liam had done all the hard work. I'd mostly clung to him and suffered my way through the series of small tunnels. The Great Pyramid had been the worst; the others were just mildly unpleasant.

When we were finished with the last, we laid the figures out on the ground outside and studied them, moving words around. When we figured it out, it read: *Head to the Sphinx Temple for your clue.*

We were like a well-oiled machine at this point. Liam and I looked at each other. Wordlessly, he grabbed my backpack and we sprinted back towards the Sphinx. It was a bit of a trot and by the time we arrived, we were both winded.

There was a flag at the entrance, and a man in a white cotton robe and turban waiting for us. The sun had come up and it was getting warmer, and I envied him his cool-seeming clothing. I took the disk with a thank you, and then retreated to read it.

"Individual Task," I read aloud as Liam dropped our packs. "One of you will go step by step and reproduce a traditional Egyptian mummy, complete with linens, scarabs, and mummification rituals. A judge will be waiting nearby to give you your next clue once you have completed the task to his satisfaction." I looked up at Liam in horror. "Please tell me we're not going to have to mummify a real body."

"This is TV, Katy. I doubt they found someone willing to volunteer for that."

Good point. I considered things, then shrugged. If it was nasty, well, I had the stronger stomach. "I'll do it."

Liam grinned. "I was hoping you'd say that."

I gave him a quick kiss and dashed into the designated area. And stopped being amused. There were six tables laid out, each one with a 'body.' A cameraman dashed forward, recording my flinch of reaction. I moved closer to the nearest table and heaved a sigh of relief when I realized that the 'person' on the table was plastic. Thank god for that. Next to the table was a scroll, and next to that was a series of tools and jars.

I considered the implements laid out before me, and picked up a small hook, then shuddered. I did not want to know what that was for.

After examining the items, I unrolled the scroll. It was done in a cheesy sort of hieroglyphic, complete with pictures detailing each step of mummification. Here was where you washed the body. Here was where you removed the internal organs and put them in jars. Here was where you shoved the hook up the nose and scooped the brains out.

I brushed my fingers over the dummy's skin…and it felt almost like real skin. It was even warm.

Ew.

I swallowed hard and looked down at my dummy. "You're lucky it's me and not Liam, mister."

A SHORT TIME LATER, I WIPED MY HANDS CLEAN AND TOOK THE DISK that the judge held out for me, feeling vaguely queasy. That had been a little more realistic—dummy and all—than I had preferred.

No sooner had I received my disk and went out to greet my partner than another team showed up—Summer and Polly. Damn. How did they constantly get to the head of the pack? It was crazy. Hot on their heels were Abby and Dean and Tesla and Brodie. Almost everyone had caught up. I didn't see the other two teams, but I was pretty sure they weren't far behind.

Off to the side, Liam waved me down and I raced over to him with the disk. We hunched over it, reading the clue quietly. "Head to the harbor of Alexandria and look for the Pharos Lighthouse," I read aloud.

"One of the seven wonders of the ancient world," Liam murmured. "Interesting. I thought it was destroyed."

I'd never heard of the darn thing. "So how do we find something that's destroyed?"

"It says to head to Alexandria," he pointed out. "Maybe someone there will know more."

We gathered up our things and returned to our waiting taxi.

Several hours later, we departed the train that had taken us to Alexandria and hailed another cab. While riding on the train, we'd borrowed someone's smartphone and had a chance to do some research on the Pharos Lighthouse—it had apparently been found under the sea and there were diving tours that could get us to where we needed to go. I suspected that we'd find a flag at one of the diving stations.

With our cab driver, we searched the bay section. I spotted the cameras before I spotted the flag, and nudged Liam. "Over there."

He nodded, and we bounded out of the cab after paying the driver. Off atop a nearby hill, I could see Chip Brubaker waiting at the finish line. This had to be the right place. I took Liam's pack as he headed to the scuba diving shop, meeting the judge with the flag.

The man handed him his task and Liam read it aloud. "Dive in the waters of Alexandria's Eastern Harbor. Search the treasure chests along the bottom of the ocean for ten coins that depict the Lighthouse of Alexandria. Once you have all ten coins, proceed to the finish line." Liam glanced back at me and grinned. "Wish me luck."

"How about a good luck kiss?"

"Even better," he said, moving toward me. Before I could take the initiative, his hand went to the back of my neck and he dragged me toward him in a quick, fierce kiss that left my knees weak.

"Good luck," I said, hugging his oversized backpack to my front, wobbly. "I'll, um, be here."

He disappeared off with the production crew, and I sat down on a chair at the dock, waiting. I could at least watch and see who else showed up and make note of the order they arrived in. Unless Joel/Derron and Hal/Stefan showed up ahead of the others, they had to be in last place. A bad flight, maybe. It didn't matter. We seemed to be safe for now.

Of course, as soon as that thought crossed my mind, I knocked on wood.

The diving shop sold snacks and cold bottles of water, and I made myself comfortable, waiting in a shady spot and eying the flag stop.

At least an hour crawled by. No Liam. No other contestants. I spun my water bottle and then purchased another and more snacks for Liam, because I knew he'd be hungry. We'd been going all morning long, and if his dive was taking this long, he was bound to be exhausted when he returned. I peered at the waters of the harbor, but didn't see anything. I'd just wait here for him to return, since Chip was so close by.

A taxi pulled up a few minutes later. To my dismay, Brodie and Tesla jumped out of the cab. They'd gotten ahead of the rest of the group. Damn it. And now I was going to have to sit with one of them. Double damn.

I nearly groaned aloud when Tesla disappeared into the dive shop, leaving me with Brodie. Figured.

My brother sprawled onto the deck next to me and rested his head on his pack. "Hey, sis." He gestured at my water bottle. "I don't suppose you'd give that to me? I'm wiped."

"They sell them in the shop, Brodie."

"Yeah, but Tesla and I are pretty low on funds at the moment." He grimaced. "She likes to spend money and we keep running out."

I eyed my brother's sweaty hair and cracked lips, and sighed, handing the water bottle to him. "You hungry, too?"

"God yes, I'm starving."

I wordlessly handed him the bag of trail mix I'd been saving for Liam. "I'd give you some money but it's not just mine."

"That's okay," Brodie said, stuffing food into his mouth and taking a huge swig of water. "You are awesome, Katy, you know that?"

I just shook my head at Brodie. "I'm your sister. I'm not going to let you die on a dumb race."

He grinned and flopped back down on his bag. "This race is pretty awesome, actually."

It was, I had to admit. I was having a lot more fun than I'd anticipated… but most of that was due to Liam. "I'm still a bit mad at you for the partner swap," I told him. "You should have talked to me first."

"I just didn't want Tesla to go, you know? I didn't realize they were going to flip us." He shielded his eyes from the sun and squinted up at me. "I *am* sorry. You're my sister. I didn't want to screw you over."

I sighed. "I know." Brodie was just Brodie. Kind of thoughtless, really impulsive, but didn't mean any harm. "So how's Tesla in the partner department?"

"She's pretty good," he said and gave me a wicked grin. "And she's pretty good at the race."

"Gross, Brodie. Just gross."

He laughed, finished his water, and then gave the empty bottle a mournful look. Jeez, how long had they been without water or anything to eat? I returned to the shop, bought two more bottles and two more bags of trail mix, then sat next to Brodie again and wordlessly handed him one of each.

My brother enveloped me in a bear hug. "I love you, Katy."

"Yeah, yeah," I said, but I was feeling a little better about me and Brodie. I gave my brother a hug back and then nudged his shoulder. "You tell Tesla to watch it on the money, all right? We don't get that much for each leg, and it's probably stupid of me to be buying you stuff since we're competing."

"Is Liam a good diver?" Brodie asked, looking a bit too interested. "Tesla says she is. If we can pass you guys, we get first place."

I had no idea if Liam was a good diver, but I wanted first place. "Don't know. How were the others doing at the mummy challenge?"

He made a face. "Dean's a machine. He was ripping through it. Polly was kind of grossed out. The other two didn't show up while we were there."

"Wow, their flights must have really been backed up. Poor guys." Two all-male teams, both delayed. They'd be neck and neck until the end—I didn't want to be in *that* race to the finish line.

He nodded. "It's gonna be one of them eliminated. I just know it."

It sure seemed that way.

A cameraman zoomed past, filming something. Both Brodie and I leapt to our feet to see who was coming.

Liam's tall body trotted down the dock, still in the wetsuit, dripping water. I gave a happy little jump and grabbed our bags, heading toward him.

"Congrats, Katy," my brother called out to me. "We'll get you next time."

"In your dreams," I called back, grinning. I gave Liam a quick one-armed hug as I met him and then pointed at Chip. "Finish line's right up there."

Liam looked exhausted, his wet hair pushed off his brow in a messy tangle. "That challenge," he breathed, "was awful. Do you know how many chests there are at the bottom of the harbor? My god. I thought I'd never find ten with coins. And then not all of the coins are lighthouse coins. You have to dig through them looking for the right ones."

My eyes widened. "Glad you did it and not me."

We raced up to top of the hill and met Chip. The finish line tape was intact, and I had to admit that it felt amazing to bust through it, hand in hand, and bound onto the mat in front of the host.

"Liam and Katy! You're the first team to arrive!"

I gave a happy squeal—even though we'd known it—and flung myself into Liam's arms. He kissed me full on the mouth in response.

Chip laughed. "Seems like your partnership is working out all right."

"Seems to be," I said, pulling my now-wet t-shirt away from my chest and wiping at Liam's dripping wet-suit.

"Well, as the winners of this leg of the race, I have an additional prize for you two." Chip gave us both a teasing look, and then produced an envelope from behind his back. "The second Ace of the game."

I stared at it, then groaned.

Damn it. Another Ace? That was the last thing I wanted. "Can't we, like, trade that in for a trip to Fiji or something?"

Chip frowned and held the Ace out. "You don't want it?"

I looked over at Liam, who took it in hand. "No, we'll take it. Better us than another team."

Chip nodded. "It's all yours, then. Congratulations!"

I tried to look thrilled, and failed.

The host glanced down at his watch. "You have twelve hours until the next leg of the race. Enjoy your stay."

We headed into Alexandria for the day. Both Liam and I were too tired to argue with the cab driver when he suggested a particular hotel that was very nice and tourist friendly. Usually that meant 'expensive,' especially if the cab driver was suggesting it. Still, the hotel he dropped us off at was decent looking on the outside, and the rooms reasonable.

As we headed up the stairs to our room, my mind focused on the conversation we'd had at the bottom of the Great Pyramid. Of Liam's sultry promise to me. Of spending the day in bed and kissing for hours. Of making love.

Of course, all of that came to a crashing halt as soon as we opened the door to the hotel room.

It was a small room, which wasn't a problem. It was also clean, and neat, and had an old TV perched atop a dresser. It also had twin beds. Two rather tiny twin beds.

I giggled. I couldn't help myself. I looked at the sight of those two small beds, and it just bubbled up inside of me. Romantic evening cuddling together? Not in those bunks.

Liam chuckled, too, and dropped his bags on the threshold. "I…guess we could ask for a different room? I didn't think to ask about the beds."

I shook my head. "It's okay. Maybe things just weren't meant to be." I grinned over at him. "You're probably pretty tired after that last leg of the race."

"Not that tired," he said in a disgusted voice, and I broke out into giggles again.

He shut the door to the bedroom behind us, and then he moved to my side. His hand stroked my cheek and then he leaned in and kissed me, his mouth moving over mine in a tender, gentle kiss. When it broke, he looked down at me. "I still want you, Katy. You still want me?"

I nodded up at him. "More than anything."

"Then I think we should push these beds together," he told me, his voice husky. "And enjoy our downtime."

I kissed him again, my hand sliding along his shirt. He'd given back the wetsuit after we'd checked in for the race, and changed back into his own clothing. I brushed my fingers under his shirt to feel his warm chest underneath. "Do you have condoms?"

He stiffened, and then gave a small curse. "No. I don't. But there's a gift shop downstairs."

"I'll wait up here, then."

He pressed another kiss to my mouth. "Be right back." He grabbed his wallet and headed out the door, leaving me alone in the room.

I studied the bed situation. They were separated by a small nightstand which boasted of an alarm clock and a lamp. I headed to it and unplugged both, then dragged the nightstand off to the opposite end of the room. Once that was done, I shoved the two beds together and considered them. Not nearly as bad, though still probably a smaller bed than would be comfortable. I didn't suppose it mattered, I thought with a smile. It wasn't like we were planning on doing a ton of sleeping today.

And just that thought made my face grow hot. I ran a hand along my pigtails, wondering if I should take them down. I decided against it, since Liam seemed to enjoy them. I slid my shoes off and opened my bag, considering my clothing. I didn't have anything sexy or fun to wear. It was all race gear. Every few days, someone in production would meet us at the beginning of the race and swap out our clothing for new, fresh ones so we never had to look wrinkled or smelly on TV. Naturally, no lingerie was included. I thought about stripping out of my shorts and just remaining in my race shirt. Or a bra and panties, but the bra I had was a sports bra and looked like something designed more for a vigorous hike than making love.

After a moment more of indecision, I stripped out of everything and slid under the covers of the now-doubled bed.

Just as I did, I heard Liam return to the door. He was talking to someone, and I ducked under the covers, terrified. Oh lord, what if one of the other racers was out there and wanted to hang out? I'd die of mortification, considering Liam was likely standing out there with a box of condoms and I was in here, waiting in bed and naked. I strained my ears, trying to hear the conversation.

"Not right now," Liam said. Then, "No. I can do an interview later. I promise. Right now I'm just really tired." Another pause. "No. No, you can't see what's in the bag."

A moment later, the door shut and Liam came into view, an exasperated look on his face. "Those cameramen are really determined. I—" His voice stopped as his gaze moved to the sight of me, waiting in the bed. A smile curved his face. "Guess you didn't change your mind."

I trailed a finger on the blanket. "Guess not. You disappointed?"

"Hell, no." Liam set the small bag down on the dresser. "But our cameraman out there thinks something's up."

I didn't know what to do about that. "Should we order a pizza or something? Maybe he'll go away if we do?"

He shrugged, then pulled off his shirt. "We can order a pizza later, if you like."

The breath caught in my throat at the sight of Liam undressing. I'd seen him in his boxers before. I'd definitely seen him without a shirt. But somehow, seeing him strip down in front of the bed while I waited in it, naked? Really brought things home.

He pulled off his pants, and looked over at me. And paused. "You look… uncomfortable."

"This is just…" I gestured at the beds, pushed together. "Faster than I normally move."

Liam stripped down to his boxers. "If you want to take it slow, I'm fine with that." He moved away from the dresser and sat on the edge of the bed, still in his boxers. "Okay if I get under the covers with you?"

I shook my head. I didn't mind. "You must think I'm being silly. You probably have girls throwing themselves at you all the time."

"I don't think you're being silly," he said, pulling back one side of the blankets and sliding under them. He slid a bit closer, but there was still a foot of space between us. "And most of those girls just want to nail anyone in the band because they're in a band. Has nothing to do with me or what I'm like."

"And what are you really like?" I asked in a quiet voice.

He thought about this for a moment, then shrugged. "Kind of like I am on this race. I like to compete. I don't like the limelight. I have an appreciation for smart, brave girls." He reached out and tweaked one of my pigtails. "And blonde pigtails."

"Brave girls?" I gave him a look of disbelief, clutching the blanket to my breasts. "You're kidding, right? Which one of us was wailing like a ninny inside of the pyramids earlier?"

"You were claustrophobic," he said easily. "Everyone has fears. You got past yours, though. Normally you're fearless, and I like that about you. I'm willing to overlook a moment of weakness in the scheme of things." He gave me a crooked smile. "As long as we never mention that mukluk incident ever again."

I laughed, unable to help myself. "You're the one that keeps bringing it up, not me."

"That's because it makes you smile," he said, and his hand left my hair to brush his the backs of his fingers along my bare shoulder. "And I like seeing you smile."

Goosebumps danced along my skin and I shivered at that small touch. I moved a little closer to him in the bed, until we were facing each other, each of us propped up on an elbow. Inches separated us, but the blankets still lay between us, a barrier.

And I reached out and hesitantly brushed my hand over his pectoral, tracing the lines of the spider-web tattoo. "Can I ask you about these?"

"You can ask me about anything," he said in a low, husky voice. His eyes remained on me, as if fascinated by my touch.

"What's the spider-web for?" My fingers moved over the lines.

He shrugged, his shaggy hair brushing against my fingers. "Was an idea I had. Kind of symbolized being caught in a web at the label and all that. When I got too frustrated with how things were going, I'd go out and get another tattoo."

And he had sleeves of them and others on his body. "You must be frustrated a lot."

Liam grinned. "Sometimes I just like the art. But sometimes, yeah. It's the best career in the world, and the most frustrating at times."

"I think every career is like that," I told him, tracing the lines of a star on his shoulder.

"Even baking cupcakes?"

I gave him a wry look. "It sounds corny, but you haven't made six dozen cupcakes for a client who then insists that they didn't want them in that shade of yellow and can you have new ones ready in an hour?"

"No, I guess I haven't experienced that," he said, and ran his fingers along my bare shoulder again.

I shivered, my nipples hardening under the blankets.

My fingers moved to the bottom of the star and noticed there was a broken heart mixed into the lines covering his arm. "What's this for?"

He glanced down at his arm and sighed. "No one important."

"Tesla?" I guessed.

He raised an eyebrow at me, the piercing glinting. "You know about that?"

"Saw it on your website." Got a little hurt by it, if I was being honest with myself. Of course, I couldn't hope to compete with her. She had history with Liam, and a connection through the band that I could never duplicate. I was a small time baker. She was Tesla Spooner, hot rock chick and star of

Finding Threnody.

He grunted, considering. "It was a long time ago, you know. I don't want you to feel weird about it."

I had to laugh at that. "You don't think this whole thing is a little weird?"

"Well, yeah." His mouth quirked. "But I don't want you to feel weird about her and me. Ancient history. I swear."

I nodded, and decided to touch one of his piercings, instead, brushing my thumb over the ring in his lower lip. "What made you get this?"

He shrugged. "I liked it. I like piercings."

I touched the stud on his eyebrow, and then the bar across the bridge of his nose. "Did this hurt?"

"Nope."

"Which one hurt the most?"

He brushed his shaggy hair back and showed me his ear. There was a bar in the cartilage of his ear, pierced from the top to a hole in the side. Instead, he pointed to the tiny hoop at the front of his ear.

"This tiny one?" I brushed my fingers along it, smiling. "It doesn't look like it would."

"This is called a tragus. Hurt like the fucking dickens. Even my dick piercing didn't hurt that much."

I stilled. "You have a...um, piercing?"

He grinned again. "Told you I like piercings."

I could feel my face getting hot again. "I don't have any."

"That's all right," he told me, and his hand slid to my waist, resting over the blankets. "I kind of like you just how you are."

"Boring?"

"Never boring," he told me. His thumb brushed over my hip, that small movement noticeable even through the thin blankets. "Different from the usual kind of girl I run into. That's all."

That was sweet of him to say. I didn't know if it was true—if the tables were turned, I'd probably think I was pretty boring. But maybe Liam liked me because I was different than Tesla. Way different. My fingers brushed along his jaw, and I tilted his face toward mine.

His lips parted as I kissed him, and I felt his tongue stroke against my lower lip, felt the piercing flick against my flesh. The man did love his piercings. I kissed him back, my tongue brushing against his as we began to kiss in earnest. My fingers twined in his hair and I held him against me, kissing in a dance of tongues. Over and over, they slicked together, forming a suggestive rhythm that made the blood pound in my veins and made my hips start to rock with the suggestion of it.

Liam didn't move, just let me kiss him. His hand remained anchored at my waist.

The more I kissed him, though, the more I wanted. His mouth brushed against mine, and his lips felt like that delicious, curious mixture of metal and flesh, and every time a piercing rubbed against my skin, it made a little flash of excitement roll through me. Kissing Liam wasn't like kissing anyone else. He was considerate, and thorough, and his tongue felt amazing against my own.

And still I wanted more than kisses.

My hand slid below the blankets, to his chest, and I brushed my fingertips over his lower belly, exploring him. The blankets were starting to slide down off of my body, and I hesitated, wondering if I should pull them back up. But Liam's gaze was locked on my face, as if suggesting that he'd move as slow as I wanted to move. He wouldn't look if I didn't want him to.

And I knew that even though I was in bed with a sexy, edgy rock star? I was still in control. He'd let me call the shots. If I wanted to stop, all I had to do was ask.

Of course, I didn't want to stop.

I kissed him again, soft and sweet, no tongue. Just a coaxing of lips. By that point, I'd shifted toward him so much that I was practically hovering over his face, my hand cupped on his stomach while the other tangled in his hair. The blankets fell down to the small of my back, and I was exposed to him.

And he still wasn't looking. I hadn't given the signal that it was okay. So I took his hand, and pulled it onto my breast.

His gaze slid down, then, to my naked breasts and exposed belly. "You're beautiful, Katy. So beautiful." Reverently, he cupped my breast, staring at it, at the small pink peak that hardened when he brushed his thumb over it. My breasts weren't large—nothing about me was large, sadly—but in his hand, my breast looked like it was just the perfect size. Small, perky, uptilted.

Liam's hand slid to my back and he pulled me against him, then rolled us over in the bed until I bounced onto my back. "I want to get a good look at you," he told me, and simply gazed down at my naked body sprawled on the bed under him as he hovered over me, propped up on an elbow. His fingers brushed over my breast, then the other.

I sucked in a breath, watching the reverent look in his eyes.

His gaze went to my stomach as if fascinated, and brushed his hand over the plane of it. "Not a tattoo on this skin anywhere. You're like a blank canvas."

I gave an awkward laugh at that. "Is that a good thing?"

"It's kinda beautiful on you," he told me, and I felt warm with the glow of his approval.

He shifted against me, and then Liam's fingers moved back to my breast, cupping it and flicking at the peak to make it harden. I whimpered at his touch, jolts of intense feeling sparking through my body. He leaned over and brushed his lips over the tip, caressing it.

I moaned, my back arching. His hard, hot form was pressing down over me, and that felt almost as delicious as the touches he bestowed on my skin.

Liam's tongue brushed over my nipple, swirling, and then I felt the flick of metal against it. I gasped as he rolled my nipple against the piercing.

He looked up at my response, looking pleased with myself. "Do you like that?"

I blinked rapidly, dazed. "How can I not?"

He shrugged, then pressed kisses over my chest, moving over to my other breast. "You'd have to tell me if you didn't like it."

I gave a low moan as his mouth captured my other nipple. "And what would you do if I asked you to stop?"

He bit my nipple lightly, which made a jolt shudder through my body all over again. "I'd be very, very disappointed."

"Oh?" My voice sounded wavery.

"Yeah," he said softly. "And then I'd just go south." And he began to kiss lower.

My stomach quivered as his mouth moved over it. He slid to my belly button, and his tongue—and piercing—dipped there. I moaned again, wriggling a little against him. My hands moved over his shoulders, touching and kneading those tattooed muscles as if unable to stop touching him, exploring him even as he explored me.

"I'd continue south," he told me in that soft voice, "until you told me to stop, of course."

And his mouth rested just above my sex.

A shiver of anticipation racked through me, and my hips flexed, as if begging for him to go lower. But he didn't, and I whimpered, not wanting to shove his head down to the vee of my sex...but not wanting him to abandon that area, either.

"What do you want, Katy?" He concentrated on my flat lower stomach, and kissed the soft skin there.

"I want you, Liam," I breathed.

"Do you want my mouth on you?"

The words left my throat, and I nodded, unable to speak.

That seemed to be fine with him, because his hand stroked along the inside of my thigh, coaxing it open. My knees fell apart, and he shifted a bit lower, his shoulders settling in between my legs. He appeared to be concentrating very intently on his exploration of me.

One finger brushed down the seam of my sex, and I let out a shuddering gasp at the simple touch, shocked at the bluntness of it—and how very wet I was.

Liam seemed surprised by it too, and raised the finger to his mouth, then sucked the moisture off of it. He seemed pleased by the taste of me, and leaned in for another taste.

I moaned again at the feel of his fingers parting my flesh, and then the first lick of his tongue against my heat. He started out small; light, inquisitive flicks of the tip of his tongue against my flesh, exploring me and tasting me. My fingers clutched at his shoulders, squeezing repeatedly, unable to do more than just that as he leisurely explored my sex with his tongue. When he hit upon my clit with his tongue, I sucked in a harsh breath, my body tensing.

He paused at that, as if considering, and then stroked his tongue over me again. This time, I felt the ball of his tongue piercing against it. A low sob of delight escaped my throat, and my hips jerked in response.

I heard his low chuckle, and then he wrapped an arm around my thigh, pinning me, and began to lick me in earnest.

I thought I'd had oral sex before? I hadn't seen anything yet. Over and over, Liam licked the hell out of me, working that piercing against my clit, stroking with his tongue and then rolling that metal ball against it in a motion that I came to crave even as it drove me wild. After a few minutes of this, he began to speed up, and my hips began to move with his mouth, slow, sensual flicks of my body that followed his tongue, increasing my pleasure.

And the moans coming from my throat? Were unearthly. I wasn't able to keep quiet; I didn't care who heard me. Liam's mouth felt too good, and I was too lost in the pleasure of it.

He sucked, then, hard; my clit pressed up against that metal ball of his tongue stud, and the twin reactions made me shatter into a million pieces. A small scream erupted from my throat, and I quivered all over, shuddering with my release. He continued to suck and press his tongue against my clit, milking every moment of my orgasm, and I writhed against him, clawing at his shoulders. "Liam," I panted. "Oh god, oh god. You can move your mouth now. I...oh god." My words trailed off into a low moan as the orgasm continued to ripple through me for long moments. I was lost in the wash of it.

His mouth lifted, and he gave a low laugh. "Katy, shhh."

I moaned, shaking my head. "Liam—"

He slid up the bed and began to kiss me again, chuckling once more. "You're loud enough that everyone's going to hear you yelling my name."

I began to kiss him back fiercely, tasting my own release on his mouth. I didn't care. I felt way too good—and way too aroused—to care. I slid my tongue against his, flicking it, even as I reached between us and grasped his cock through the thin material of his boxers.

This time, the low groan that split the air was his.

"Liam," I breathed against his mouth. My hand gave his cock a stroke through the fabric. "Do I get to explore you, now?"

"I didn't get to finish you," he told me with a groan, and then his lips were desperately kissing mine. Between kisses, he added, "Never even touched your legs."

"They're short," I told him, and stroked his cock again, my grip resting at the thick root of him. "You're not missing much."

"I don't know," he groaned against my ear, eyes closed tight as I stroked him again. "They'll probably look pretty good on my shoulders."

Just that mental image made me wet all over again, and I moaned, kissing him again. My mouth slid to his neck, and I spotted one of his tattoos and began to lick the flesh there, fascinated by it.

He groaned, his arm looping around my back and holding me to him. "God, you're good at that."

I gave his cock another stroke with my hand, pleased at his words. My tongue danced along that tattoo, and then I licked and sucked at the skin there, liking the mark I left on his skin. It wouldn't be apparent because of the tattoo, but if you looked closely enough, you'd see it. And that made me hot all over again. I left him another, just because I liked the look of it.

He moved back over me, hips sliding between mine, and we began to kiss again. His mouth pressed against mine, hot, hard and desperate with need. My hand on his cock was trapped between us, and it rubbed against my flesh as he ground his hips against me.

"Why don't you remove my boxers?" He told me, licking against my lips.

I did, but not before tracing the head with my fingers...and stopped.

He was pierced there, too. Two balls, one atop the head, and one underneath.

I gasped at the sight. He'd told me about it, but I'd been unable to picture it. Seeing it, I gave the head of his cock another rub, checking things out. I traced him with my fingers, marveling at the stud there. "You really do like piercings."

"I really do," he said, and sucked on my lower lip. "I bet you'll like it, too."

Mmm, I just bet I would. When his hips rolled against mine again, I slid my hand away, moving to his backside. I cupped his tight ass through his boxers and ground my hips against his cock, loving the friction of his flesh against mine, separated only by a thin layer of cotton.

He pumped against me again, the hard bar of his cock sliding along the vee of my sex. I wrapped my legs around his hips and pushed against him, need still boiling through me, wanting more.

"Lose these," I told him, tugging at the waist of the boxers. "Want to feel you against me."

"I can do that," he murmured against my mouth before kissing me again. The angle of his body shifted, and then The boxers slid to the floor. I linked my legs behind his back again, and this time, when he slid along the hot vee of my sex, I was able to feel every inch of him.

It was heaven. I dug my fingers into his shoulders, clinging to his body. "Oh god, you feel really good."

"Katy," he breathed, and pushed a little deeper, until his cock was separating the lips of my sex and sliding between them. The head butted against my clit, and I felt the rub of that piercing.

A shuddering gasp escaped my throat.

"Need to get the condoms," Liam told me, his voice tight.

I slicked my tongue over his mouth, pumping my hips against his. "Then get them."

He chuckled. "You've got to let me go, first." And his hand slid along one of my legs that were locked at his waist.

I gave a mock pout and released him. "Hurry back."

"Oh, I plan on it." He bounded off the bed and moved to the small bag, tearing open the box he'd bought. I watched him from the bed, all hot and bothered, admiring his naked ass (no tattoos there) and the small dual dimples at his lower back, his lanky shoulders that seemed to form a large triangle. He turned back to me a moment later, condom rolled on, his cock jutting...and bright purple.

I giggled. I couldn't help it. "Nice...color?"

"Yeah, yeah." He climbed back into bed and on top of me. "They only had colored condoms in the gift shop. I'm saving pink for a reward for later."

I threw back my head and laughed, picturing that.

Immediately, Liam began to kiss my exposed neck. "You shouldn't laugh at a man's cock. It doesn't do wonders for his ego."

"Your cock is just fine," I told him, dragging my fingers through his silky black hair as he pressed hot kisses on my neck. "And it feels great so far."

"Flatterer," he murmured against my collarbone, then slid his cock along my sex once more, lubricating it with my wet flesh.

I moaned at the feel of him sliding against me. "Whatever it takes to get you inside."

In response to that, he poised his cock at my entrance, and then pushed deep. And then held there.

I sucked in a breath, my eyes going wide as I tried to process the sensation. Liam felt large inside me, thick and delicious, but the thing that had made me breathless? The rub of that piercing, even through the condom. That odd, strange stud that had rubbed along my walls as he pushed his way in....and had nearly driven me out of my mind.

"You okay?"

I nodded, clinging to his shoulders. "Do it again?"

He pulled back, and then thrust slowly, watching my face. Then, his hips began to make small rocking motions, back and forth, inside me. Short, fluid little thrusts designed to rub that piercing.

I moaned and wrapped my legs around him, raising my hips with his movements. "Oh god, that's good. Oh, *god.*"

He chuckled at my reaction and leaned in to kiss me again, hips continuing to rock against my own short, jerky movements. "It's called an apadravya."

I bit my lip to bite back the rather animalistic groan rising in my throat Was apadravya a foreign word for *drive you fucking mad with pleasure?* Because it was. Every stroke of his cock inside me was just a little bit wilder than I was used to, and that strange little piercing rubbing against me was driving me wild. I dug my fingers into his back and began to raise my hips harder, encouraging his strokes to become rougher. "More."

Liam pulled back and thrust into me so hard that the entire bed bounced.

I screamed. Oh damn, *yes.* I threw my head back and gave myself over to the sensation, eyes closing. There was nothing but Liam's body rocking over mine, his cock thrusting deep inside me in rough, hard motions that I loved, and that infernal piercing that I wanted to claw out of his body and rub up against at exactly the same time.

"No," he said softly, and grabbed my hand. "Look at me, Katy. I like it when you look at me." He pressed my hand back over my head, pinning me to the bed and pinning me against him.

Like I was going anywhere? Not when this felt so incredible. I opened my eyes and watched him as he thrust into me again, concentration and intensity in his dark eyes. It felt incredibly intimate, feeling him thrust into me while I stared up at him, his mouth hovering inches from my own.

And as he pressed my hand to the bed, his fingers jerked in a strange motion, and I realized he was trying to tap out a frantic beat on my hand. Our rhythm in the bed had inspired him, maybe. Or maybe he could never get away from the music, but the intensity in his eyes was making me lose what little control I had.

I felt the tension rising in my calves, and gave a loud whimper as I felt my body start to lock up with pleasure. The next orgasm was cresting fast, and I didn't want this to be over. I clenched my internal muscles around him, trying to fight the sensation, to extend this crazy pleasure just a bit longer.

He bit out a curse and slammed into me, harder, as if surprised by my response.

And then I lost any hope of control. I cried his name out again, and my release flooded through me like a tidal wave.

Liam thrust into me again, hard, and those fingers pressed down as if in an intense cord, his face tightening, eyes closing, and I realized he was coming, too. I watched him as he did, awed by the expression on his face. For a moment there, it almost looked like it had when he'd been doing the guitar solo in the video.

And I couldn't help it—I giggled at that thought.

His eyes flew open, and a sated half-grin curved his mouth. "What?" he panted.

I ran my hand down his sweaty chest, still feeling the aftershocks of our lovemaking even as he relaxed against me. "I was just thinking that your o-face looks the same as your guitar solo face."

Liam snorted and rolled to the side of me, pulling off the condom. He tossed it into the nearby garbage and then cleaned off with a towel he'd brought, then dragged me against him. "Anyone ever tell you that you need to quit laughing at a guy when he's coming inside you?"

"Nope," I said smugly, and then teased him. "Usually they're thinking, 'holy shit, Katy, that was amazing.'"

"It was," he said, and kissed my shoulder.

And really, how could I refute such a sweet thing? I curled up against him, enjoying the feel of his naked flesh against mine. God, he felt good against me.

He pressed another kiss to my neck. "You got quiet. Thinking about the race?"

"I haven't thought about the race in at least a half an hour," I told him lazily. "Though I guess we should be spending this time planning."

"I've got a plan," Liam said, pressing his mouth to the soft skin on my arm. "I figure we have at least one more round we can squeeze in, as long as you let me get my stamina back. Then, we shower. Then, we sleep for a few hours before returning to the starting line. And that's about as far as my plan goes."

As plans went, it was an excellent one. "I like the way you think." I ran my hand along his arm. "Plus, this gives me the chance to see how you look in pink."

"I aim to please."

Chapter Eight

"What did Katy and I do last night? None of your business. Turn off that camera." —Liam Brogan, Turkey Leg of The World Races

WE HAD TO LEAVE FOR THE FINISH LINE IN THE MIDDLE OF THE night. It sucked, but my internal clock was so incredibly messed up from bouncing around Europe that I probably would have been tired no matter what time we left. Holding Liam's hand and sneaking kisses when we thought the cameras weren't looking, though? Kinda helped my mood and I didn't mind that it was two in the morning, local time.

We'd stopped to snag cups of coffee and headed back out to the dock at Alexandria, where the starting mat was. It overlooked the harbor, and I stared down at it, feeling the air ruffle my hair as we waited for the clock to tick down to our start time. "Who do you suppose got booted?" I asked Liam.

He thought for a moment. "Joel and Derron, I think. They were big guys and I'm betting one of them had trouble with the pyramids, too. Those were some cramped spaces."

I shuddered at the memory.

"Two seventeen am," an assistant announced, and tapped a watch. On cue, our cameraman hovered, light shining in our faces. A local came forward, camel reins in one hand (nice touch there, *World Games*) and our disk in his other.

"Thank you," I murmured to him and took the disk with a small smile. As was our usual, I turned it over and Liam read over my shoulder. "Make your way to Canakkale, Turkey. There, look for the marked car lot at...." I wrinkled my nose at the unpronounceable street name, and then skipped it. "You will find five marked vehicles and your next destination. You have one hundred and ninety-eight dollars for this leg of your journey." I looked up at Liam. "Is it just me, or are they giving us a lot of money?"

"How so?" He took the disk from me and pulled off his backpack to slip it in.

I thought back to the prior seasons I'd watched, frowning. "I don't know. I just seem to recall that on a lot of the shows, no one ever got much money for each leg of the journey."

"Maybe we're going to expensive places," Liam suggested.

Or maybe they want us to keep getting hotel rooms, I thought, but didn't say it aloud. That was just Cranky Katy being cynical all over again, no doubt. I'd keep my suspicions to myself.

Plus, I liked getting a hotel room with Liam. It was kind of a win-win as far as I was concerned. I just hoped my parents didn't watch our season of The World Races. Ugh. I tried not to think about that. The last thing I wanted was my parents to see me hook up with a rock star while in a game.

Once we arrived at the marked car lot, I counted the marked cars that were left. All five. "We're still in the lead," I told Liam. "But we shouldn't be." All five teams that were left had been on the same flight, though separated into different parts of the plane. Liam and I had snagged two seats in the very front, while Brodie and Tesla had been in the back of the plane. Too bad for them. The Olympians—Summer and Polly—and Joel and Derron sat together on one row. They put their heads together and I knew they were plotting on how to overtake the lead. It worried me a little...until Dean and Abby got the seats behind us. Seeing them made me feel better, and we'd planned on following each other out to the next destination so we could tackle our tasks together.

But at the airport? We'd gotten separated when our cab driver had stopped for gas and we'd had no way to flag down Dean and Abby and let them know. They'd zoomed on past while we'd waited at the gas station, and I'd felt first place slip away. Liam hadn't been concerned, though. He'd only squeezed my hand and then pulled me in for a long kiss while our driver went in to pay.

And I found I couldn't be all that concerned about last place, either.

Still, it was weird to get to the car lot and realize we were the first ones there. Had everyone else gotten lost? We paid our taxi and picked out our car, settling in even as the cameraman sat in the passenger seat to film us. Liam sat in the front seat and I slid into the back, picking up the packet of paperwork back there.

It was the next clue. I tore open the paper seal attached to the map and began to read. "Make your way to the village of Hisarlik, just outside of Tevfikiye. This is the site of the ruins of the ancient Homeric city of Troy. There, you will meet a Greek soldier at The World Races flag who will give you your next clue."

"Off we go, then," Liam said, and our little car sped out of the parking lot.

THE RUINS WERE NOT ALL THAT DIFFICULT TO FIND, OR THAT IMPRESsive. I guess I'd been expecting some sort of massive city, but it was really just a bunch of half dug-out hills, tumbled stones, and areas that had been roped off that we weren't allowed to see. Nothing at all like Pompeii, and since we'd just come from there, they paled in comparison.

There was an enormous fake Trojan horse at the entrance of the ruins, though, and sure enough, the flag and The World Races station was there. Liam parked the car and we bounded out, racing for the flag.

Our next disk was handed to us. A team task, and one that didn't surprise me, given the five stations and blocks of colored wood set aside. Our team task was to build a duplicate of the Trojan Horse. Once we had our wheeled contraption built to the specifications of the Greek soldier supervising the task, we had to push it across the ruins on the marked path. Once we'd arrived at the end of the path, we'd receive our next disk and clue.

We set to work, heading for the pile of wood that had been colored black to match our team shade. As we did, I glanced around at the four other piles that still had no one working on them. "Liam," I said quietly. "While we're the only ones here, should we talk about the Ace?"

He picked up one of the four wheels on our mat of pieces and examined it, glancing over at me. "What about the Ace?"

"There are only three more eliminations," I told him. "Should we make a team decision on who we want to use it on?"

He gave me a serious look. "Katy," he murmured, moving closer so no one could overhear us. Not that it mattered. We were wired and mic'd for sound. Had been the entire trip. "The only team I think worth saving that would help us out is Abby and Dean. But…"

"But," I agreed. There was that whole 'Tesla and Brodie' thing. "So basically we can either play the Ace to be nice and save Brodie and Tesla if we need to, save Abby and Dean to try and propel ourselves ahead, or be dicks to everyone and not use it at all."

"Heh. That about sums it up."

I considered, then sighed. "Abby promised me that if she got an Ace, she'd use it to save us."

"Did you promise the same thing back?"

"No. It didn't come up in conversation. But I'd feel bad if we had an opportunity to save them and we didn't."

"Well," Liam told me, handing me the wheel and then picking up another, considering it. "The way I look at it, someone's feelings are going to get hurt. We can use it to push ourselves ahead in the game, or we can use it to salvage relationships outside of the game."

"And what if the Ace means another split?" I hated the thought of it.

"It won't."

I shielded my eyes from the sun and squinted up at my partner. "How do you know that?"

"Because splitting us up made good TV." He leaned in and gave me a firm kiss on the mouth, ignoring the fact that the cameraman hovered merely feet away. "Splitting us up again robs them of a lot of romantic scenes. Tesla and Brodie, too. They won't part us."

I blushed and handed him the wheel back. "So what do we do?"

"Whatever you want to do," Liam told me, his expression serious. "I'm leaving it up to you."

"Up to me?" I hated the squeaky note in my voice. "Why me?"

He squatted by the pieces, sorting through the jumble, the wheel still in his hand. I knew we should have been working on the task, but I wanted to get this squared away.

"It's up to you," Liam told me, picking up a painted dowel rod and comparing it to the hole in the center of the wheel he was holding, then discarding it. "Because it won't bother me either way. Dean's a good friend, but he won't hold a grudge if we don't save them. But I know you and Abby are close. As for Tesla?" He glanced up at me and grinned. "I don't care if she's mad at me after the race, but Brodie's your brother. You gotta do whatever you gotta do. The Ace is your choice."

"Well, you're definitely a different partner than Brodie," I grumped, squatting next to the pieces with him. "He wouldn't have asked for my opinion."

"I should hope I'm a very different partner than Brodie," Liam said, and wiggled his eyebrows at me.

I blushed beet red. I was pretty sure the camera caught it, too. "I think I'm going to save Abby and Dean. They've worked with us. It'd be unfair for us to leave them out to dry."

Liam nodded. "Sounds good to me."

WE HAD THE BOTTOM HALF OF OUR WOODEN-HORSE-ON-WHEELS constructed when a flood of cars suddenly showed up in the parking lot. I snapped a board into place, then grimaced as I watched the other four teams charge forward. "Looks like everyone caught up," I told Liam.

He grunted, continuing to work on our horse.

Abby and Dean trotted up to the challenge mat next to ours and began to work on their horse. I glanced over at her. "What happened?"

"Our cab driver was an idiot," she told me. "He took us over an hour in the wrong direction and then tried to charge us for it." She made a disgusted face and pushed her sweaty curls off of her forehead. "Luckily, I pitched a fit and got us out of it."

"The good news," Dean leaned in to tell me with a grin, "was that apparently everyone else was following our cab. Which is why we're all late except you two."

I glanced at the other teams. They all looked pretty annoyed. Brodie's forehead was set in frustrated lines, and I felt a twinge of pity for my brother. He wanted to win this race so badly and they were not doing well at all. I squashed the pity, though. Brodie wouldn't help me if the tables were turned.

"Hand me that piece?" Liam told me, interrupting my guilty thoughts. I automatically handed it over to him and began to work on our horse once more.

The arrival of the other teams spurred us on, and a few short minutes later, we had used all of our wood and had a rather rickety-looking horse completed. There was a handlebar on each side for us to push on, and Liam and I pushed ours forward, heading for the marked path.

It was like pushing a shopping cart that was full of sand and held together by string. The thing creaked and groaned as if it were dying with every bump, and the tail wobbled like it was going to fall off. We pushed through the maze of walls and ruins, grimly determined. To my relief, our Trojan Horse held together and we crossed the finish line of the marked path.

The Greek soldier was there in his corny costume, and gave us our disk with a flourish. We took it from him with a nod, and quickly read the back. *Take a train to Nevsehir. From there, take a bus or taxi to Cappadocia, Turkey. Make your way to the Goreme Open Air Museum to receive your next challenge.*

"A train?" I asked, surprised. This was the first train we'd been instructed to take.

"Maybe they want us all to bunch up together again," Liam guessed. "Come on. Maybe if we hurry, we can catch an earlier departure."

He put his hand out for me to take and I clasped it, racing alongside him as we ran through the ruins and back toward the parking lot, heading for the car. As we did, we passed the others, still working on their horses. No one looked close to done, though everyone stopped and looked at us as we ran past, cameraman racing next to us.

"Hey, Katy!"

I turned, dropping Liam's hand at the sound of my brother's voice.

Brodie was on the far side of the horse, and he was frowning. He waved me over as if he wanted to talk to me. I hesitated, looking back at Liam.

He'd stopped too, and was watching me.

"Brodie wants to say something to me," I told my partner in a low voice.

Liam glanced at the cars, then back at me, clearly impatient but trying to hide it. "He might be trying to slow you down, or get information from you about the horse so he can get ahead of the others."

That did sound like my brother. I looked over at him again. "What is it?" I called back.

Brodie gave me an exasperated look and waved me over again, not wanting to say whatever it was aloud. He was definitely up to something.

I shook my head and gave him an apologetic look, then grabbed Liam's hand again. We raced back toward the cars and jumped back into ours. I pulled out the maps, studying for the nearest train station. "We should probably head back into Canakkale. The city's big enough that any train station would be there."

"Gotcha," Liam said, easing the car back onto the highway.

I glanced back out the rearview window. Brodie was watching us leave, even as Tesla knelt on the ground, piecing together the horse. My brother didn't look upset, just thoughtful.

And I wondered what it was he'd been trying to tell me.

THE TRAIN TO NEVSEHIR WAS A SLEEPER. I EYED IT SKEPTICALLY, CONSID-ering that we were the only ones in our small compartment. Either we'd had some serious luck, or this was another 'tweak' by the race runners to give the couples on the race some more alone time.

"Don't you find it suspicious that we keep getting stuck alone together?" I asked him as we set our backpacks down.

"Suspicious, yes. Unpleasant? Not in the slightest." He leaned in and pressed a kiss to my mouth. "Besides, you heard the lady at the train station. We could have taken a fourteen hour bus ride. Let's just count our blessings."

He had a point. The lady at the train station had tried to convince us (repeatedly) that we should have gone by bus. It would be much faster, she told us. It would leave much earlier than the train, which left at the end of the evening. But the race had said train, so we took the train.

I eyed the tiny bunk beds in the sleeper car. Perhaps I was too suspicious after all. Those didn't look exactly big enough to get frisky on. "I suppose." I glanced down the hallway of the train car as other passengers moved past. It was late at night and I didn't see too many people around. If there was anyone else on the race in this car, they weren't out and about. "Do you think the others got on this same train?"

"Without a doubt," he told me. "I can't imagine anyone spent hours building that horse."

I nodded. He had a point.

"Come on," Liam told me, shutting the door and hanging a 'do not disturb' placard outside. He wiggled his eyebrows at me suggestively. "You have to be tired."

"Are *you* tired?" I asked in a light voice.

"Exhausted," he told me, his voice husky as he sat down on the lower bunk and tugged me between his legs. "I was just thinking we should lie down and relax."

I arched an eyebrow at him. "So I guess this means I get the top bunk?"

"Bottom."

"And where are you sleeping?"

"Oh, were we talking about sleeping?" His hand slid down to cup my ass. "I think, perhaps, we're talking about two different things, my lovely pig-tailed Katy."

"Mmm." I ran my thumb along his lower lip, then grazed it over his piercings. "Maybe you should be more specific as to what you were thinking of."

"I was thinking," he said, flexing those delicious fingers over my buttocks. "That maybe I'd climb into this bed and you'd squeeze in next to me and we'd see what color condoms we had in store for today."

I laughed softly at that, my fingers moving to brush his shaggy hair out of his eyes. "That doesn't sound like a bad idea to me."

"I think it's a fucking awesome idea, personally," he said, and leaned in, pressing his face between the valley of my breasts. "Because I haven't been able to get you out of my mind all day."

Just like that, all the teasing in me vanished, and every nerve ending flared to life. I sucked on a breath, my fingers tightening on his scalp as he nuzzled between my breasts, then kissed the curve of one through the fabric.

"Want to take this off?" Liam asked me, tugging at the hem of my shirt.

Did I ever. I ripped it over my head, exposing my belly and the ugly sports bra they'd given all the contestants. I quickly dragged the bra over my head as well, my torso bare.

Liam leaned in again, brushing his lips over my breastbone and then kissing the now-naked curve of my breast. I shivered, leaning against him, my eyes closed as I enjoyed the sensations. His mouth nipped at my skin, a languid trail to the tip of my breast.

I sucked in a breath when his mouth latched on to my nipple and he rolled it against the piercing on his tongue. A little moan escaped me as his hand slid to my other breast, his fingers plucking and playing with my nipple as his mouth worked the other in tandem. He felt so good against me, and I could feel my pulse racing at his touch, desire centering between my legs in response to his touch. "God, Liam, your mouth."

"And here I've always thought my fingers were the talented ones," he murmured against my breast, then bit lightly at one nipple even as he tweaked the other.

I whimpered, my knees going weak, and I sagged against him, clinging to his broad shoulders.

"Such pretty breasts, Katy," he murmured. "So small and perky, just like you."

"I don't know if you should be telling a girl that her breasts are tiny," I told him, then sucked in another breath when he nipped at the underside of my breast with his teeth.

"I like their size," he told me. "A perfect mouthful." And he slowly licked my breast, that piercing flashing against my skin.

I moaned, pressing up against him. "I want to lick you, too."

"But I'm enjoying licking you so much," he protested, flicking his tongue over my aching, hard nipple. "You wouldn't want to take that away from me, would you?"

"Never," I breathed, and my hand slid between his legs, stroking his cock through his clothing. He was already rock hard against my hand. "But I never got my turn to lick this."

He groaned then, and his hand left my breast, both of them moving to the waistband of my pants and tugging them down my legs. "Want you naked, Katy. Naked and sprawled under me right now."

Just the mental image of that drove me wild. I shoved at my clothing too, pushing them to my ankles and kicking them aside. I was naked then, and my hands tugged at his black race t-shirt, wanting to feel his naked flesh against mine.

"Help me get changed." He jerked at his shirt even as my hands went to the studded belt he wore.

I slid to my knees and tugged the buckle apart, then undid his fly. His cock pushed out against my hands, straining through his boxers, and I couldn't resist. I leaned down and rubbed my mouth against him through the thin cotton fabric of his underwear.

He jerked to a stop, groaning. "Ah, fuck, Katy. You're distracting the hell out of me."

"Am I? Gosh, that's a shame." I leaned in and grasped the waistband of both his jeans and his underwear, dragging them down until his cock was freed. "You're really going to hate it when I do this, then."

And I put my mouth on the head of his cock.

Liam groaned like a man in pain, so loud that it made me giggle, and I shushed him, wrapping my hands around his thick, hot length. "If you don't keep quiet, I'm going to stop."

He bit his lip, eyes closing, and leaned back against the tiny bunk. His hand moved to my hair, but didn't push me forward. Didn't do anything, just rested there.

But I was feeling heady with power and arousal. I was making Liam lose control, and eating it up. I moved in a little closer, until my bare breasts were pressing against his thighs, my nipples scraping against his legs. This was a major turn-on for me. I wrapped my fingers around his cock and ran my mouth over the thick head of him, exploring him with my tongue. Beads of pre-cum formed, and I licked them away as they appeared, then took the head into my mouth and lightly sucked, feeling those piercings with my tongue.

The breath hissed out of his throat, and his hand clenched in my hair.

"Sensitive?" I asked in a sultry voice.

"You could say that." He sounded like he was gritting his teeth.

I rolled my tongue over one of the piercings, then the other, and then took him into my mouth again. I didn't take him deep into my throat—I didn't know enough about how that would work with his piercings—so I just licked him like a lollipop, over and over again, with my clenched fist stroking his hard length occasionally.

He groaned again, and he tugged at my hair, trying to drag me away from his cock. "Katy," he panted, "You have three seconds to get on that bed."

"Or what?" I purred, but I was so slick with need that my flesh was rubbing back and forth when I pressed my legs together, and I wanted him deep inside me. So I crawled onto the bed and flipped over to my back, watching him.

He got up and opened his bag, and I watched in fascination as he pulled out a condom—blue this time—and rolled it carefully over his cock, adjusting it around his piercing. And then he glanced over at me and gave me a wicked, wicked look that made my entire body shiver with anticipation.

Liam pounced on me in the next second, sliding between my thighs. I flexed them against him in encouragement, but instead of sliding inside me, he got to his knees and grasped one of my thighs, pushing it back until my foot was in the air. Then, he pressed a kiss to the side of my foot and placed it on his shoulder. The movement stretched me wide, and I moaned with arousal, anticipation getting the better of me.

He ignored my needy sounds, placing his cock at my entrance with slow, deliberate care. I tensed, waiting for that delicious slide home, but it didn't come quite yet. Instead, he held there. His hand moved to my sex and his thumb grazed against my clitoris.

My choked gasp of pleasure echoed in the small room. My entire body tensed, ready to slide right into orgasm. This would take no time at all—I was already so turned on I was practically writhing against his hand.

Then, he pushed inside me.

The strangest little mewing sound came from my throat, involuntary. And then Liam was pressing forward, his mouth moving to capture mine even as he stroked deep. My leg was stretched onto his shoulder, my knee mashed up against my breast as he leaned in to kiss away my moans. And he began to thrust. Not hard, but quick and fast, and I felt each one deep inside me, stretched and exposed as I was.

I moaned again, the sounds muffled by the thrust of Liam's tongue in time with his cock. The sensations were driving me wild, and I couldn't keep quiet. Soft, whimpering little gasps escaped me with every thrust of his cock as he rocked into me, over and over again. I was wild with pleasure, and that orgasm that had been so close? Spiraled out of control within moments, and then I was crying out, heedless of his quiet shushings, the kisses that tried to drown me out. My entire body was locked around his as pleasure overtook me, and a moment later, overtook him.

When I came down, I realized that Liam had collapsed on top of me, breathing hard, just as spent as I was. The only sound was our mingled, rapid breaths and the constant steady hum of the train as it moved along the tracks.

Liam groaned once more, then leaned up to kiss my mouth in a hard, insistent claim. I kissed him back, dazed. That had been amazing.

"Is it wrong of me to hope that we have a private train car on every leg of the race from here on out?"

"Nah," I said in a shaky voice, curling up against him when he rolled next to me on the narrow cot. I'd kinda been thinking the same thing.

* * *

THE GOREME OPEN AIR MUSEUM LOOKED LIKE SOMETHING OUT OF the Flintstones. Buildings of rock with square windows had been carved out of the side of the cliff. It was really interesting, but not half as fascinating as the colorful hot air balloons we'd passed on the way here. There was one waiting on the ground nearby, and I gave it a wistful look. We didn't have time to do something like that.

Liam tugged at my hand when I headed toward the stone building, turning me away. "I think I see the flag over there, in that field."

To my delight, he pointed at the hot air balloon. Sure enough, there was The World Races flag, and someone already in the nearest balloon, waiting. "Oh my gosh, do you think we get to go up in the balloon? How freaking cool is that?"

Liam chuckled at my excitement. "I take it you want to do this one?"

I gave a little bounce of pleasure. "Can I? Do you mind?"

"Not at all," he told me, and leaned in to give me a private smile. "Have fun. I'll be here when you get back."

I gave him a happy, enthusiastic kiss, not even caring that we were being filmed anymore. What did it matter? Liam was a great guy, and gorgeous. Who cared if the world was going to see us kissing?

I sprinted for the brilliant purple and yellow balloon, leaving my heavy pack with Liam and carrying only my necessities—my ID, some money, and of course, the Ace. As part of the race rules, we were never to let those leave our sight.

I bounded to the mat and gave the man at the flag a smile of thanks as he handed me the disk, then read it quickly. *Take a ride in the hot air balloon and look for clues as to where you are to head next. Each hot air balloon ride lasts one hour and holds two players. If you do not see the message on your first ride, you must get back in line and wait to ride again.*

A bit of anxiety clenched my stomach. What if I didn't find the message on the first round? We might be here all day. I looked back at Liam, but he only waved at me, clearly not seeing my distress. No sense in worrying about it, I told myself, and got into the basket of the balloon.

A player was already there, seated and waiting on a small bench inside the basket.

Brodie.

He grinned at the sight of me. "Hey there, sis."

"I see you got here ahead of us," I told him, taking a seat next to him. I couldn't even be mad about it. Everyone had to take taxis from the train station out to Goreme. It was entirely possible that he'd beaten us out here, though I hadn't seen Tesla. "Where's your partner?"

"Probably ran off to find a restroom," he told me. "She's got a killer hangover from last night."

Spending all their money on drinking? Figured. Maybe that was another reason the producers kept giving us so much money per leg. They wanted Tesla to get wasted. Lovely. My opinion of the show dropped a few notches as I sat down next to Brodie.

A cameraman got onto the balloon as another assistant handed us each binoculars.

"Can we share answers?" Brodie asked the assistant.

The man shrugged. "Not against the rules."

I gave Brodie a sour look. He was assuming I'd share with him? Because I had to suspect that if it was the other way around, it wouldn't happen.

As the balloon lifted off, I hung on to one of the basket's bright red railings—the hot air balloon equivalent of a chicken bar. We lifted into the air, and no one said anything for a long time, the sound of the burner flame echoing in our ears. The ride was surprisingly smooth, and before long, the ground was mere specks below us. My breath caught in my lungs at the wonder of being so high in the air, weightless and free. It was incredible. The countryside of Cappadocia spread out below us, all rusts and brown rock formations and craggy valleys.

At my side, Brodie turned and got to his feet, putting his binoculars to his eyes. I did the same, not wanting to be shown up by my brother. Strange how we'd started this race as partners and ended up as rivals.

"So if you see the message, you gonna share?" Brodie asked me.

I glanced over at him, but he hadn't looked away from his binoculars. He continued to scan the ground, as supremely confident and utterly casual that my answer would be a positive one. Which irritated me. I ignored him.

"Katy?"

"I haven't decided," I said after a long minute.

"Are you serious?"

"This is a race for two hundred and fifty grand, Brodie. Why should I hand it over to you? That kind of money buys me a lot of advertising for a start-up business, you know."

"Yeah, but this was my dream, not yours, Katy. You know it's not about the money. We can split the money if we win. Either one of us." He leaned in. "You know what I want out of this more than anything."

Publicity. Fame. His fifteen minutes. And if he won, he'd get that much closer. And if I stepped all over him on the way to the money, I'd ruin his dream. Ugh. My stomach twisted, and I couldn't really blame it on the balloon ride. "Brodie," I sighed. "I can't just think about me in this. You know if it was just me, we could talk it out. But Liam's my partner in this."

"So I hear," Brodie said in that brotherly tone of voice. "And I want you to be careful around him, Katy."

I rolled my eyes and put down my binoculars. "Are you serious, Brodie? You of all people are going to lecture me? You, that's been hooking up with Tesla Spooner for this entire race? Who couldn't wait to be her partner? Who wanted to be with her so bad that you ditched me at the first opportunity?"

"I didn't know the Ace was going to make us flip partners, Katy." Brodie threw up his hands in disgust. "How many times do I have to say that? You think if I'd have known that, I'd have screwed you over? You're my little sister. I care about you. I honestly just thought we'd save them for another round, and, you know." He gave me a dopey grin. "Tesla'd be appreciative."

"Yuck, Brodie. Just yuck."

"Hey, you asked." He nudged me. "You scan that side, and I'll scan this side."

I did, turning back to the rocky hills of Cappadocia. There was nothing that could be written anywhere on these hills, I determined, but enjoyed looking anyhow. The balloon ride was incredibly peaceful, and I was happy that Brodie and I seemed to be back firmly on brother-sister ground. I liked my brother, even though he was a bit of a selfish brat at times. And if he hadn't been a brat, I wouldn't have gotten the chance to spend all this time with Liam. It had worked out really well, actually.

And I smiled to myself as I scanned the countryside. It had worked out wonderfully, if I was honest with myself. And Brodie just wanted to get ahead in the race. There was no harm in that. At least he hadn't asked me for money.

"See anything?"

"Not yet," I told him. "Nothing that even looks like a message."

"Me either. Keep looking."

I did, obediently scanning the countryside with the binoculars.

"Hey, Katy?" Brodie said after a few more minutes.

"Hmm?"

"So...what are you and Liam planning to do with that Ace?"

I sighed. "Leave it alone, Brodie."

"Oh, come on," my brother said in a pleading voice. "You and Liam have been hovering around first place for several legs now. Tesla and I have a good leg, and then we drop all the way to the back of the pack again depending on whether or not she's having a good day or a bad day. And guess what kind of day she's having today?" There was an unpleasant tone in his normally cheery voice.

"A bad day?" I said, trying to hide my gloating and failing.

"She's hot, but man, she's really high maintenance. You can ask Liam about that." Brodie sounded a bit disgusted with his partner. "She drinks like a fish, insists on using all of our money, and she's horrible with a freaking map."

I chuckled. "Is she good at anything?"

A pause, and then Brodie gave me a sly grin. "Well, yeah. She's pretty good at *something*."

My face flamed. "Yuck again, Brodie! I did not want to know that."

"You asked!" He reached over and tried to give my head a brotherly noogie. "So, come on. Are you going to help your brother out?"

I turned back to my side of the balloon, scanning for the message. "Shouldn't we be looking for the clue?"

"I found it about five minutes ago, actually."

"What?" I yelped, rushing over to his side of the basket. My stomach heaved when the thing lurched in response, and the others in the basket glared at me. I clung to the chicken bar and raised my binoculars again. "You saw it and didn't tell me?"

"Well," Brodie said. "That's why I wanted to talk about the Ace."

I scanned the hills behind us with my binoculars, but could see no hidden messages, no nothing. Crap. Double crap. I'd lost the message and Brodie was going to hold it over my head. "I can't believe you!"

"Like you said, it's a race for two hundred and fifty grand, Katy."

"You really, really suck."

"And you have the Ace."

I resisted the urge to fling my binoculars at my brother's head. "So you're blackmailing me? Is that it? If I don't give you the Ace, I'll end up in last place because I'll have to go up again. But if I do give you the Ace, I'm helping you win. What exactly am I supposed to do here, Brodie? Either way, I lose."

"You should give me the Ace because I'm your brother," he said, his face earnest. He gave me a puppy dog look. "And Tesla hasn't done her challenge yet. You know whatever it is, she's going to suck at it. She's hung over like hell. And then we're going to be last, and I'm going to be eliminated." His face, so similar to mine, drew into sad lines. "It doesn't matter if you go up twice in this stupid balloon. I'll still be the one going home at the end of the day."

"Brodie," I began.

"You don't need it," he pleaded with me. "Liam's a great partner. And even if he wasn't, you never wanted to win. Not really. But I have to win, Katy. I have to stay on the show for as long as possible. And I can, if you give me the Ace. Think of what good TV it'll make—a secret brother/sister alliance."

I wavered. "It's not exactly secret if we work together. People kind of expect that, don't you think?" But that 'good TV' comment had me thinking, and thinking hard. I could save my brother and make him happy, get the clue from Brodie and ensure Liam and I stayed at the front of the pack, and the sneaky exchange would make good TV.

Except Liam would be mad that I'd given away our advantage. He wanted to win. And he hated Brodie.

And I'd promised Abby that I'd save her if it came time. Abby, my best friend on this race, and the one who'd really helped us out from day one. Not Brodie.

But Brodie was my brother. And he had the clue I needed.

I pulled the Ace out of my pocket and held it out to him. When he reached for it, I snatched it out of his grasp. "Just a second. I need you to make me a promise, first."

His eyes lit up. "What's that?"

"I promised Abby and Dean that we'd save them. If they get into danger and you don't, I want you to use it on them."

"Done," Brodie said quickly. He reached for it again.

This time, I smacked it into his hand, feeling uncomfortable as I watched his fingers curl over that important packet. He stuffed it into his pocket and then enveloped me in a boisterous hug. "You're the best, Katy. You know that?"

"Yeah, yeah," I murmured, but I hugged my brother back. Liam had said it was mine to use as I judged, after all. Maybe he wouldn't be too mad about this.

Maybe. Or maybe he'd be pissed that I'd given Brodie and Tesla the chance they needed to push ahead. He wanted to beat Tesla, and he wanted the money. He also hated Brodie.

Ugh. I got anxious just thinking about all this. "So are you going to tell me the clue?"

Brodie dragged my smaller form against him and noogied the hell out of my head. "You know I would have told you either way, right?"

"Jerk," I said, squirming out of his grasp. And no, I hadn't, but it was good to know now. "Just tell me the dang clue."

He pointed at a section of the distant hills. "There's a circle with several race flags set up over there. I imagine we'll pass by it again when we come in to land the balloon. And there are words spelled on the ground. 'Time for your partner to get oiled up.'"

"Oiled up?" I stared at the area Brodie had mentioned, but couldn't see anything. "I bet you're looking forward to that."

"You have no idea," he said with a dreamy grin.

Yuck, again. I elbowed Brodie...but then I imagined Liam all oiled up, and my grin was probably as dopey as Brodie's.

Sure enough, I saw the area Brodie had mentioned when we circled back. My brother hadn't been lying, which I was thankful for. I raced out of the balloon and back to Liam, who had both of our bags on his shoulders. Tesla was stretched out on the ground, a shirt tossed over her eyes as she either napped or tried to kill her hangover. I stepped past her and flew into Liam's arms. He grinned at the sight of me, spinning me around.

"How was it?"

"Spectacular," I told him, though I couldn't quite muster an enthusiastic smile. Giving the ace to Brodie was bothering me, though it did appear that he hadn't been lying about his partner having a bad day. I nodded back to Tesla's prone form. "What's with her?"

"Hung over," Liam said, leaning in to whisper it, and then nipped at my ear. "You find our clue?"

"I did," I told him. "Come on."

As we left, I glanced back at my brother and Tesla. She still hadn't moved from her spot on the ground, though Brodie was slinging backpacks onto his back. And I felt a twinge of pity for my brother.

They were still at the head of the pack at the moment. Maybe he wouldn't need the Ace at all. Maybe all my worrying was for nothing.

WE ARRIVED FIRST AT THE MAKESHIFT STADIUM. IT HAD BEEN SET UP like a Greek amphitheater amongst the rocks, but at the center was a large circular grassy area, and a row of five, burly men in stiff leather pants. Off to the side was a small changing tent. This was going to be the oiled up challenge? Weird.

Liam left our packs with me, and I sat down on them and drank a bottle of water as he bounded to the flag. He glanced over at me as he received the disk, and then began to read. And then groaned aloud, looking back at me. "Turkish Oil Wrestling," he called at me.

I gave him a thumbs up. "Go get oily!"

He raced to the changing booth, grabbed something from the ground, and disappeared inside the booth. I glanced around, looking for Brodie and Tesla. The stadium was only a short walk from where the balloons had landed. They should have been here by now.

A moment later, Liam stepped out of the booth, wearing the strange pants. They were thick, the material bulky, and reminded me of old fashioned football player pants. It looked as if they were made of leather. He wore no shirt, and I could see the tattoos dancing along his skin, his arms dark with black lines.

He grinned at me, rubbing a hand on his flat belly, and then moved toward the row of waiting men. He pointed at the first one and the man stepped forward. They both moved into the grassy circle.

I tilted my head as the cameraman stepped past, zooming in, and the judge moved forward, a carafe in hand. He began to pour the oil over the thickly muscled chest of the short, stocky man directly across from Liam—his opponent—and then on Liam's chest. His opponent reached forward and began to spread the oil on Liam's chest. Liam hesitated, then awkwardly returned the gesture.

My jaw dropped a little, and I leaned forward, fascinated by the two men as they oiled each other up. Then, they stepped forward. As they did, two other men came out and demonstrated the proper way to wrestle.

I tilted my head even more when one man stuck his hand down the other's pants and hovered over him, squatting.

That was…weird.

The man continued to hold the other man by his pants. It was also apparently legal, since the judge nodded approval at the pair, and they got up and clapped hands in a sporting gesture.

Oookay.

Then it was Liam's turn.

The judge blew the whistle and stepped back. Liam immediately moved into a fighting stance, all oily muscles and slick tattoos, and I admit, I got a little turned on just watching him move.

It didn't last long, though. His opponent gave him a minute, then quickly flipped him with a well-placed leg. Oily arms grappled and slid against each other, and then Liam landed hard on the ground, the other man over him.

And the man shoved his hand into Liam's pants to pin him.

I couldn't help it. I giggled.

Liam shot me a glare, his face flushed with irritation. Clearly not high on his list of fun challenges. I smothered my laugh and tried to look sympathetic.

The judge shook his head and blew the whistle. "No. I'm sorry," he told Liam. "Try again."

The man let Liam up, and my partner got to his feet, adjusting his pants and brushing the long black hair out of his face. He shook himself off, then gave a nod of readiness.

The judge blew the whistle again.

It was clear that the wrestler Liam faced was trying to go easy on him. He held his hands out, ready to counteract a move, but he also wasn't exactly being aggressive. He waited for Liam to move, and then when Liam lurched forward, grabbed him by the pants and slammed him to the ground again.

This time? I winced. That didn't look like fun. Liam wasn't quite sure how to handle his oily opponent. He rubbed his gleaming shoulder and rotated it, as if the muscles ached, and dragged himself back to his feet again.

Someone ran up beside me. A backpack dropped and Brodie flopped down beside me. "Hey."

I watched as Tesla dropped her pack next to Brodie and stepped forward to receive her clue. This was her challenge. Oh, this was *not* going to go well for them.

Brodie squinted and watched as Liam went down for the third time. "Did that dude just shove his hand in Liam's pants?"

"Turkish oil wrestling," I explained. At least, I hoped that was part of the schtick and not just an overly handsy wrestler.

"Ah," Brodie said, as if that explained everything.

"So what took you guys so long? You left the same time we did."

"Tesla needed a few minutes to recharge her chakras," Brodie said in a deadpan voice. "She insisted on doing some yoga to align her spirits or some shit."

"Seriously?"

He twirled a finger near his ear, indicating his partner's insanity. "She's lucky she's hot."

"Yeah," I said in a snide voice. "It's so much better to have a hot partner than a capable one." Speaking of hot partners…I looked over at my greased-up rock star and felt a familiar quiver in my loins when he grappled the man he was wrestling, his muscles flexing. Oooh, he was getting better at this.

A moment later, he flew over the man's shoulder and thumped onto the ground. The man turned him over and shoved a hand down his pants again.

Liam cussed under his breath.

Brodie howled with delight, clearly enjoying Liam's discomfort.

I shoved my brother. "Shut up, already."

"Maybe you should have done this one, Katy," Brodie said, but it was loud enough for Liam to hear. He glanced over his shoulder at us, and the look on his face was narrow-eyed.

"Quit being a jerk," I told my brother, and clapped my hands to encourage Liam. "You've almost got it," I called to him. "Just ignore everything but your opponent."

"Holy mother," Brodie breathed, and I turned to where his gaze was centered. Tesla had moved out into the ring with her opponent, dressed in her yellow team sports bra and a pair of the odd leather pants. The judge seemed to enjoy pouring the oil on her, and her opponent ran slick hands over her, looking rather pleased that he'd gotten the job. The other wrestlers were watching her get oiled up, too.

And then the whistle sounded, and she faced off with her opponent. Tesla danced around him, bobbing and weaving in light motions that surprised me. Maybe when she had her chakras aligned, Tesla was light on her feet. Or something. Either way, she managed to slid behind her wrestling partner and almost pinned him to the ground before he grabbed her and flipped her over.

The moment Tesla hit the grass, Liam hit again.

On the next round, though, she got it. My jaw dropped as I watched Tesla slide over her opponent and shove her hand down the man's pants. And that guy looked like he was enjoying it. Yeah, he probably hadn't been trying too hard to fight her off. Who'd want to fend off a beautiful oily woman that wanted to get her hands on you?

"Winner," the judge announced, and handed Tesla her disk.

"Yeah!" Brodie leapt to his feet, pumping a fist in the air. "Hot damn, way to go, girl. You rocked that."

"It's because her opponent wanted to be touched by her," I grumped. "He wasn't exactly running away."

I winced as Liam slammed into the ground again. Tesla hadn't been that much better than Liam, or faster. It seemed like her wrestler had gotten the 'go easy' memo, though, and Liam's hadn't.

"Or maybe she's just got a bigger set of balls than Liam, there," Brodie said with an obnoxious laugh, and grabbed his crotch at Liam just as my oily rock star was picking himself up off the ground.

With an angry snarl, Liam launched himself at Brodie, flying across the arena.

Tesla backed away even as I shot to my feet.

Brodie tried to push Liam away as he charged, but Liam was covered in wrestling oil and shirtless. There was nothing to grab but slick, ropy muscle. As I watched, Liam gave Brodie a hard shove, and when Brodie sprawled backward, Liam flipped him onto his stomach and shoved his hand into the back of Brodie's pants, grabbing his underpants in the world's largest wedgie.

It was basically the same move that the Turkish wrestler had done to him, over and over again.

"Who's got the bigger balls now, huh?" Liam said in a low voice.

"You fucking son of a bitch!" Brodie flailed, fists flying.

The judges rushed forward to break up the fight. I ran to Liam's side, putting my hands on his oily chest. "Hey," I murmured, wide-eyed. His chest heaved with angry, rapid breaths. "Calm down," I told him. "He's just trying to get under your skin."

"Your brother," Liam heaved between breaths, "Is a fucking dick."

I couldn't argue with that.

Liam's dark gaze turned on me and he leaned in. "We're not helping them in this race. I'd be happy if they went home tomorrow."

I said nothing. Liam would flip out if he found out I'd given Brodie the Ace. So I didn't admit it. What he didn't know wouldn't hurt him, and this was a bad time to confess. I ran a hand over his oily chest, trying to soothe him. "You're doing great," I murmured, ignoring Brodie's shouting on the far side of the judges that separated the men.

Liam seemed to calm a bit under my touch, though he still looked furious at Brodie.

A production assistant came up to one of the judges a moment later and whispered something. The judge nodded, and approached Liam and I as Brodie and Tesla headed off with their backpacks, presumably to the finish line. The man handed us a disk. It was bright red, with a big "6" on it.

"You have incurred a six hour penalty for fighting," he told us gravely. "You must wait here for six hours after your task is completed before you can receive your next set of directions."

"Six hours?" I protested. "Why did Brodie only get two hours for fighting previously? That's not fair."

"Two hours for every punch thrown."

Liam's jaw tightened.

I hid my disappointment. Six hours? We were going to get eliminated for sure. But it was what it was. I gave Liam's chest a pat. "Don't worry about it," I told him. "Just finish the task. You're doing great."

He looked down at me, then leaned in and gave me a hard kiss, his piercing scraping against my cheek. Then, he stalked inside the ring and faced his opponent again.

It only took two more tries before Liam managed to flip his opponent. Once the man was down, he seemed to concede the fight, and let Liam shove a hand into his pants and pin him.

I whooped and cheered as Liam finished, and the production assistant set a stopwatch. Liam gave me a rueful grin and moved to my side, dragging

me against him. I didn't care that he was oily, and sweaty. He was delicious.
When he kissed me again, I kissed him back.

"I'm sorry," he told me.

"For what?"

"For losing my temper," he said, his voice gruff. "I've pretty much cost
us the race."

I gave a shrug, feigning lightness. It wouldn't do any good to berate him.
"The way I look at it, we've got a nice vacation in Acapulco to look forward
to instead of sleeping in airports."

"Mmm," he said. "Do we get to share a bed?"

"Absolutely," I told him, rubbing a hand on his chest. "I'll even be the
one to oil you up next time."

He sighed and pulled me close, just as the next team pulled up. We
watched the two Olympian women race forward, our hearts sinking. They
hadn't been that far behind Brodie and Tesla, and the balloons carried two,
which meant another couple should have been hot on their heels.

That left one more couple an hour after them. No one was going to be
six hours late.

We were totally eliminated.

I LAY ON THE GRASS, LIAM'S HEAD RESTING ON MY STOMACH, AS WE
waited for time to pass. Idly, I toyed with his hair and we stared up at the
brilliantly blue skies of Cappadocia, watching the occasional balloon float
past.

"This place is really pretty," I said softly.

"Mmm." Liam's eyes were closed, and I couldn't tell what he was thinking.
We'd been more or less silent for the past few hours, simply waiting. Abby
and Dean had come and gone, Summer and Polly had come and gone.
There was one more team—Joel and Derron—and we hadn't seen them
anywhere, which made my stomach jumble into knots as the hours passed.

Liam had put his clothing back on over his oily chest, and his black
shirt stuck to his skin, but there was no place to go to wash the oil off.
We had to sit at the location and wait for our penalty to be over. It didn't
matter anyhow, I told myself. We'd be heading to the loser lodge shortly
and would have all the time in the world to shower.

We'd been here for hours on end. I didn't know how much time had
passed—the race didn't allow us phones and neither Liam nor I had a watch

set to the correct time since we jumped time zones so often. Someone would just tell us when our penalty was over, so we waited.

And waited.

And waited.

Which was why I was so surprised when I heard the sound of running feet. I turned idly and glanced down the path that had led to the challenge.

Joel and Derron had arrived.

I sat up, knocking Liam's head from my stomach, and he rolled away, surprised. We both stared at them as Joel moved forward to do the challenge and Derron came to sit next to us.

"I'm surprised to see you guys," he said, beaming at us. He looked thrilled. Of course he was. We were still at a challenge, hours after it should have been done. "What happened?"

"Six hour penalty for brawling," Liam said, glancing up at him.

"Brawling?" Derron's eyes widened and then he grinned. "Don't tell me. Brodie?"

"How'd you guess?" Liam asked, even as I stiffened in my seat on the grass.

"He and Tesla have been planning on trying to break your game for a while," Derron said. "Told me all about it last flight because we sat near them. Said you're too zen, so he was trying to get under your skin. Figured if he rattled you he might get the advantage."

My jaw dropped. My brother was a low down, sneaky jerk. He'd been sweet and apologetic to me while plotting behind my back the entire time. That little jerk.

Liam snorted. "Yeah, well, it worked."

Derron grunted. "He's kind of a shit." He glanced over at me. "Sorry. I know he's your brother."

"No, it's okay," I told him, feeling more than a little irritated at Brodie. "He *is* a shit." And he was totally going to hear a mouthful when I caught up to his ass.

He'd deliberately goaded my partner to try and get us eliminated from the race. And then as soon as he got me alone, what did he do? Played on me to get the Ace.

And I'd fallen for it. I felt like an idiot. I gave Liam a guilty look. Maybe it'd take a while for the Ace thing to hit the air. By that time, hopefully he'd have cooled down and he wouldn't freak out.

Though if he did freak out, I couldn't blame him. I'd fucked this up pretty good.

"So what happened with you guys?" Liam asked Derron. "You're hours behind everyone else."

"I couldn't find the stupid signal," Derron said, his face edging into unhappy lines. "I had to ride that damn balloon four times. Finally found it right under my nose." He shook his head. "I thought I'd cost us the race...."

His words trailed off but I knew what he'd meant. He thought he'd cost them the race until he saw us still sitting here. I glanced over at Joel as he emerged from the changing tent, all hard, compact body and stocky legs. He was a soldier, and incredibly fit. I had no doubt he could do this challenge easily. Judging from the smug expression on Derron's face, he thought the same thing.

The judge cleared his throat. "Liam and Katy?"

We leapt to our feet, all tension returning. "Yes?" I squeaked, my voice sounding ridiculous as I straightened.

"Your penalty is over." He held out the disk. "You may continue on to your next task."

I gave Liam a look of excitement, and he grabbed our bags as I raced for the disk. I glanced over at Derron, who'd gone stiff with frustration, his gaze on his partner in the ring. He wouldn't look over at me. That was for the best, since I couldn't hide my excitement.

As Liam came to my side, I read the disk. "Make your way to the finish line for this leg of the race. Return to the Goreme Open Air Museum and look inside for Chip Brubaker."

"Come on. We need to run it. We gotta make up time," Liam said, grabbing my hand just as the judge blew a whistle. Joel had just finished the task. *Already.*

We exchanged a look, then ran for the museum as if our lives depended on it. Liam's hand clasped mine so tight that I thought my knuckles would break, but I couldn't say that I wasn't doing the same to him. We rushed back to the Air Museum and circled the grounds, looking for the finish line.

"There!" I spotted it just as Joel and Derron turned a corner behind us. Liam cursed and we surged forward.

We got to the finish line seconds before Joel and Derron did.

Chapter Nine

"Is it wrong to be so intensely attracted to someone like Katy and hate her brother so very, very much?" —Liam Brogan, Cambodia Leg of The World Races

Twelve hours later

"MAKE YOUR WAY TO THE ANGKOR WAT TEMPLE GROUNDS IN Cambodia. There, you must search the grounds for the marked mat and receive your next clue. You have thirty two dollars for this leg," I read aloud, then glanced up at my partner. "Guess thirty two dollars won't get us another hotel room."

"Now that's a shame," he said, leaning in to lightly kiss the tip of my nose. "I'm still bummed about this last round."

We hadn't had enough money saved to cover food and a room, so we'd opted on eating. Liam had taken a quick shower at a local hostel and we'd catnapped in chairs at a movie theater. Not the most restful of options, but cheap with our limited money. Of course, it meant that we hadn't been able to have more alone time together. We'd had to settle for furtive kisses and groping in the dark of the movie theater.

And I'd originally thought I'd be fine with us not getting more privacy, but it turned out I was totally lying to myself. Every time Liam looked in my direction, I got all hot and bothered once more, imagining his mouth on my skin and his cock sinking deep inside me, filling the ache between my legs.

It didn't seem that I was the only one affected by this. Liam constantly touched me, his fingers brushing against my skin, as if he needed those quick, soft touches to anchor him. And of course, those touches just made me all fired up all over again. I got caught up imagining his tattooed body over mine, my hands gliding over the black lines on his arms—

"—Travel agency," Liam murmured in my ear.

"Huh?" I blinked back to reality, my dirty daydreams instantly disappearing.

"We should find a travel agency," Liam repeated. "See what flight gets us closest to Angkor Wat."

"Oh. Yes. Of course." I tucked the clue under my arm and took the hand he offered me, and we sprinted away from the starting line to a nearby row of cabs.

An hour later, we arrived at the airport and booked flights to Siem Reap, Cambodia. We'd just missed the prior flight a half hour ago, and ours wouldn't leave for another hour.

We were still firmly in last place, and the other teams would have at least an hour jump on us thanks to the flights. And that was on top of the several hours we'd had to wait out for our penalty.

Liam sat down on the floor at the airport and patted his side. I moved next to him and curled up under his arm, pillowing my head on his shoulder and trying not to think of the logistics of things. "We're screwed unless there's a miracle of some kind," I told him, ignoring the camera-man that hovered nearby and taped our cuddling.

"Mmm. We'll catch up," Liam told me, his fingers idly playing with one of my blonde pigtails. "Don't lose faith."

"I won't," I told him, linking my fingers in his free hand. My other traced the lines of one of his tattoos, even as he stroked my hair and then my shoulder. Crap, now I was getting all turned on again. "I just worry that we're going to get booted before we even get started."

"We'll have a chance," Liam told me. "Worst comes to worst, we can just trade the Ace to Abby and Dean for a chance to get ahead or something. I bet they'd do it."

I said nothing, my stomach giving an awful clench of dismay. For once, I was glad that we were the last ones at the airport, because then no one could tell my partner—my sexy, gorgeous, hard-working partner—that I'd screwed us both and given the Ace to my lying brother.

ABBY, IT TURNED OUT, WAS RIGHT ON THE MONEY WITH HER ADVICE. Make good TV? The producers will knock themselves over trying to save your asses.

We arrived at Siem Reap on schedule, got in the marked car left for us, and drove out to the Angkor Wat temple grounds. We blew through the first challenge—counting devas listed on the temple walls. It was time-consuming, but not too awful. As we counted, we'd also seen a group of musicians at the center of the temple, and Polly from the Olympian team working on a task. She finished up just as we approached, racing past us to return to her partner.

The first individual task? To select one of the traditional Cambodian musical instruments and learn to play a tune for the nearby judge. Liam had taken the task, and one of the instruments was a stringed instrument—a krapeau. Within a short time, he managed the strings, was humming the melody, and played it for the judge, who handed us our next clue.

That one had been almost too easy.

For my task? We'd had to turn around and race back to Siem Reap and head to a nearby restaurant, where Khmer Cuisine was served. The second individual task was there, and as soon as I saw that it was at a restaurant, I knew the producers were rigging things to get us to stay. I was the only one on the race that had culinary school experience. If there was a challenge I was going to excel at, it was going to be cooking.

Sure enough, when we arrived at the restaurant, I saw that not only was Summer there, working on the challenge, but Brodie and Abby were both there as well. We'd caught up with the other teams somehow.

"Good luck," Liam told me, and gave me a quick kiss before I dashed to my table.

For this challenge, my clue read, *you have a table full of traditional Khmer ingredients. You must taste the provided dish to determine how to prepare it and then make it from scratch. A judge will taste your dish to determine if it has been made properly. Once you have completed both dishes to his satisfaction, you will receive your next task.*

I sat down at the only empty table—right next to Abby, who gave me a queasy smile. Her table was torn apart, ingredients spread and sprinkled everywhere, and both of her 'taster' dishes half eaten. I picked up the first one and studied it, blanching. "Are these ants?"

"They are," she told me. "And they taste every bit as nasty as you'd think."

"Lovely," I said, and gave Liam a grateful smile when he dropped a bottle of water off at the corner of my table. Good man. The other plate seemed to be full of wiggly tentacles on a stick. Okay, that was not nearly as bad. I'd just think of that as the local calamari dish.

As soon as I sat down, Brodie got up and sprinted to the exit, his task completed. Damn. Well, that was all right. The other two teams were still here. I studied my table ingredients, and didn't recognize many of the spices or herbs. The easiest thing to do would be to taste the dish, then taste each spice until I figured out which ones it had been made with, and go from there. Steeling myself, I grabbed a pair of chopsticks and took a tiny bite of the ant mountain. It was bitter tasting, but there were spices mixed in, and it wasn't so terrible as long as I didn't think about what I was eating. Lemongrass, I decided. There was lemongrass in there, and garlic. I took another bite, contemplating. Lemongrass, garlic, and something else I couldn't identify.

Abby took one look at me, and swigged more water, clearly having issues with the challenge. "I am not so good with insects."

I set the plate down and licked the tip of my finger, then stuck it into a plate of what looked like spices. It was hot and unpleasant, and I swigged more water. Not what I was looking for. I did notice a bit of greenery at the corner of the table, broke off a small blade, and chewed. There was my lemongrass, at least. I pulled my bowl of 'fresh' ants closer and set the lemongrass next to it, contemplating my next spice.

"You guys are doing really well," Abby told me, leaning in to whisper. "Making good TV?"

"Guess so," I said, and couldn't resist a blush. I pointed at the lemongrass at the corner of her table. "You need some of that."

She tore off a handful and shook her head. "This is going to be it for Dean and I, I think. If you turn in the wrong dish, they make you start over, which means you have to keep tasting over and over again, and my stomach can't handle it right now." She patted her lower belly. "Maybe in another seven months."

My eyes widened and I forgot all about eating. "You're pregnant? Are you supposed to be racing? Isn't this dangerous?"

She grimaced and swigged more water. "Keep it down. I haven't said anything to Dean."

I glanced over at her husband. There was a look of concern on his handsome face, brows furrowed as he watched his wife chug bottles of water. But he clapped his hands and gave her a supportive thumbs up when she looked over at him. "You're doing great, baby," he called out. "Don't get discouraged."

"Why are you on a game show if you're pregnant?" I asked, leaning in to taste another one of my spices. Ugh. Bitter as hell, but possibly in the ant dish. I set it aside in the maybe pile.

"I didn't realize I was. By the time I did, it was too late to back out. You know I hate these sorts of shows, right?" She shook her head and shuffled a few of her spice dishes, contemplating the mess of cooking on her table. "I swore I'd never be on another one of these things, but Dean's coach passed away a few months ago and he's been in a funk. He needed a distraction and when they called and offered, I thought it'd be a good idea." She scrunched up her face and tasted the ant dish again. "I didn't figure out about you-know-what until a few days before the race, and by then it was too late to change my mind. I figured it couldn't hurt anything, right? But I didn't think I'd be eating spicy bugs, either." She shook her head. "I can't keep them down, which means we're done."

"I can help," I told her.

"No, you need to play to win. If you can do this fast, catch up with your brother and I'll try and beat Summer." She gave me a crooked grin. "And if I don't, I'll just hope for the Ace if you're game."

Oh god, that damned Ace. I swallowed hard. "Um, Abby…"

She studied her plates, not paying attention to me. "I don't know which is worse. The ant pile or the squid on a stick."

"Abby," I told her quietly. "I haven't told Liam yet, but…Brodie blackmailed me on the last leg and I had to give him the Ace."

Abby stared at me a long moment, and then the side of her mouth curled into a smile.

"I'm so sorry," I told her. "I know we had a deal, but he's my brother—"

"Oh, girl." She waved a hand and set her plate down. "Do not worry about that in the slightest. I'm only here for Dean. I don't care if we leave today, though he'll be disappointed because he likes to win."

"I feel awful. Liam's going to be so mad when he finds out."

She leaned in again and tapped my arm. "Let me give you another piece of advice, Katy. This is a reality TV show, but it's not reality in the slightest. There's a difference between making good TV and making good friends, and I've done this before. I know the difference." She smiled wider. "I think of you as a friend, and this race won't change that. But Brodie's your brother, so if you have to save his ass, that's what you do. I don't think he'd be as understanding." She winked. "I don't know if you noticed, but he really, *really* wants to win."

I snorted and chewed a green leaf, then spat it out. Disgusting flavor and not what I was looking for. I shuffled the bowls again. "Yeah, I noticed."

"So don't you worry about us," she said, mixing her ingredients and then picking up her chopsticks with a resigned face. "If he gets all bummed, I'll just tell him about the baby."

From across the room, Dean cupped his hands to his face and called out, "Less gossip, more eating, Abby."

She waved a hand at him, dismissing his words. "I'm eating, I'm eating."

"You're the best, Abby," I told her.

"I know," she said loftily, then gave me a curious look. "How is Liam handling the whole Ace thing? I thought he hated Brodie."

"Uh, I haven't told him yet." I winced. "After that fight, I'm kind of afraid to. But if it comes down to Liam or Brodie, I don't know what to do. Brodie's my brother and he wants to win this more than anything. And Liam..." I sighed. "I'm not sure what Liam is other than my partner."

"It's hard to say," Abby said, her voice sympathetic. "Like I said, this is reality TV, but it's not reality. You're great together right now, but who can say what happens after the race? Dean and I lucked out, but it wasn't easy. I hated him for a long time, simply because of what I'd been led to believe."

"I know," I told her. I suspected that once Liam and I were apart? He'd go back to his rock star lifestyle and I'd go back to Katy Short, unextraordinary baker. It wasn't like we had a future. He probably spent most of the year on tour. I spent most of the year in the kitchen, working on recipes and baking to orders. Besides, Liam and I barely knew each other outside of this race. It wasn't like we had any hope for a long term.

But...I really liked him.

Which was bound to get me hurt.

I pushed those thoughts aside and tasted ingredients, combining them with my ants. When I thought I had the right spices, I handed my bowl to the waiting chef, who cooked everything up and then handed it back to me. I tasted it, then tasted the other bowl. Close, but not quite. Was it close enough? I tasted again, wincing when something squished between my teeth. Next to me, Abby gagged again, and that made my stomach turn once more. She wasn't making this easy, that was for sure. I set aside the bowl and worked on my squid dish, which wasn't as bad. There were less alternately crunchy and squishy bits. Instead, the entire thing was slightly rubbery and tasted of lime and some sort of extremely spicy herb that seemed familiar enough. I combined ingredients, tasting, then handed my bowl over to be cooked.

This time, the squid tasted almost exactly like the sampler dish. I put it aside and tweaked my ants, even as Summer sprang to her feet, her disk in hand, task completed. The two Olympians cleared out and then it was just me and Abby.

Shit. I could help her, but if I did, I might be eliminating myself. And it was clear she wasn't doing well with the challenge. She kept adding cracked pepper to hers, and I was pretty sure that I hadn't tasted cracked pepper in either of my dishes.

I adjusted the amount of lemongrass in my dish of beef, ants, and noodles, and handed it to the chef again, who cooked it once more and then handed it back. I tasted and tried not to think that I had a belly of squid and ants at this point.

Perfect. I waved the judge over, who came and tasted both of my dishes. He took a long moment, sampling both, then when I was about to burst from nervousness, he nodded and handed me my disk.

I charged up from my table, excited, even as Liam sprang forward, both of our bags in his hand. I looked back at Abby, still seated at the table, and on a whim, I arranged the bowls of ingredients into two rows of what I'd used, making it obvious as to which ingredients were for which. She gave me a grateful look as we sprinted away to read our clue privately.

As soon as we were outside, Liam grabbed me and pulled me close in a tight hug. "I'd give you a kiss but you've been eating ants for the last half hour."

"I don't blame you," I told him, and flipped the disk over to read the instructions. "Make your way to the Amansara Hotel in Siem Reap, and look for the finish line."

"We're still in this," Liam told me. "Come on."

The drive to the hotel was a tense one, and I read directions out to Liam between constantly looking out the window, checking for Abby and Dean's marked car to pass us. We'd made up time, but I didn't know if it had been enough. Abby and Dean could have left moments after us and took an alternate route to the hotel, and we still might be the last ones to arrive. We'd made up so many hours, but you never knew in this race.

When we pulled into the parking lot, Liam slammed into the first parking spot he saw, and we jumped out of the car, leaving our bags behind. I ran to his side and took his outstretched hand, and we raced into the hotel, looking for the finish line. His hand clenched mine tightly, and that somehow felt right that we'd cross this line together, hand in hand.

When we crossed the finish line, Abby and Dean were nowhere to be seen. Chip smiled at us, and spread his hands in a munificent gesture. "Welcome, Liam and Katy! You are team number three and still in this race."

I threw my arms around Liam's neck, hugging him tight.

Just as I did, the door opened and Abby and Dean rushed in behind us. I saw Abby's face fall when she spotted us, and I slid down from Liam's grasp, guilt washing over me. Dean's eyes narrowed but he kept a friendly smile on his face, able to hide his emotions a lot better than Abby did.

"Abby and Dean," Chip said in a grave voice as they stepped onto the mat next to us. "You are the last team to cross the finish line. Unless someone plays an Ace, I'm sorry to say that you will be eliminated."

I bit my lip, feeling acutely uncomfortable. I moved a little closer to Liam, staring straight ahead and not looking at the team next to me. I didn't want to see the understanding disappointment in Abby's face and the frustration in Dean's. They'd been good friends to us the entire race and I was about to screw them.

"Liam?" Chip prompted.

"Katy and I discussed it," Liam said, his arm sliding around my waist. "It's her decision. I won't push her one way or another. And whatever she chooses, I support her."

Chip gazed at me. "Katy?"

I felt like the world's biggest asshole. "I'm sorry," I whispered.

I didn't play the Ace. I couldn't. I'd given it to my brother, our biggest rival and enemy.

"I'm sorry, Dean and Abby, but you've been eliminated."

"It's okay," Abby said, her voice cheerful. "It's been a good run, and Dean and I did this just for fun, anyhow."

"Every day, I wake up and I feel like I've won," Dean said. I pictured him pulling Abby into a hug as he often did in quiet moments, but I didn't dare look over at him. "Just because I have her at my side. No regrets here."

"No regrets," Abby emphasized, and it felt like it was for my benefit more than anything.

And then the production crew stepped in and ushered Dean and Abby away for post-game interviews, and I was left with my partner and the host.

"The hotel has generously offered to let you stay here during your break," Chip told us in a too-smiley voice. "I'm sure you two would love some alone time, so I'll let you get to it. You can just check in at the front desk."

"Thanks," Liam murmured. "I'll get the keys."

When we got up to our room, Liam set down our backpacks against the wall and turned to me. "You want to tell me what you were thinking back there?"

I crossed my arms over my chest, unhappy and numb. I'd just screwed over our friends. "It's complicated."

"I don't understand you," Liam said in a low voice. He dropped into a chair and stretched his legs out. His hands rubbed his face, and he seemed incredibly weary. "Was it strategy?"

"Not really," I told him. "I just…couldn't."

"They wouldn't split us up again. We make good TV."

"I know."

"So…why?"

I shrugged uncomfortably. *Because I gave our Ace to Brodie, because I thought he'd changed and he's my brother. Turned out he was just using me.* But the words wouldn't come out of my throat.

"Do you know something I don't? About the Ace? Is there something bad that happens if we play it?"

I shook my head. "I know what you do."

"Then I really don't understand," Liam said, a hard edge to his voice. "It's not that you didn't play the Ace just now. If it was strategy or you had a plan, I could understand it. But not playing it just to not play it? That just seems cruel to me, and I thought we were friends with them."

"We are," I said softly.

"Then why?"

I bit my lip. "I...I don't have it anymore."

"You...what?" He gave me an incredulous look. "Where did it go?"

My stomach gave an unhappy gurgle. I wasn't sure if it was stress or all the ants I'd eaten this afternoon. Either way, I felt like I was going to throw up. "I gave it to Brodie."

Liam's face grew hard. His eyes were cold and unfriendly as he studied me. "You...gave it to Brodie." He said it so flatly that it made me wince.

"He was in last place and he was in trouble," I explained.

"And he's your brother," Liam said slowly. He tilted his head at me, as if seeing me for the first time. "And he really, really wants to win."

"He does," I agreed.

"And you don't care about winning."

I shrugged. That had been my story the entire time, hadn't it? I didn't care about winning nearly as much as I cared about cashing out for that twenty grand. So why was I fighting so hard to stay in the game? I supposed it was because I didn't want to disappoint Liam.

Unfortunately with the way he was looking at me at the moment? We'd moved past disappointed and straight to furious.

"So. Has all of this been a set-up, then?"

It was my turn to be confused. "What do you mean, a set-up?"

He gestured expansively. "All of this. Splitting up. Romancing me and romancing Tesla and then working together behind our backs. Is all of this a set-up to push your way to the win?"

My jaw dropped. "What? No!"

"Really? Because that's not what I'm seeing. I'm seeing someone that was mad that she was partnered with me, and then kissed me out of the blue not a day later. And I couldn't figure it out." He gave a wry snort. "I mean, you didn't act like a groupie. That I know how to handle. And here I thought you were just a nice girl having fun. Maybe the pigtails fooled me. But those aren't you either, are they? It's all for the show. Everything."

I ran a hand over my pigtails and shook my head. "You're wrong."

He put his hands up, as if to stop my argument. "Just tell me one thing. Did he promise to split the prize money with you if you helped him?"

I was silent, rather horrified. Brodie *had* promised to split the prize money. "It's not what it looks like, Liam—"

"Fuck." He shook his head. "I can't believe you fucking slept with me just to win some money."

I grabbed one of the pillows off the bed I sat on and threw it at his head. "I didn't sleep with you for some prize money, you asshole."

"Then why did you?"

"I thought I liked you. I guess I was wrong," I said bitterly. "You're kind of a dick."

"Yeah, well, you're kind of fake."

"Fuck you."

"Have you been throwing challenges?"

"Have I *what*?"

"Throwing challenges. You know. So your precious brother could catch up."

"Are you kidding me?" I thought my jaw couldn't drop any lower. I was wrong. "You really think I've been throwing challenges?"

"I don't know what to think anymore."

"Gee, if my memory serves me correctly, someone on this team's been sucking at challenges and it wasn't me." I tapped my finger on my chin as if mockingly contemplating things. "Who sucked at oil wrestling? Who sucked at eating mukluk? Actually, I should be asking you if you were throwing challenges—you're the one that started fighting at the oil wrestling and made us lose six hours!"

The look on his face could have iced a glacier. "I attacked your brother because I didn't like the way he treated you. I see now I was misguided and it was all just to fuck with my head. I'm sorry I bothered."

My jaw worked silently. I could think of nothing to say. The hurt spiraling through me—and the anger—was too intense. "You're wrong about me."

"Yeah? Prove it, then."

"How?" I snapped at him. "No matter what I do, you think I'm helping my brother out."

"Don't fuck us in the challenges in this last leg. If we win, I'll know you weren't lying. If you throw the challenge just to let your brother get ahead? I'll know where things really stand."

"Fine."

"Fine, then."

"All right."

He glared at me, then shook his head, getting to his feet. "I'm not staying in here tonight. I'll find someplace else to crash."

"Whatever," I yelled after his back.

He slammed the door and I was left alone in the hotel room. I flopped back on the bed, utterly furious.

Throwing challenges? Working with my brother behind his back?

I'd have been utterly furious...except that the more I thought about it, the less innocent my part in things seemed to be. How was it that I'd had the best intentions and still gotten screwed in this?

And how was it that I'd had the attention of a guy that seemed utterly perfect for me...and managed to somehow mess that up?

Abby was right—this wasn't reality, and it was messing with my head. I was ready for this race to be over so I could go back to my real life. At least there, I knew how things stood. There, rock stars with delicious tattoos and sexy piercings didn't romance me and drag me into bed, or trace tiny circles on my arms as I leaned against him. No one was so attuned to being with me that he had to touch me all the time.

That was reality.

This? This was just a dream that had turned into a nightmare.

Chapter Ten

"Everything's all wrong. All wrong, and I don't know how to fix it. All I know is that I don't know if I can trust Katy, and that makes me so goddamn miserable I can't stand it. I'm in love with her and I don't know if I'm being played for a fool."—Liam Brogan, Final Leg of The World Races

LIAM DIDN'T RETURN TO OUR ROOM THAT NIGHT. I DIDN'T SEE HIM again until it was nearly time for us to depart, and he met me on the mat, thin-lipped and frowning in my direction.

"Hi," I said softly as I took my place on the mat next to him. "Where'd you sleep?"

He shrugged. "Didn't sleep. Just needed to get my thoughts together."

"Oh." I studied him. He looked more than tired, he looked…done. Like all the fun had gone out of this and he wanted to be anywhere but standing next to me. Which hurt. "You know, Liam—"

"Let's just race, okay, Katy? I don't feel like talking right now."

I forced myself to put on a carefree smile. "Sure. Whatever."

An assistant ran up, tapping her watch. "Time to go." She handed us our clue and we watched the cameraman approach. When he gestured for us to begin, I offered the clue to Liam. Normally I was the one that read them, but that was back when we were a happy little team.

Not when I was Katy, Scheming Sister From Hell.

He nodded at me. "You go ahead."

"Gee, thanks." I flipped The World Races disk and peered at the writing. It was dark out, the middle of the night. "Make your way to Betsy Ross's House in Philadelphia, Pennsylvania. This is the last leg of the race. You have one hundred dollars." I pulled the money out and brightened, smiling at Liam. "This might be the first place we've gone where we didn't have to exchange anything."

"Let's just head to the airport," he said, putting his hands on his backpack straps and walking forward.

My face fell. Was he going to be like this for the rest of the trip?

If so, this was going to quite possibly be the longest leg ever.

It definitely felt like the longest flight ever, I thought to myself as we sprinted off the plane some thirty hours later. Two layovers and more hours in an uncomfortable airline seat than I could imagine, but we had landed at our final destination. All three teams were on the same flight—Summer and Polly had been at the very back of the plane, and Tesla and Brodie had been toward the front. Liam and I got the last two seats and had spent every leg of the flight separated.

I'm sure that made him happy.

It was awkward, though. We'd gone from awkward, unhappy team to fun, happy couple, right back to awkward, unhappy team. Liam didn't talk to me during layovers, even though we sat next to each other. He just put his earbuds in and began to tap a beat out on his bag, lost in music and looking everywhere but at me.

I tried not to let it bother me too much. The others had given us a few curious looks, but no one came over to chat except for Brodie, and I'd chased him off. The last thing I wanted was to sit down and have a long pow-wow with the brother I was supposedly in cahoots with.

At least we'd finally landed. I was the first racer out of the plane, and had to stand around and wait for my partner. Brodie and Tesla raced past with a smirk, but Liam wasn't too far behind.

"Let's get a cab," was all he said to me.

"Fine."

Cabs were easy to find at the airport, at least, and we ran to one just as

Brodie and Tesla's cab pulled out ahead of us. "Do you know the way to the Betsy Ross House?" Liam asked the cab driver, tossing his bag into the trunk. I shrugged out of my pack and moved to set it in the trunk next to his, but to my surprise, Liam took it from my hands and placed it next to his. At least his chivalry remained in place.

"Yep," the cab driver said easily, then eyed the cameras. "You guys in some kind of race?"

"Yes," I told him, sliding into the back seat. "Can you drive fast?"

"Lady, you ain't seen fast," he told us as he moved back to the front seat. He got in and adjusted the rearview mirror as Liam sat next to me and closed the door to the cab. "You look familiar."

"I get that a lot," Liam said, but didn't offer an explanation.

"Buckle in," the cab driver told us. And then we peeled out of the airport. The lurch of the car flung me, headfirst, into Liam's lap—I hadn't finished buckling myself in. And my chin went right into his crotch.

Warm hands helped me upright. "Careful," Liam murmured. His grip seemed to linger on me for a moment longer than necessary, and then his hands went to the belt. "Like he said, buckle in."

"Getting there," I whispered, feeling a bit breathless and hot at Liam's touch. Maybe all wasn't lost between us. Maybe he'd had a chance to stew on his doubts and realized that I wasn't leading him on.

But Liam didn't say anything else, and I sighed and buckled myself in.

A short time later, we pulled up to the Betsy Ross House just in time to see Brodie and Tesla disappear inside. We were right on their heels.

"Wait here," Liam told the cab driver as he grabbed my hand and we raced after the yellow team. The Betsy Ross house was a quaint little woodsy courtyard in the middle of the city, an old-fashioned flag fluttering on one wall. There was a large tree in the front and several small cafe tables, but no World Races mat. It had to be inside.

We made our way inside, and sure enough, at the front door stood a woman dressed in a white cap and old fashioned clothing. She smiled at us, disk in hand. The disk was labeled clearly with "Individual Challenge."

I looked at Liam. "You or me?"

"I'll do it," he said, and stepped onto the mat.

"You sure?"

"Can't think that Betsy Ross was famous for eating disgusting things," he murmured, and cast a sideways look at me. "We'll be fine."

I nodded, but felt a little easier. Liam didn't seem to be as angry. Guarded, yes. Angry, no.

"Betsy Ross was the creator of the original American flag," Liam read aloud. "Outside of this building, you passed by a replica of the original flag. In the next room, there are two hundred and thirty seven incorrect replicas and three correct. Find a correct flag and return it to the judge for your next clue." He turned and looked at me. "Wish me luck."

"Good luck," I told him softly.

He opened the door to the room and stepped inside, and I caught a glimpse of hundreds of flags, a cacophony of red, white and blue stripes. I winced in sympathy. The flag might be easy to identify if you knew what you were looking for, but digging through all of those? They'd start to look the same after a while.

"You can go to that room and wait," the judge told me, gesturing at a door at the far end of the small room.

I nodded and stepped through the doorway. There was a small side room with three chairs lined perfectly in a row.

And sitting in the middle one? My brother.

That meant that Liam was against Tesla in this task. That also meant that I'd be against Brodie in the next one.

And if I didn't outperform my brother? Liam was going to think I threw the challenge.

I groaned at the sight of my smiling blond brother. I was totally hosed.

"Nice to see you, too," he told me.

"You screwed me in this game, you know," I told him as I thumped to the seat next to him.

"How so?"

Did he really not know? I gave him an incredulous look. "The Ace."

"Oh." He shrugged. "You didn't have to give it to me."

"You blackmailed me! You deliberately withheld information and then blackmailed me to get it after you'd promised you'd work with me. What was I supposed to do?"

Brodie grinned and leaned over to noogie my head. "Don't be mad, Katy. I'll buy you some cool stuff with my prize money when I win the two hundred and fifty thou. It's the least I can do to say thank you."

"I don't want you to promise me money," I sputtered. "My partner already thinks we're in cahoots. He's furious."

"Is he, now?" Brodie seemed really interested in that. "Good. So does this mean you're going to throw the next challenge?"

"No! Are you kidding me?"

"Come on. He's already mad. And I'll make it worth your while after I win, I promise."

"Just shut up, Brodie. It's not even up for discussion."

"Suit yourself." But he wouldn't stop smiling, which infuriated me more.

I crossed my arms over my chest and slouched in my chair, irritated as hell at him. "I hope Liam blows Tesla away in this challenge and you have to eat our dust for a change."

"Won't happen," Brodie said smugly.

Ten minutes later, the door opened. Both Brodie and I sat up, alert and waiting for our partners to return. I gave a whoop of delight when I saw it was Liam, and nearly launched myself into his arms. "So fast? You did awesome!"

He grinned at me and displayed the next task disk that he'd won. "Guess I have a better memory than I thought."

I took the disk from him, and noticed Brodie's interest. I shoved it under my shirt so Brodie couldn't sneak a peek at the writing on the backside. "Let's get out of here," I told Liam.

He nodded, and his hand went to the small of my back, instinctively moving closer to me.

"Don't forget what we agreed, Katy," Brodie called after me.

I gasped. That lying sack of shit. I turned and confronted him. "Nice try. I didn't agree to anything with you."

"Uh huh," he said, and winked exaggeratedly.

"Bullshit," I told him, and turned back to Liam. "He's full of it."

But Liam only gave me a speculative look. "Let's just get in the cab. We don't want to lose our lead."

Damn it. Why was I even trying? Liam wasn't going to believe me, no matter what.

I STOOD OUTSIDE OF THE SMALL STOREFRONT AND READ THE SIGN TO make sure that I was at the right place, then read the clue-disk again. "Go to the Pretzel Factory. Inside, you will find trays of dough waiting for you. You must twist 200 pretzels Philly-style and then hand them to the baker. The baker will then hand you a large box of finished pretzels that you must deliver to a nearby office. There, you will receive your next task." I turned and looked at Liam. "Wish me luck."

"Luck," he said softly.

I didn't know what to think of that response. He didn't touch me, and his voice was flat. I stared at him a long moment, then shrugged and headed inside. I couldn't read him, and it was bothering me. He'd shut down completely and it hurt me more than I cared to admit.

"Hi," I said as I walked in. There was a judge there, waiting on the mat. It was a woman with blonde hair, a chef hat, a green apron, and way too much lipstick. "I'm here for the challenge."

She gestured at one of the nearby tables and a cameraman scooted out of the way as I approached it. There were three massive tables laid out in the kitchen, all three covered with big bowls of dough and trays. I was the first one there, and I eyed the tableau, sizing it up.

The judge hurried to my side. "Let me show you how this works." She took one of the bowls and fed the dough into a strange looking machine. As I watched, it pushed out a long tube of dough, and she picked it up and began to weave it into the pretzel shape. She moved fast—so fast I was dazed watching her—and immediately picked up the next length of dough, then began to braid it, too. I watched her do three of them before she turned the machine off, gave me a thumbs up, and then returned to the mat.

All right, I guess that was all the demonstration that I was going to get. I flicked the machine back on again and waited for the first tube of dough, then snatched it when it came up. Immediately, it squished and lost its shape, and I yelped, trying to push it back into a semblance of shape. By the time I'd wrangled my dough into a mangled figure eight, looked nothing like hers, and the machine kept spitting out tubes of dough. I groaned and slapped my ugly pretzel down on a nearby tray. I'd save that pile for rejects.

It took me sixteen pretzels before I figured out what I was doing, and sixteen more before I started to get any sort of speed with it. My shoulders cramped because I was concentrating so hard that every muscle in my body was tense. But my pretzels weren't looking like rejected limp doodles, so that was a win. I filled the first tray, exhausted, and counted.

Thirty two out of two hundred. Dear god, it felt like I'd been here forever.

To my annoyance, Brodie strolled in a moment later, breathless. Damn it! He'd caught up. I had lost whatever advantage Liam had gotten us. And unless I sped things up on this challenge, Liam was going to think I blew it on purpose. Frustrated, I wiped my brow, ignoring the flour I got on my face, and continued to work on my pretzels.

Brodie strolled past my table, eying my handiwork. He looked at my tray, grinned, and then moved to a table across from mine. The judge hurried over and started the pretzel-dough machine for Brodie, demonstrating three pretzels to him.

I paused for a moment, watching him as the machine began to spit out dough, and couldn't help but grin when he confidently grabbed the first tube of dough…and it fell apart in his hands.

I smirked and returned to my pretzels, twisting the next one slowly into shape.

The room grew quiet, nothing but the sound of the machines whirring. I twisted a few more, noticing that I was getting better at this, if not faster. I sneaked a peek over at Brodie, since he was being so quiet. My brother stood over his tray, but his gaze was on my hands as I twisted my pretzel, and I could see that he was clearly trying to copy my much slower movements.

That jerk. He was going to profit off of my hard work? Again? Not likely. I tossed down my pretzel and grabbed a few of the big metal trays, propping them up so they formed a shield.

"Hey, not fair," Brodie told me, a whiny protest in his voice.

"Neither's cheating off of me," I retorted. "You've screwed me enough in this game, thanks."

"Katy, I'm supposed to win, remember? That was our deal."

"No," I hissed. "You think I agreed to that, but I didn't. We were supposed to be a team, remember? Except you threw me away for the hot rock chick and didn't give a shit. And ever since then you've been trying to sabotage me."

"I have not!"

"No? Remember that whole Ace thing?" I twisted the next pretzel viciously and noticed that it actually looked closer to the demonstration pretzel. Huh. Maybe angry pretzeling was the way to do it. "Or maybe the whole 'gee, Katy, don't forget what we talked about' thing?" I mocked his deeper voice.

"Oh, come on. I was just having fun."

"Yeah?" I slapped another pretzel down on the tray, noticing viciously that his pretzels looked like shit. "It's not fun for me, Brodie. You don't seem to care about my feelings at all."

He snorted. "I didn't realize you were going to be such a baby about it."

"Liam's pissed at me, Brodie!" I twisted hard, then laid the new pretzel next to its brothers before scooping the next long tube of dough off of the machine. I was almost keeping up with it now. "You think I'm going to be happy about that? I happen to really like the guy."

"He doesn't need to win," Brodie countered. "He's rich."

"So's your partner. You're still trying to win."

"You know I want to win!"

"Yeah, well, I want Liam," I yelled at him. "And you fucking ruined that for me, so thanks a lot."

"Language," one of the cameramen hissed at me. "We're still filming."

I sighed and yanked another piece of dough in my direction, pleased to see that Brodie was still trying to watch me, but my table was shielded. Good. And he was still on his first tray. Double good.

"He's a rock star, Katy," Brodie said, and I recognized the tone of voice. That was his whole 'big brother knows all' voice. The patient, almost too-knowing, too-smug tone of voice that I normally tuned out. Today? It got on my damn nerves. "You know just as well as I do that we won't see him or Tesla again after this race."

"Well, you made sure that was the case, didn't you?" I said bitterly. "Black-mailing me for the Ace was pretty low."

"I don't get why you care so much," he said, and for a moment he sounded genuinely confused. "You said you just wanted the money. You'll still get the same amount for second place as you would for last."

"Would you give up on the money?" I bellowed. "It's not about that for me. Not anymore." I was getting a throbbing headache just trying to reason with Brodie. Why was I even trying? "You know what? Never mind, Brodie. Just never mind."

Summer rushed in a moment later, her eyes wide. She grinned happily at the sight of us. "I could hear you two yelling down the block. Led me right to this place."

"Only one of us is yelling," Brodie said in a sulky voice.

"Fuck off, Brodie," I said in my sweetest voice, and stuffed another pretzel in the tray.

"Language," the cameraman said again, and we fell quiet.

Everyone twisted in silence for a while, the tension in the room utterly palpable. I couldn't help but notice that once Summer got set up with her table, Brodie propped up a few trays and made his own fort so she couldn't copy his hand motions. I peeked over at Brodie, and was discouraged to find that he'd started moving quite a bit faster than I'd hoped. If his pretzels looked halfway decent, he was going to make up a lot of time.

I finished the tray I was on and counted pretzels. Ten more. I got nervous at that, my hands shaking as I rapidly twisted and squished the pretzels into the proper shape. And then I was done. I leapt up, waving for the judge.

She strolled over to my table as if in slow motion and I twisted my doughy, flour-covered hands so I wouldn't reach out and shove her toward my table. As I hovered, she counted, and then nodded. "That's two hundred."

I hopped with excitement. "Now I do a delivery?"

She nodded and moved back to the mat. A large box of hot pretzels was waiting, painted black for my team color. It was about the size of a large ice-chest, and I hoisted it up, frowning. It was bulky and awkward to hold.

"You need to wear a delivery hat and apron," she told me cheerfully, and produced a boat-shaped hat with a big plastic pretzel on the front, and a plastic apron.

I set back down the pretzels, took the clothing from her, slapped the hat on and tied the apron around my waist. "Address?"

"Independence Hall," the woman said in a sweet voice. "Good luck."

"No street?" I didn't know where that was. This was Philadelphia—what if there were four different Independence Halls? "No directions at all?"

"No." Her smile remained in place.

"And I can't take a cab?"

"You have to walk."

Figured. I hefted the box and headed for the exit, trying not to panic. And here I'd thought twisting pretzels would be a challenge. I should have done the stinking flag task—Liam had been out of there within moments. Me, I'd spent the last hour twisting dough into knots and now had to hike across town with an enormous box of pretzels.

As soon as I emerged from the pretzel shop, I was greeted with polite clapping. "Good job, Katy," Polly called, and Tesla clapped her hands.

"Thanks," I said, touched by their encouragement. I squinted into the bright squinting sunlight and glancing over at my partner. Liam leaned against a wall, his pose utterly casual. But he was clapping, his hands slowly moving together, his gaze on me.

Did he hear me arguing with Brodie?

Our eyes locked for a long moment. Liam didn't speak.

Guess not. Feeling awkward, I hefted the box. "I have to deliver this before I get the next set of instructions."

"Good luck," Liam called as I turned to leave.

I glanced back at him, then hurried down the street. The hall surely couldn't be that far away. I just had to find it, and I had a lead on the others.

I'd been mistaken about one thing, though—the hall wasn't close. And all too soon, the Katy-curse came back to haunt me. I went down a few streets, asked for directions, followed the directions I'd been given, and twenty minutes later, was hopelessly lost. Downtown Philadelphia was kind of crazy. There was an enormous amount of buildings all clustered together, and I had no idea where I was going. Not only that, but the box was getting heavier by the moment. Why on earth did the five foot tall, direction-challenged girl get the task that involved delivering a heavy box?

Frustrated, I grimly hefted the getting-heavier-by-the-minute box onto my shoulder and kept walking, only to realize I'd passed by the same tree twice now.

I was lost.

And this was the final leg.

And Liam was going to think that I was doing this on purpose so Brodie could win.

I admit, I panicked. I ran to the nearest building. I'd just ask for fricking directions, if that was what it took.

There was a small coffee shop nearby, and I hefted the box under my arm, pulling the heavy glass door open. Someone was coming out at the same time as I was going in, though, and nudged my box. It fell to the ground, pretzels spilling everywhere.

I gave a small scream of dismay. "No!"

"Sorry," the man in a suit said, holding a cup of coffee. He watched me as I knelt over the pretzels, and then turned away and left, as if it wasn't important to help me. Dick.

I hurriedly scooped pretzels back into my box, trying to place them back the way they'd been neatly stacked. That was a losing battle, though, and by the time the box was full, I still had twenty pretzels sitting on the ground and couldn't close the lid. Frustrated, I mashed pretzels and tried to stuff them back into some semblance of order. Pushing the pretzels back into place took another five minutes of my time, but I couldn't leave any of them behind. Once the lid was back in place, I headed into the deserted coffee-shop. "Do you know where Independence Hall is?"

The guy behind the counter peered at my hat, then stared at the cameraman trailing me. "You on TV?"

"Something like that," I told him, impatient. "Independence Hall?"

He waved a hand. "Back that way several blocks."

"I just came from there," I exclaimed.

"Well then, you're heading in the wrong direction. Go back that way a few blocks. You can't miss it."

Can't miss it? Apparently I had. Heart sinking, I wondered if the delivery location had been closer than I'd thought. I'd gone at least eight blocks by now, maybe more. Hefting my box again, I murmured a thank you and headed out the door.

Two hundred and fifty thousand dollars was on the line, and I'd gone the wrong direction. Two hundred and fifty *thousand*.

And I'd screwed us because I was no good with directions.

The box seemed to get heavier with every block I jogged. I couldn't afford to walk at this point. Who knew how much time I'd lost by going the wrong way? When I'd gone a few blocks again, I stopped and asked for directions once more. I got the same thing—a few blocks in this direction. You can't miss it.

I arrived at Independence Hall twenty minutes later, having missed it again and gone in a circle. By that time, one of the handles on my box had broken, the bottom of the box was sagging, and I was near tears. At the front of the massive, historic hall stood a man in front of the doors, dressed in a George-Washington-style coat and a powdered wig. He stood on the World Races mat and gave me a pleased nod when I thumped my worn box of pretzels down on the ground. "Very good. Here is your next task."

I took the disk from him, weary and defeated. I wanted to lay down on the ground and give up, but I owed Liam an explanation.

Not that he'd believe me. This was the most critical task, we'd had a huge lead, and I'd blown it. The moment that Brodie had come running back before me? He'd assume the worst.

And there wasn't a thing I could do about it.

I jogged back to the pretzel restaurant, my heart heavy. We'd lost. We'd lost the race. We'd come so close and I'd blown it. I'd said that I hadn't wanted the win, but I lied. I totally lied.

Because right about now? I was sick that we'd lost everything. Second place got the same money as last place.

But that was okay. I'd keep my cool and not let anyone know how disappointed I was. How much it hurt to have everything blow up in my face in the eleventh hour. How much it hurt to not have Liam at my side at the end. I'd been warned that it wasn't a real relationship, but my heart hadn't listened so well.

And now I was in too deep.

And that hurt. A lot. It hurt worse than the ache of losing.

When the pretzel restaurant came into sight, I saw Liam leaning against the wall, every muscle in his body tense despite his casual pose. His black hair was shaggy, nearly covering one side of his face. Polly stood off to one side, scuffing one of her sneakers. Brodie was nowhere to be seen.

They'd already left.

Liam spotted me and got to his feet, and Polly looked my way with only mild interest. Her gaze was glum, and I realized that she knew they'd lost. The fighting spirit had gone out of her.

"Welcome back," Liam said in a low voice, approaching me as I rushed forward. He carried both of our backpacks again.

Like nothing was wrong when everything was wrong.

I burst into tears.

Liam's eyes widened and he moved toward me, pulling me against him. "What's wrong?"

"I…got…lost…" I choked out between sobs. "I fucking ruined us and now you hate me."

"What?" He glanced around and noticed Polly watching us curiously even as he hugged me closer. His hand splayed on the back of my head and he pulled me in for a tender kiss on the forehead. "Come on. Let's get in the cab and we can talk on the way to the next task."

Unable to speak beyond my hysterical weeping, I handed him the disk. I hadn't even bothered to look at the next task. What did it matter?

With me still tucked in his arms, Liam led me around the corner. A taxi waited there, along with one more, presumably for Polly and Summer for when they finished their task. Liam tossed our bags into the back seat, and then gestured for me to get in. I slid into the car, wiping tears miserably from my face. A moment later, he was in the car and shut the door. He leaned in and showed the driver the clue. "You know where the Rocky Stairs are?"

"Everyone does," the driver said, pulling away from the curb.

"Perfect. Thanks, man." Liam sat back and then pulled me against him again. When I wouldn't meet his gaze, he put his fingers under my chin and tilted my face toward his. "Tell me what happened."

"Muh-my pretzels spilled everywhere," I sobbed. "And I got lost and went in the wrong direction and I couldn't find the place and everyone knows I'm really bad with directions but I kept looking because I knew you would think I was throwing the challenge but I wasn't, and I don't want Brodie to get ahead at all, I just want us to get back to being cool and I wouldn't even let him see how I twisted my pretzels because I didn't want you to think I was helping him and—"

"Shhh," he told me. "Katy. I know you didn't help him. It's okay."

I looked up at him in surprise, wiping my eyes again. "How do you know?"

He gave me a crooked grin. "Tesla peeked in and said you were hiding your pretzels from Brodie so he couldn't cheat. She was really annoyed about it, too."

I gave him a tremulous smile.

"And we couldn't help but overhear everything you guys were yelling at each other," he told me in a low voice, his thumb stroking across my lower lip. "Turns out your brother blackmailed you, huh? You should have said something."

I took a shuddering breath. "I felt stupid. Like, he used me. And I gave him the Ace and then you guys fought, and I felt like I couldn't tell you. I'm not exactly proud of it."

"You should have told me." He leaned in and kissed me, light and lovely, on the mouth. "I'm not a heartless beast, you know."

"No, but you were mad and you thought I was working with Brodie to fuck you over."

"That's my own hang-up," Liam admitted. "Remember I told you Tesla and I dated once upon a time? That was pretty much how it ended up. She lied and saw other guys behind my back. So I guess once I heard that, I kind of got blinders on and assumed the worst."

"Well, that's not my problem," I told him with a sniffle.

"No, it's not." He gave me a sheepish look. "And I wanted to say I'm sorry."

"Thank you," I told him softly.

He leaned in and kissed me again, his tongue stroking over my parted lips. I felt the stud of his piercing glide along the seam of my mouth, and I opened for him, letting him flick against my tongue as we deepened the kiss. It was apology and comfort and desire all at once, and I melted into his arms. He broke the kiss a moment later and smiled down at me. "Forgiven?"

"Forgiven," I agreed, sliding my hands under his shirt to caress his bare skin. "Not that I suppose it matters, since we've lost the race."

"We'll finish strong," Liam told me, wrapping his arms around me and hugging me close. "No shame in second place." He leaned in. "And with you in my arms? I've already won."

Those three sweet words did a lot to soothe my worries, I admit.

"WE'RE HERE," THE CAB DRIVER ANNOUNCED.

I looked up from where I was snuggled against Liam's chest. The minutes had flown past, and though it wasn't a long drive, I'd enjoyed every moment of it, wrapped in his embrace, his hands touching my face, my hair, my skin as if he couldn't get enough of me. All the while, he hummed a wordless tune under his breath. I wasn't sure if that tune was for me or for him, but it was pleasant nevertheless.

"Thank you," Liam said, handing the man some money. "You don't have to wait."

I started at that, then realized…this was the last stop. He wouldn't have to wait because we were done with the race. Mouth dry with a sudden burst of anxiety, I grabbed my bag and handed Liam his, and we piled out of the cab. As we emerged, Liam held his hand out for me and I took it.

To my surprise, he lifted our twined hands to his mouth and kissed the back of my hand. "We didn't start this as a team, but we'll end it as one."

I smiled at him. "I'm just sorry we couldn't win."

"I'm not," he said. "I got a lot more out of this race than just a paycheck."

I felt my entire body flush with the heat of those words and we headed forward.

As soon as I saw the Rocky statue, I laughed to myself. This was why this place was referred to as 'the Rocky Steps.' A large statue of Rocky Balboa was off to one side and we passed it, heading toward a massive series of steps led to the pillars at the front of the museum. I vaguely remembered a scene from the Rocky movies where he'd jogged up them.

At the base of the steps, there was a *World Games* mat, a series of boxes off to each side of the judge waiting there. I squinted at the top of the stairs—Chip Brubaker waited there, along with a fleet of cameras and a finish line tape that was intact.

Midway up the steps stood Tesla and Brodie, moving slowly as they carried a yellow mini-Trojan horse on a litter.

"They're not done with the last task," Liam told me, surprise in his voice. "No one's won yet."

I blinked at my brother and his partner, unable to believe it. Sure enough, I watched as Tesla dropped the front of the litter, spilling the Trojan horse to the ground. She put her hands on her knees, panting, and I watched a look of frustration contort Brodie's face.

This wasn't done yet.

I gave Liam an incredulous look, and as one, we both broke into a sprint and raced to the judge's mat at the bottom of the stairs.

"Welcome to the last leg of The World Races," the judge told us in a low, smooth voice. It was a woman this time, dressed head to toe in the colors of the race, the big planet logo of *The World Races* emblazoned across her chest. She proudly held out the last clue disk.

I disentangled my hand from Liam's and took the disk with shaking fingers and flipped it over, reading it aloud softly. "Welcome to your final task. For this task, you must take the marked litter and, one by one, take a series of objects to the top of the steps and place it on the numbered mats designated for your team. Each of these objects represents a leg of the race, and you must put them in chronological order. Once you have placed your object, return to the bottom of the stairs for the next one. When you have placed all eight objects in order, the judge will give you your final token. When you have that token, you may cross the finish line."

"That shouldn't be too hard, then," Liam murmured into my ear, his breath tickling my skin. "We can do this."

"We can," I agreed, excitement pounding through me. I shrugged off my backpack and tossed it next to the series of large black boxes and the litter that was off to one side. The pink group of boxes was untouched—Summer and Polly were still at the last challenge. Off to one side, the yellow boxes were demolished, all but two opened. They were close to the end, then. If we worked hard, we could do this. "Come on."

We opened the first box. It was a replica of a sphinx. "This one's Egypt," I told him. "Not first."

"We need to find Greenland," he told me, opening the next box. "Here, this is it." He tossed the lid of the box aside and I moved to view it. It was a wooden replica of a sled, about three feet long and complete with wooden dog at the front, all painted in black. Cute. Liam began to pull it out of the box and then grunted. "Jesus, it's heavy."

I moved to help him and was surprised at how freaking weighty the thing was. "Did they weigh it down with lead bricks or something?"

It took both of us to drag it over to the litter, and I grabbed the front, Liam with the back. I grunted indelicately as we hoisted it into the air. The thing weighed a fricking ton. No wonder Tesla and Brodie were still doing this challenge.

As a unit, we moved forward, and since I was in front, I set the pace. I started out charging up the stairs, but that quickly gave way to a steady, slow climb. You couldn't move fast with the heavy litter, and the stairs seemed like and endless procession. It felt like it took forever to get to the top, and by the time we did, my hands and shoulders were burning. We barely passed Tesla and Brodie on the way up, and my brother didn't seem worried. As soon as we got to the top, I knew why. They already had five of their eight objects at the top. It was a disappointing sight to see, but I forced myself to concentrate on our team. What Brodie did no longer mattered. It was all about Liam and I.

We headed over to our marked mats, and I noticed that there was a grid set up like a tic-tac-toe board, with a big *World Games* globe logo in the center. Each of the empty squares were labeled one through eight, and we headed with our litter over to slot one, and dumped our sled. I was breathing hard and disgusted at how difficult this was. This last challenge was going to come down to sheer strength. Frustrated, I glanced over as Brodie and Tesla dumped their latest object onto their yellow mat, studying them.

Sled, an enormous book, a chandelier, a temple replica, a sphinx, and as I watched, they put down an enormous stringed instrument like the kind Liam had played in Cambodia. I squinted, something about that not seeming right to me.

"Come on," Liam encouraged me, and we grabbed our litter and headed back down to the bottom.

Going back down was leagues easier than heading up, and we trotted back down the stairs in record time. We headed back to our boxes and I leaned in to Liam. "Next leg was Ireland."

"I remember," he told me, prying open the next box. "You kissed me just for the hell of it."

I laughed, feeling warm. "Do you remember all the legs in order by the stages of our flirting?"

"I do," he said, and his face was serious as he looked over at me. "I got to put my hands all over you in Paris, then we had a mini-date in Pompeii. Went all the way in Egypt after you clung to me in the pyramids. Night two in Turkey, and then we fought in Cambodia. Waste of a perfectly good twelve hours in a hotel room, if you ask me."

I chuckled. "That was all you."

"I know it was," he said, and grimaced. "This box is the wrong one," he told me. "Cambodia wasn't until the seventh leg." And he showed me the stringed instrument.

Something pinged my memory again, and I squinted up at the top of the stairs, where Brodie and Tesla were descending back down to the bottom, their empty litter at hand. I looked over at their boxes—two remained. And Cambodia was seventh...

I turned and grabbed Liam's arm as he opened the next box, my fingers digging in to his skin. "Brodie and Tesla made a mistake," I whispered at him. "They've got the order wrong."

"They do?"

I nodded. "When we go up again, look at their mat."

His eyes flared with excitement. "I guess now that they don't have anyone to copy off of, they're forced to rely on their own brains."

"Then Brodie and Tesla are screwed," I told him with a grin. "My brother's a lot of things, but brains is not his strong suit."

"We need to hurry," he told me, heading for the next box and prying the massive lid off.

I thought for a minute, then leaned in. "What if we leave the item in the box and take it up the stairs? The rules didn't mention anything about that. Brodie and Tesla won't be able to see what we've got in what order, and so they won't be able to copy off of us once they figure out that they've done something wrong."

Liam grinned at me. "Sneaky. I love it."

"Let's do it, then," I said, opening the next box.

It took a few more before we found the large book that signified our stop in Dublin and the visit to the University Library. We left it in the box and hauled it up the stairs, going as fast as we could despite our cramping legs. There were only seventy-two steps (I counted) but it might as well have been three hundred. We dumped our box and raced down for the next one. After that was a chandelier, for the opera house in Paris. As we headed up again, we passed Tesla and Brodie, who were on their way back up with their next object. They were slowing down, their faces covered in sweat. I couldn't blame them—we were on our third pass up and this task was killing my legs. But we couldn't afford to slow down. Not when victory was this close.

My heart hammered in my chest as we dropped off our box, and then took the box containing the small temple up the stairs. Once we got to the Trojan horse, my legs were cramping and moving slower and slower. Liam's face was shining with sweat, his black hair sticking to his brow. I was exhausted, but sheer adrenaline kept me going.

As soon as we dumped our Trojan horse, I watched, my entire body tense, as Brodie and Tesla called over the judge. The woman picked through their pieces, then shook her head. "No. Try again."

I bit back my squeal of excitement. They had it wrong. There was time to fix this. We could still win.

We headed down the stairs at breakneck speed, and I watched as Brodie's gaze moved to our still-boxed objects. *Nice try, big brother,* I thought to myself. There was not going to be any copying off of my hard work today. Liam and I were both gasping for breath by the time we made it up the stairs with the stringed guitar-thing from Cambodia. I glanced over at Brodie's mat, and they had maneuvered things again, the Trojan horse now occupying the completely wrong spot.

"I'm sorry, no," the judge said again, and I smiled to myself to hear Brodie swear.

Excitement made our feet pound down the stairs, even though we were exhausted at this point. We grabbed the last box and hauled it onto the litter with weak, trembling arms.

"One more, Katy," Liam encouraged me. "We can do this. We can."

I nodded, saving my breath for the climb up those horrible stairs, and we continued forward. Each step felt enormous, and I counted them off in my head. Twenty steps, and I was gasping like a fish out of water. Thirty steps, and my sweaty hands were slipping on the wooden beams of the litter. Fifty steps, and my legs were cramped so tight that every step felt like knives. But I kept going, and Liam hadn't slowed down a bit. Sixty five steps, and we were close enough to see Brodie and Tesla standing over their mat. My brother had his hands twisted in his blond hair, and he looked utterly frustrated. Tesla had her tattooed arms crossed over her chest, giving Brodie a furious look, as if it was his fault. I felt a twinge of pity for my brother. Just a twinge.

And then we were up to the top of the stairs. I stumbled, my legs giving out on me, and we crashed to the ground.

"You okay, Katy?" Liam was immediately at my side, the litter forgotten. He helped me to my feet, his hands strong and sure as he grasped my arms.

"I'm fine," I wheezed. "Let's finish this."

We grabbed our litter and dragged it over to the final place on the mat, just as Brodie and Tesla waved the judge over again.

I held my breath as the judge considered their puzzle board. Then, she shook her head and I thought my heart would burst. "I'm sorry, no."

"Over here," I croaked. "We're ready."

The judge headed over, and I heard Brodie curse again. A cameraman came over to hover as Liam lifted the lids on the boxes and set them aside, then moved toward me. His strong arms went around my waist, and I leaned heavily on him, exhausted. My every nerve was tight with anxiety, though, and I couldn't take my eyes off the judge as she studied our puzzle. I knew we had things right. Liam knew. Had we mistaken something, though?

"Their stuff is still in boxes," Tesla called out in a whiny voice. "That's not fair."

"There's nothing in the rules that says you can't do that," Liam said. "Just to take it up the stairs and put it in the right spot."

"That's cheating," she shot back.

"You're just jealous that you guys weren't smart enough to do it," I retorted.

She gave me a narrow-eyed glare that I ignored, leaning heavily on Liam. My gaze went back to the judge, who had paced around our boxes again.

After a long, tense moment, she reached into her jacket and withdrew a bright green disk. "That is correct. Congratulations."

Liam gave a whoop and grabbed me by the waist. I shrieked with excitement, wrapping my arms around his neck as he spun me around.

"The disk," I laughed happily, wiggling out of his grasp. "Get the disk!"

He set me down, pressed a hard, sweaty kiss to my mouth that was so fierce that I could feel his lip piercing digging into my skin. Then he snatched the disk from the judge, grabbed my hand, and we raced toward that unbroken finish line.

Cameramen hovered, filming us as we headed toward that long piece of tape, and the host was clapping with excitement. We crossed the line and I felt the plastic snap as we pushed through it.

"Congratulations, Katy and Liam," Chip boomed as The World Races theme music began to play loudly and confetti rained down on top of us. "You are the winners of this year's *World Games!*"

Liam looked at me.

I looked back at him.

He grinned.

I flung my arms around Liam's neck once more and pulled him to me in another long, hard kiss.

Chapter Eleven

"Where do we go from here? Towards a happy ever after, man."
—Liam Brogan, Post-Races Interview

THE TWENTY-FOUR HOURS POST-RACE WERE A BLUR OF ACTIVITY. Liam and I were thoroughly interviewed on every angle of the final leg of the race, and then we did a new series of press junkets. A check was presented to us, on camera, and Chip gave a long speech about the challenges of the race and recounted the many tasks we'd performed.

I didn't hear a word of it. I simply clutched that oversized check, in a daze.

Two hundred and fifty thousand dollars. One hundred twenty five thousand dollars each. Holy shit. Brodie was going to be furious at me. I told myself that I didn't care, but he was my brother. I cared even though he'd played like a jerk. He'd hate that he came into second place. Absolutely hate it.

The others that had been kicked off the race at one time or another met for a big wrap party in Philadelphia. Everyone had been flown in, and they all took turns hugging me and Liam. Abby was delighted for us, and Dean didn't seem nearly as upset at losing as I thought he might be, which meant that Abby had probably told him about the baby. Either way, it was good to see them again, and I hugged them both for a long, long time.

Tesla wasn't speaking to me or Liam. Brodie gave me a quick hug of congratulations and then disappeared into the crowd again.

We hadn't had a minute to ourselves since the race had ended. By the time the interviews and the wrap party were over, it was extremely late at night, and the crew had assigned us separate hotel rooms. I collapsed into mine and fell instantly asleep, exhausted from endless days of globetrotting and worry. As I fell into bed, I briefly wondered that Liam hadn't come to find me. Or were we over now that the race was?

It's reality TV, but it's not reality. Abby's warning rang in my mind over and over again.

She'd been right all along. Maybe Liam figured that now that we were done with the race, me and him were done as well. It did seem like a natural place to break, I thought wistfully, if one wanted to break things off.

I didn't, but I wasn't the only one in this relationship, of course.

"Katy Short?" Someone pounded at my door. "Are you awake?"

I sat up, pushing my messy hair out of my eyes, disoriented. I'd been dragged from an incredible dream about Liam and Egypt and the hours we'd spent in the hotel room exploring each other. Waking up and finding myself in my lonely bed? Not the best way to start the day.

I went to the door and opened it, staring blearily at the production assistant there. "Yes?"

"Your ride to the airport leaves in twenty minutes. I'm here to make sure you get there."

"Oh. Okay. Give me a few to shower and get ready." I shut the door again when I saw her nod, and then dragged myself to the shower, trying to wake up. I still felt hung over from the race.

When I wiped the foggy mirror and stared at my reflection, I considered my wet blonde hair. This was the first day in a while that I wouldn't have to wear my hair in pigtails because the race had mandated it. Running my fingers through it, I grabbed a clip and just twisted it into that. No fuss, no muss. Back to normal Katy all over again. Race Katy was going to be a memory soon enough.

And I thought of Liam again. Would I have time to say goodbye? I dressed quickly, shoving my things into my bag. We'd had to travel light for the race, so luckily I didn't have much to pack.

When I opened the door to my room, though, I was surprised to see Brodie there. "Hey, sis," he said cheerfully. "You up?"

"I am," I said in a wary voice. This cheerfulness after losing the race? That wasn't like Brodie. My brother was known to sulk for days on end. "You going to the airport with me?"

"Well, I was supposed to, but I came to say goodbye."

"Goodbye?"

He grinned again, unable to contain his excitement. "The producers met with me last night. They liked me so much on The World Races that they want me to be on *Endurance Island*, which starts taping in two days. So I'm flying from here directly out to the filming location. Isn't that awesome?"

"Wow, that is. I'm surprised, honestly."

He laughed. "Because I played like a dick? Apparently the production crew loved that. They don't have nearly enough villains for good TV so they're throwing me onto *Endurance Island* in the hopes that I can stir things up there, too. And they even mentioned the show *House Guests*."

"*House Guests?*"

"You know, the one where they stick a bunch of strangers in a house together? Apparently they're about to do an all-star version in a few months, and they're considering casting me." He gave me an excited hug. "Isn't this amazing?"

"It is," I murmured, still dazed. "Wow. I'm really happy for you, Brodie. Things are looking up. You're not mad that I won?"

"Oh, I'm annoyed I didn't win," Brodie admitted, and gave me another brotherly noogie that I barely escaped. "But Tesla totally fell apart in that last challenge and she drove me crazy. As soon as she started whining about going up the stairs, I knew we'd lost it."

I said nothing, ignoring Brodie's revisionist history. Tesla's whining hadn't lost the challenge for them—their lack of puzzle skills had. But whatever got my brother through the day. "Speaking of Tesla, how's she taking the loss?"

Brodie shrugged. "Don't know. I heard they flew all the other teams out about two hours ago."

My jaw dropped. "They...what?"

"Yeah. I didn't get to say goodbye, but that's fine." He grinned. "I knew it was just for the show anyhow."

But I was still reeling in shock. All the other teams were...gone? Liam hadn't come to say goodbye? Had we just been for the show, too?

I feel like I've already won, Liam had told me in that last cab ride. I blinked rapidly, fighting back tears. "Oh."

"Sorry you didn't get asked to go on *Endurance Island*, Katy. They told me they only had room for one person." My brother gave me a mock-sad look that told me he was trying really hard not to be excited, but failing.

I waved a hand idly at that, my chest still aching at the thought of Liam flying out without even bothering to say goodbye to me. "I don't want to be on *Endurance Island* anyhow. I just wanted enough money to give my business a boost."

"Well, you've got it," he said cheerfully.

I did. I had the money and the win. I just didn't have the guy. I should have been thrilled.

But instead, I just ached.

A HALF HOUR LATER, THE CAB DROPPED ME OFF AT THE AIRPORT AND I headed inside, ticket in hand. Being in the airport again after all the running around of the past few weeks made me instantly tired, and I couldn't seem to muster any enthusiasm as I headed to my gate. It felt weird to sit down at a gate and not have a cameraman hovering to tape my every movement. I slumped in my chair and tried not to think about how weirdly lonely it felt to be on my own for the first time in weeks.

Maybe the loneliness was because I'd been discarded romantically? I kept telling myself that it wasn't important. My brother had been callously dumped by Tesla and wasn't upset because he'd known it was short-term. I told my brain that I shouldn't be upset, too. But I couldn't help it.

I had stupidly fallen for a guy that hadn't even wanted to be my partner in the beginning. Unhappy, I stared off into space, resisting the urge to tap my fingers on the bag like Liam had, always with a melody in his head.

Whispers and giggles drove me out of my reverie. "You think that's really him?" someone said nearby.

I glanced up.

Two girls were giggling, and one had her phone out and was videotaping something in the distance.

"Go ask him for his autograph," another girl whispered, and more giggling followed.

I craned my head, trying to see what they were staring at. To my surprise,

Liam Brogan, lead guitarist of *Finding Threnody*, was heading my way, a backpack slung over one deliciously tattooed shoulder, his shaggy hair falling over his brow, piercings gleaming in the sunlight streaming through the airport windows.

And he was heading directly for me.

I got up from my seat as if in slow motion, staring at him, drinking in his tall, delicious form, the dark eyes, the wicked glint in his gaze, the sensual mouth that I loved to kiss.

He ignored the girls filming him and the stares he got, and came to stand right in front of me. His gaze moved over my hair, and his mouth quirked into an amused grin. "No pigtails?"

"I'm done with those for now."

"Shame," he said, and the word was so low and husky that it made me quiver. "I kind of liked those."

I blushed. "You're still here? I'm kind of surprised."

"Why? You never came to say goodbye."

My jaw dropped. "I...Brodie said—" I snapped my mouth shut and groaned. "God, remind me never to listen to my brother again." I rubbed my forehead, just thinking about the headaches that came with being related to Brodie. "He told me everyone else flew out hours ago."

"Not me," Liam said. "I was waiting to talk to you, but you never came."

"It wasn't because I didn't want to," I told him softly, and to my horror, my eyes filled with tears. "I just thought that we were done because the race was done."

Liam's arms went around me, and he pulled me closer. "Now when," he whispered huskily, "have I ever given you that impression?"

My hands slid around his waist and I splayed my fingers on his back, enjoying the play of muscles against my hands as I stared up into his face. God, he was gorgeous. I could eat him up with a spoon. No wonder all these girls were ecstatically taping him. "But you're a big famous rock star and I'm nobody."

"You're Katy Short," he said with a grin. "Smart, determined wearer of pigtails and winner of The World Races. And I happen to be in love with you."

My breath caught in my throat. "You are?"

"I am," he said, and leaned in to brush the lightest of kisses over my mouth.

"I love you too," I breathed against his lips.

And then he kissed me, harder, and I felt his tongue swipe into my mouth and my knees went weak. This felt like a dream.

He broke off the kiss and nuzzled me, his hands sliding to my ass and cupping me against him. "So what are your plans?"

"I have no idea," I told him honestly. "I guess I see what a cash influx of one hundred and twenty-five grand can do for my business."

"How about a vacation?"

I laughed at that. "You didn't get enough travel in over the past few days?"

"I wasn't thinking about traveling," he told me, brushing a lock of stray hair off of my brow in a tender motion that made my heart ache. "I was thinking you and me on a solitary beach house for about a month or so. We can sleep late, eat meals that aren't airport food, and pretend that the outside world doesn't exist."

That sounded like heaven. My hands tightened around his waist. "I'd love to, but don't you have rock star stuff to do? Like go on tour?"

"Tour's over," he told me. "The band's breaking up. Tesla actually just finished recording her first solo album. The label just hasn't announced anything yet. They're waiting for the show to air. It's all been agreed upon with the network."

I gaped at him. "Your band broke up? Oh my god, I'm so sorry."

"I'm not," he said bluntly, and he gave me a grin that didn't seem unhappy at all. "Tesla was miserable to work with and I have the connections now that I can do what I want. And I like song-writing. So if I take six months off to just write a bunch of songs, it's no big deal."

"It isn't?" I breathed the words, barely daring to hope.

"Nope. And then," he shrugged. "We see where it goes from there."

"What if it goes well?" I asked him. I couldn't help myself.

He smiled. "Then we see if you want to move to LA or I want to move to…where did you say you were from again?"

I laughed. "Oklahoma."

He grimaced. "Okay. Or we see if I can move to Oklahoma. Either way, I want to be with you." He leaned in toward me again, his mouth hovering over mine, almost kissing. "If you want to be with me."

"Always," I told him softly, and then pulled back. "But I have two conditions."

His pierced eyebrow rose. "Oh?"

"One—no pretzels."

Liam laughed. "I think I can manage that."

"And two, you're in charge of directions." I grinned.

"I don't foresee that being a problem," he told me, and his hands squeezed my ass. I heard the girls nearby titter, no doubt catching every moment on their smartphones. I didn't care. "So you want to be with me even though I'm not going to be a big shot rock star anymore and just a songwriter?"

"I want to be with you always," I told him, sliding my arms up and around his neck to pull him down to me in another kiss. "I think this partnership has real, long-term potential."

"I agree," he told me, and kissed me again. "Best partner in the race."

"Best," I breathed against his lips.

And then we kissed all over again.

About Jill Myles

JILL MYLES is the pen name for *USA Today* Bestselling Author Jessica Clare. As Jill Myles, she writes a little bit of everything, from sexy, comedic urban fantasy to zombie fairy tales. As Jessica Clare, she writes erotic contemporary romance. She also has a third pen name (because why stop at two?). As Jessica Sims, she writes fun, sexy shifter paranormals.

Too many pen-names to follow? Sign up for Jill's newsletter and you'll receive notices of new releases under all three pen names, along with a coupon for a free read.

You can visit Jill/Jessica's website at www.jillmyles.com

Jessica Sims'
MIDNIGHT LIAISONS

Where the paranormal go to find a date...

BEAUTY DATES THE BEAST

WANTED: Single human female to join charming, wealthy single male were-cougar for a night of romantic fun – and maybe more.

Me: The tall, sensuous, open-minded leader of my clan. You: A deliciously curvy virgin who's intimately familiar with what goes bump in the night. Must not be afraid of a little tail. Prefer a woman who's open to exploring her animal nature. Interest in nighttime walks through the woods a plus.

My turn-ons include protecting you from the worst the supernatural world has to offer. Ready for an adventure? Give me a call.

DESPERATELY SEEKING SHAPESHIFTER

WANTED: Supernatural single seeks sexy she-wolf to help him bear all.

Me: A strong, silent type who doesn't care much about the creature comforts. You: Sweet as honey. No such thing as too big or too small—you're just right.

Let's take things slow. I'll start as your bodyguard, but hopefully soon I'll shift into your mate. You need a man who's born to be wild, and I'm ready to protect you from all the wolf pack can throw in your direction. Don't be afraid of your animal side. Show me yours, and I'll show you mine.

"Funny, sexy, and lively." —Publishers Weekly

AVAILABLE NOW IN PRINT AND E-BOOK FORMATS
www.jessica-sims.com

43849708R00111

Made in the USA
Charleston, SC
10 July 2015